Also by Sage Blackwood

JINX: THE WIZARD'S APPRENTICE

JINX'S MAGIC

SAGE BLACKWOOD

Quercus

First published in 2014 by HarperCollins Children's Books US,
10 East 53rd St, New York, NY10022

First published in Great Britain in 2014 by Clays Lts, St Ives plc

Quercus Editions Limited
55 Baker Street
7th Floor, South Block
London W1U 8EW

A CIP catalogue reference for this book is available
from the British Library

ISBN 978 1 84866 273 5

10 9 8 7 6 5 4 3 2 1

For Deborah Schwabach
and
Jonathan Schwabach

through the fire

Contents

1

An Encounter with No Werewolves

It wasn't that Jinx didn't like people. It was just that sometimes he had to get away from them.

He was no sooner out of earshot of the campfire, breathing in the deep, green strength of the forest, than he heard a single tree's voice.

Stuck. Trapped. All is lost.

Jinx hurried through the underbrush, weaving around great moss-covered trees and stumbling over roots.

The cries came from a beech sapling. A mighty pine had fallen, crushing the beech to the ground.

Jinx grabbed the sapling and yanked, but couldn't free it. He could hear it murmuring its despair. *You waited and* waited for a chance like this, for a big tree to fall so that you could grow toward the sunlight, and then *this* happened. It was hard to be young in the Urwald.

Jinx wrapped his arms around the rough, pitch-splattered pine trunk and tried to move it. He couldn't shift it an inch.

Oh. Right. He was a magician.

Jinx drew the Urwald's lifeforce power up through his feet. He levitated the fallen pine a few inches.

Free! Free! said the sapling. *Sunlight!*

It swept upward, its leaves brushing Jinx's face.

Jinx was feeling a sense of accomplishment—the tree might someday grow as tall and stout as the giants around it, thanks to him—when he suddenly sensed a deep golden hunger nearby. He turned his head slightly to the left . . . and was eye to eye with a werewolf.

Jinx froze, terrified. It was no good doing a concealment spell—the werewolf had already seen him. There was no time to scream for help—the werewolf was only a few yards away.

It was wearing spectacles.

As Jinx stared, the werewolf licked the end of a pencil and wrote something in a small notebook.

"Why did you do that?" said the werewolf, in growly but perfectly good Urwish.

"D-do what?" said Jinx. He hadn't known werewolves could talk. He'd been stalked by werewolves, clawed by werewolves, and very nearly eaten by werewolves, but they'd never exchanged pleasantries.

"Levitate the tree." The werewolf's pencil was poised over the notebook. "Do you consider yourself a magician?"

Was it good, or bad, to be a magician, as far as werewolves were concerned? Probably bad. Jinx tried to calm down. The werewolf licked its lips hungrily, which did not help Jinx calm down.

"Er," said Jinx. "H-how do you feel about magicians?"

"I am very fond of them," said the werewolf.

"Oh," said Jinx. "Well I—"

"As long as they're young and tender. Stringy old witches and wizards disagree with me." The werewolf touched his midriff and winced.

There was chattering overhead. Jinx looked up. A chipmunk sat on a branch, tail upright, and watched Jinx and the werewolf with interest.

"It's, er, late in the year for chipmunks," said Jinx, in what he hoped was a light conversational tone.

The hackles on the werewolf's neck rose. "Unsympathetic magic approaches. Excuse me."

He tucked his notebook away—Jinx didn't see where—and slunk off.

Jinx felt relieved . . . for half a second. Then he became aware of a cold blue hole piercing the great green lifeforce of the Urwald.

He turned around. Two elves stared at him. They were

blue, with silver-white hair, and they glowed slightly. Jinx had seen elves before, but never up close. The feeling that came from them was cold, not like winter or ice, but cold like a dark, faraway place that has never seen either.

At least the werewolf had been *alive*. The elves were . . . something else. Not dead, because "dead" has something to do with "alive," and Jinx had a feeling that elves did not.

One of the elves opened its mouth, and a sound came out like a cat being dragged backward through a drain.

The other elf, who Jinx guessed was a lady, answered— a snarly, hairball-hacking sound. Jinx was ordinarily good at languages, but he wasn't even sure this *was* a language.

"What?" said Jinx.

"Doesn't listen very well," said the female elf, switching to Urwish. "Not as well as he's supposed to."

"I do too," said Jinx, annoyed.

"Aren't you supposed to be the Listener?" said the male elf. His voice rang like iron dropped on ice.

"I don't know about 'supposed to,' but yeah," said Jinx.

"He has no idea what that means, Dearth," said the lady. "Are you telling me our brilliant Bonemaster couldn't kill *that*?"

"He did kill him," said Dearth. "More or less. But it didn't take. Bottle spell, you know."

"And now look at it. What a poor excuse for a flame."

"The Bonemaster hasn't come into his power yet," said

Dearth. "Not really. More than this one has, of course. But he isn't yet strong."

"They're a curious pair," said the lady. "Why choose an old man and a boy?"

"Choose, choose," said Dearth scornfully. "No one is chosen. The wicks choose themselves. It's always been that way."

"Who chooses themselves for what?" Jinx demanded.

"Should we kill him?" said the lady.

Now this was going too far. Jinx tried to summon the Urwald's lifeforce . . . and found that he couldn't. He was trapped inside the cold blue hole the elves had brought with them. The lifeforce was outside it.

"It's completely unnecessary, Neza," said Dearth. "And our Bonemaster can't become truly strong without him. There have to be two wicks. It was ever thus."

"But if the Bonemaster kills him, we reign supreme," said Neza.

"Reigning supreme can be a great deal more trouble than it's worth," said Dearth irritably.

"Well, this one doesn't know who he is. That's all we need to know," said Neza. She made a dismissive little gesture at Jinx with her nose. "You won't remember this, Flame."

She waved her fingers, and Jinx was engulfed in a maelstrom of silver-blue sparks. The sparks filled his eyes and got up his nose. He batted at them, trying to clear them away—

"Jinx!" Someone was calling his name. That was his name, wasn't it? He felt confused. His nose itched. And there was a girl in a red cape coming through the woods.

Oh. Of course. Elfwyn. And how could he have forgotten his own name?

"What are you doing up here?" she asked.

"I was just . . ." Jinx looked back at where there had been—something, hadn't there? A chipmunk? Yes, he was pretty sure there had been a chipmunk.

"I was just thinking," he said.

"I thought I heard you talking to someone."

"The trees probably," said Jinx. He didn't talk to the trees aloud, but he was too embarrassed to say he'd been talking to a chipmunk. *Had* he? He didn't remember.

"I was worried," she said. "You shouldn't go off by yourself. There could be werewolves, you know."

Something tugged at Jinx's memory, but he couldn't think what.

"Nah, I'm fine," he said. "There are no werewolves around here."

2

An Ill Wind

They were traveling the Path—Jinx, Elfwyn, Reven, and the wizard Simon Magus. Jinx was fond of all of his companions, at least in theory. Elfwyn was a sensible girl who suffered from a terrible curse that forced her to answer any question truthfully. Other than that she was good company. Reven was—well, Reven was probably a king, and certainly dangerous.

He was also good at stuff Jinx was not so good at, like fighting, and talking to girls. Jinx sort of admired Reven for these things, but not aloud.

Then there was Simon . . . who had *said* he'd let Jinx go to the edge of the Urwald without him. The problem was (and Jinx only knew this because he could see other people's feelings) that Simon didn't want to let Jinx out of his sight. And this was because a few months ago Jinx had fallen off a hundred-foot cliff and gotten, if you wanted to be perfectly accurate, killed. It was only good luck on Jinx's part and good spell work on Simon's that had kept the situation from becoming permanent.

Ever since then Simon had tended to hover, and to watch Jinx more closely than people really need to be watched when they're almost thirteen.

It was a warm day in late fall, and a strong wind sent brown leaves scuttering along the path. Jinx walked a little behind his companions, and the trees spoke to him.

The Terror, they said. That was what they called Reven. *The Terror is still here. Why is the Terror still here, Listener?*

Because of Simon, said Jinx. *I'm trying to take Reven out of the Urwald, but Simon keeps taking us to visit all these witches and wizards, asking them all—*

Tell the wizard Simon you must go. To the forest edge. Yes, very soon, Listener. Tell him.

Right, because he really listens *to me.* Jinx didn't bother to say this, because trees seldom understood sarcasm. *I'll try.*

Suddenly a ripple of alarm ran through the trees, then surged to a torrent of terror.

The trees cried out a warning.

Danger. Death. Destruction. Flee, Listener!

8

Jinx hurried to warn his friends. "Run!"

"From what?" said Simon. "If there are monsters, we'll do a concealment spell."

"We can't hide!" said Jinx. "There's a clearing near here—we can make it if—"

Simon stopped in the middle of the path and scowled. "There is not a clearing near here."

"Yes, there is," said Jinx. "Will you listen to me for once?"

Jinx could see the clouds around the wizard's head—Simon was afraid. That surprised Jinx so much that for a second he could only stare.

Then the fear slipped away behind the blank white wall that hid some of Simon's thoughts. In the same instant the forest darkened. A blast of wind tore through the trees, sending the branches creaking and groaning overhead.

"Told you," said Jinx.

"Told me what?"

"It feels like there's a storm coming," said Elfwyn.

"It's a huge storm!" said Jinx. "Like a thousand drag-ons. Only wetter."

"A storm? All this fuss is about a *storm*?"

Jinx could've shaken Simon with frustration. "It's a *killer* storm. It'll be here in a few minutes."

"Then I expect we'll get wet," said Simon.

"We'll get dead," said Jinx. "The clearing's half a mile

north of here. We can make it if we run. This is a really monstrous storm. It can tear your limbs off!"

Reven looked up anxiously at the creaking branches. "Perhaps we should listen to Jinx, good wizard."

"I'm not taking orders from my apprentice," said Simon. "If I change my mind about that, I'll let you know."

"There *is* another path up here," said Elfwyn. "How did you know there was a clearing, Jinx?"

The sky had turned steely gray. The wind roared like thunder, and then rushed overhead. A branch snapped and hit the path just behind them. Elfwyn grabbed Simon's arm and hauled at him. Reven stared at the branches thrashing all around them.

"Come on!" Jinx grabbed Simon's other arm. "Move!"

"Let go of me," said Simon.

Suddenly Jinx felt the hairs on his neck stand on end. A thick bolt of lightning ran from the ground to the sky and back, pink and crackling, and a tree beside the path lit up, shooting sparks. There was a loud *BANG*. Jinx heard screaming—the others wouldn't, of course—and the tree snapped, halfway down the trunk. For a moment the fractured tree stood wavering atop its stump.

"RUN!" Jinx yelled.

They ran. The tree came crashing to the path behind them, so close that they stumbled forward from the force of the impact. They turned up the new path and kept running. The rain arrived, sheets and blankets of rain, barrels and cauldrons and lakes of rain.

The houses in the clearing were dim gray shapes through the downpour. Elfwyn ran to the nearest house.

"Not that one!" Simon cried.

A branch came crashing out of the forest and knocked Simon sprawling. Jinx and Reven struggled back to help him—Elfwyn was pounding on the door.

"I'm fine," said Simon, getting to his feet. "Get into the flippin' house, why don't you."

A mighty burst of wind whipped into the clearing and swept them all *smack* into the side of the house. Jinx tried to move, but the wind crushed him right back against the wall, flat as a leaf. Simon grabbed him and dragged him to the open door.

Then they were inside, the door was safely closed and barred, and there was firelight and the smell of things cooking. Outside, the wind howled like a thousand werewolves. Things crashed against the outer walls, but the house barely trembled.

A sharp-nosed old man sat at a table, dunking bread into a bowl of stew. Jinx was suddenly hungry.

"You're dripping water all over the floor," said the old man.

"We can't help that. It's raining," said Elfwyn.

"Why are you wearing a dress?"

"Because it's what I have, of course," said Elfwyn. "Why wouldn't I—"

"Not you." The old man waved a bread crust at Simon. "Him."

"It's not a dress," said Simon. "It's a robe. Is that all you have to say? Jinx, all of you, go stand by the fire and dry off."

"What do you need a robe for?"

"Robes are what wizards wear," Simon said between clenched teeth. "You three, hang your coats on the chairs."

"They'll drip all over the floor," said the old man. "Here, what are you doing in my cupboard, boy?"

Jinx felt a jolt of real horror when he realized that it was Simon being called "boy." He half expected the old man to be set aflame or turned into a toad, but Simon just got some wooden bowls and spoons out of the cupboard and clunked them down on the table.

"Where's the bread?" said Simon.

"In the breadbox, of course, where it always was." The old man had gone back to eating. "Take it all, don't worry about me. It's not like it matters whether I starve in my old age."

"Whatever finally carries you off, it won't be starvation." Simon ladled stew from the pot hanging over the fire. "Here, you three, sit down and eat."

"My stew's not good enough for you?" the old man demanded of Simon.

"It's got meat in it."

"Of course it's got meat in it, that's the point."

It was goat stew, with peas and lumps of potato. Jinx tried it. It was pretty good. There was nothing rotten or nasty—quite unlike the food you usually got in clearings.

"Still playing wizard, are you?" said the old man.

"Yup." Simon had taken off his sopping robe—he had regular clothes on underneath—and was wringing it onto the hearth.

"I tell people you died of plague."

"That's thoughtful of you," said Simon. "I expect they wonder where the wagonloads of potatoes come from in thin winters, then."

"These yours?" The old man gestured with his bread again.

"No." Simon gave Jinx, Reven, and Elfwyn a thoughtful look. "Well, yes, the younger boy's mine."

The old man hitched his chair around and looked hard at Jinx. Jinx looked back. He could see the cloud of gray-white, smug satisfaction that surrounded the man like a second skin. Whatever happened, Jinx suspected, this man would only see it through that cloud, through what it meant to him and what he could get out of it. Now he was sizing Jinx up through the cloud, and Jinx hated it.

"Hmph. Well, at least he's not wearing a dress."

"I left it home," said Jinx.

The old man ignored him, but Simon glared. Apparently

it was all right for Simon to be sarcastic, but not Jinx. Figured.

"The mother must've been pretty dark," said the old man.

"Must've been," said Simon. "Do you have any cheese?"

"Why don't you just look around till you find it? Is she dead?"

"Yes," said Simon. "Is this all the cheese you have?"

"If I'd known you were coming I'd've baked a cheesecake. What'd she die of?"

"Elves," said Simon.

At the word "elves" something stirred in Jinx's memory. He wondered if he should say something to correct the colossal misconception that was being formed here. A glance at Simon told him he should not. Simon's thoughts were a box of whisper-thin light green glass that might shatter at any second, which would lead to flames and toads and all sorts of horrible things.

Simon whipped a knife out of his pocket and stabbed the cheese viciously.

Outside, the storm raged. The window shutters rattled and shook. Elfwyn and Reven exchanged nervous glances and went on eating.

"Some storm," said Reven, in the overcheerful tone of someone trying to pretend everything was normal. "It's even worse than that one that blew us to the Bonemaster."

"I wonder if the Bonemaster has anything to do with this storm," Elfwyn murmured.

"He can't," said Jinx. "We destroyed most of his power."

"Unless he's escaped," said Elfwyn. "And found a way to get more power."

"Storms just happen," said Jinx.

"That lightning was amazing," said Reven. "That bolt that almost hit us—I never knew lightning was pink."

"Some of it's blue," said Jinx. "Like the flash right before it that stretched across the sky, and there were eight branches of lightning coming down to the treetops from it—"

He stopped, confused. Reven and Elfwyn were staring at him.

"We didn't see that," said Elfwyn. "Because we were under the trees, not on top of them. And so were you."

"Maybe I just looked up and saw it," said Jinx. But no, he knew he had seen the sea of swaying treetops, and lightning rippling and dancing across it.

"I think you're turning into a tree," said Reven. "Forsooth, you see what the trees see. You'll be sprouting leaves next."

Simon and the old man were still arguing.

"If you'd stayed here and married Friddelotta—"

"Don't start that." Simon hacked at the cheese as if he

was decapitating an enemy. "Just don't."

Reven coughed. "I'm sorry, sir, we haven't been introduced. I'm Reven, and do I have the honor of addressing Simon the Wizard's esteemed father?"

"Esteemed? The brat hasn't visited me in fifteen years."

"Twenty. His name is Egon," said Simon.

Jinx was surprised. He'd always assumed that Simon, like Jinx and almost every other Urwalder old enough to tie their own shoes, was an orphan.

Reven bowed and said all the polite things that you probably had to say if you'd been raised at King Rufus's court and didn't know any better. Jinx went back to eating.

"What's it like?" Elfwyn asked him, very quietly.

"What's what like?"

"Being able to"—she dropped her voice even quieter—"talk to the trees like that."

"Strange," said Jinx. "It's started happening when I don't expect it. And I mean it's not always really talking. Sometimes it's just sort of being there."

"Like a tree," said Elfwyn.

"You could've done real well out of Friddelotta," said Egon. "Her father was cooked by a dragon, you know. She inherited nineteen goats."

"Lucky her." Simon turned to the door. "Is the wind letting up a little?"

"No," said Elfwyn.

16

"You could've been a big man in goats by now, is what I'm saying," said Egon. "But instead—all this hocus-pocus nonsense. Wearing purple dresses. Dancing around in the dark with witches."

"I have never—"

"Is that why you never get lost anymore?" Elfwyn asked Jinx.

"Yeah," said Jinx. "But I didn't get lost all *that* much before." Well, okay, maybe he had once last summer, in a situation that had perhaps involved an uncomfortable amount of troll. But nowadays . . . it was something about the root network. He always knew where he was.

"This all changed since you, um, fell off the cliff?" said Elfwyn.

"Yeah. I guess." They were still talking very quietly, though it wasn't really necessary because Simon and Egon had started shouting at each other.

"Come on, all of you," Simon snapped. "We're leaving."

He went to the door and unbarred it. The wind smashed into the room, tearing the door out of his hands. Reven grabbed the old man out of the way as the table and chairs flew across the room and hit the far wall. The flames in the fireplace shot up and out, licking the ceiling beams. Jinx, struggling not to be blown into the wall himself, quickly sucked the fire out of existence with a thought.

"Will you help me get this flippin' door closed!" Simon yelled.

Jinx, Elfwyn, and Reven fought their way across the room, climbing the floor. It took all four of them to wrestle the door back into place and bar it.

"You're a disaster, boy," said Egon. "I've always said that."

"It's true you've always said that," said Simon. "All right. I suppose we're staying the night. Put the fire back, Jinx."

3

Cold Oats Clearing

The next morning the storm was over. When they went outside, the first thing Jinx heard was the forest mourning. And he saw why.

Great trees lay everywhere across the clearing. Some of them had smashed into houses. And farther into the forest, more trees had fallen.

"Was anybody killed?" Reven asked.

"Thousands," said Jinx.

"What?" Reven rippled purple-green alarm at him. "Where? How do you know?"

Jinx blinked and shifted his mind into people-thought. "Thousands of trees. I don't know about people."

"People are what matters," said Reven.

"Right," said Jinx absently. He walked to the edge of the forest. The path they had come up yesterday was obliterated now by fallen trees. And Simon had wanted to stay out in the storm!

The forest murmured about the storm—how it had come shrieking down from the Boreal Wastes, cutting a slash of death, and finally howled its way out of the Urwald to the south.

"Come and help, Jinx," said Elfwyn. "This woman has a tree on her house."

"I don't know what *you* can do about it." The woman had a thin, moany voice. "It's a huge tree, and you're just a little bit of a boy."

Jinx bit back an angry retort. After all, the woman did have a tree on her house, and that would upset anybody. It had smashed through the thatched roof and broken part of one thick, timbered wall.

Jinx backed up to the very edge of the forest. He concentrated hard, and drew on the Urwald's lifeforce.

There was a creak as the tree came loose from the house and rose slowly into the air. It was heavier than the pine he'd lifted before. He drew on more power. Now the tree floated easily. Jinx went over and took hold of it—his fingers sank into the rotten wood—and swung it free of the house. He let go and cut the levitation spell. The tree thumped to the ground.

The woman looked at him with a mouth like an O.

"Now put the house back together," she said. Instead of thank you.

"I can't," said Jinx. "Sorry. Ask Simon."

Simon was standing on a rooftop, summoning the pieces of a broken chimney.

A teenage girl came running up. "Friddelotta, how did you get the tree off your house?"

"The wizard boy did it," said the moany woman. "But he won't fix the house."

The girl looked at Jinx with nervous respect. "Will he take the trees off our house?"

"You could ask him," said Jinx, annoyed.

"My name is Hilda, sir. Would you please to come and take the trees off my mother's house?"

Jinx would have thought Hilda was making fun of him if he hadn't been able to see the shape of her thoughts. She was perfectly serious, calling him sir. Weird.

"Sure," he said.

Jinx spent the next several hours levitating trees and pieces of broken building. He tried not to let Simon see him doing it. Simon didn't know how much power Jinx had, and Jinx didn't want him to find out.

Simon was doing all sorts of magic that Jinx had never learned, sticking broken walls back together, summoning far-flung thatch and bits of smashed crockery that stuck themselves back together as they flew.

"No doing anything about the goats or chickens," said Elfwyn, coming up beside Jinx. "They're probably miles away by now."

"If they're alive," said Reven. He had his trusty ax and was getting ready to chop up one of the fallen trees.

"Wait!" a woman cried. "Leave that for the wood-cutters."

"I don't mind doing it," said Reven.

"It's safer if the woodcutters do it."

"It's all right," said Jinx. "The trees that are in the clearing, the Urwald says it can't eat anyway."

Simon grabbed Jinx and pulled him aside. "Jinx, don't be weird."

"The forest said—"

"Yes, I'm sure it did." Simon hustled him along the edge of the clearing. "But you're already strange enough. These people are going to talk about you. Let's not make it worse, eh?"

"But—"

"Now. You want to explain to me what you're doing?"

"Helping," said Jinx. "The same as you."

"Uh-huh. Levitating enormous trees off of houses. Where'd you learn to do that?"

"You taught me to levitate stuff," said Jinx. "Remember?"

"Oh yes, I remember. I remember you had great difficulty levitating a pebble, and even more difficulty levitating a cup, and—"

"I got better at it," said Jinx.

"Clearly."

Jinx hoped that was going to be the end of the discussion, but then it took an unexpected turn.

"When you were in the Bonemaster's castle—did he give you anything?"

"Of course not," said Jinx. Except for the occasional whack on the head.

"Did you take anything from him?"

"Yeah, your life, in a bottle, remember?"

The dark cloud around Simon's head grew lightning streaks of fury. Even though Jinx knew that they were aimed at the Bonemaster and not at him, they still made him nervous.

"Look at me," said Simon.

Jinx did, and immediately found he couldn't look away. "Don't do magic on me!" He pulled his eyes away from Simon's with an effort.

"Did the Bonemaster do anything to you? Other than kill you?" said Simon.

"He didn't really kill me," said Jinx. "I fell."

"Look at me and say he didn't do anything to you."

Jinx glared into Simon's oddly yellow eyes. "The

Bonemaster didn't do anything to me. Okay?"

Simon nodded. There was purplish perplexity around him, as if he hadn't seen something he expected to see, and didn't understand what he *had* seen. "Good. Keep the talking-to-trees thing a secret."

Oh, Jinx had plenty of secrets. His whole head was full of secrets. There was the fact that he'd regained his ability to see people's thoughts. That was a secret from everyone except Elfwyn, which made it a very precarious secret. Then there was the fact that he could draw on the Urwald's power—that was a secret from Simon. And Elfwyn's curse, which he had to keep secret out of common decency. But he couldn't see why *this* had to be secret.

"It's useful to be able to talk to the trees," he said. "People need to know what trees think. And it got us out of the storm."

"Yes, into a far worse fate," said Simon.

"Is that really your father?"

"Obviously."

"But *you're* not really *my* father."

"Of course not. What, you want blood relatives? They're such a great joy. You want *my* relatives?"

"You have more?"

"Half the people in Cold Oats Clearing." Simon made a waggly-fingered gesture at the men, women, and children busy thatching holes in roofs and reattaching doors to door-posts. "Uncles and cousins and things. Bunch of idiots."

"You told me not to call clearing people—"

"These ones are idiots. Trust me." Simon scowled. "Do the trees say anything about the Bonemaster?"

"They don't really talk about the Restless much. Um, the Restless are people and trolls and like that."

"Well, supposing you ask them."

"No! Not right now. That would be awful."

Simon puffed green bewilderment, so Jinx explained, "It's like if your whole family had just been killed and I asked you—"

"To stop dancing for joy?"

"You don't mean that," said Jinx. "Anyway the Bone-master's all locked up. You put wards around his castle."

"What do you think I've been doing for the last two weeks, boy?"

"You've—we've *all* been walking around from one magician's house to another," said Jinx.

"Correct. And what have I been asking these witches and wizards to do?"

"Help you strengthen the wards around Bonesocket."

"And why, in your wildest imaginings, do you suppose I might be doing that?"

"I guess because the wards aren't strong enough?"

"And what have they all been saying to me?"

Lots of stuff. Much of it so rude that Jinx felt repeating it to Simon would be hazardous. "That they don't want to," Jinx summarized. "And that the Bonemaster isn't their problem. Do you think he could escape from the wards?"

"Of course he can escape the wards. He's a magician. All he needs is power."

"But we destroyed his power," said Jinx.

"The Bonemaster may have other ways of getting power."

Something about the words *Bonemaster* and *power* tugged at Jinx's memory, but he didn't know why. He had a mental image of elves standing in the woods. Some dream he'd forgotten, maybe.

"Like what?" said Jinx.

"I don't know." Simon pressed his lips together and stared out at the clearing, his thoughts a dark gray cloud of worry. "I need to go to Bonesocket and see what he's doing."

"Now?"

"Now struck me as an excellent time," said Simon. "Though last week would probably have been better. Right. We'll say good-bye to your friend Reven-the-king, collect the girl, and head back."

"I promised the trees that I would take Reven out of the Urwald."

"Well, I certainly wouldn't expect you to put my wishes ahead of the trees'."

"They're petrified of him. They call him the Terror."

Simon gave Jinx an odd look. "The trees do?"

"Yeah."

"That ridiculous boy is a greater danger than the Bonemaster?"

"I guess he is if you're a tree," said Jinx.

"As it happens, I'm not. Did the trees say why?"

"They just have this really bad feeling about him. Something he might do, I guess."

"I see," said Simon. "The trees have a feeling. Very well. You can escort king-boy as far as the edge of the Urwald. Then you're to turn around and come back immediately. No sightseeing along the way. I need you home to help me deal with the Bonemaster."

"You mean you're letting me go?" Jinx had expected more of a struggle.

"Unless I change my mind." Simon reached in his pocket. "Here. You'd better take this with you."

Jinx saw the flash of gold in Simon's hand and was annoyed. "I've been out on my own before. I can take care of myself."

"Yes, I was very impressed last time. We practically had to carry you home in a bucket. Take it, or you're not going anywhere."

Jinx took the gold bird. It was a piece of Samaran money, called an aviot, and Jinx knew that Simon had bespelled it so that he could keep an eye on Jinx . . . at least when Simon was home and remembered to look in the Farseeing Window. Angrily, Jinx stuck the bird in his pocket.

"And drop the attitude. I suppose you're at a difficult age."

Jinx thought that was a bit much coming from Simon, who had been *born* at a difficult age. He started to say so, but then he saw warm blue clouds of worry around Simon's head. The wizard was very close to not letting Jinx go at all. And the trees wouldn't like that. So Jinx kept his mouth shut.

Reven bowed, of course, taking his leave of Simon. "Farewell, good wizard. Thank you for your hospitality. I'm sorry not to have met your lady wife."

There was a little ripple of red pain from Simon at that. Sophie had gone through the magic door into her world, Samara, months ago, and hadn't returned. Jinx wished she would. He was very fond of Sophie.

Simon grunted. "Well, if you get into trouble, come back. The door knows your name." He turned to Elfwyn. "Yours too. But you'll be coming back anyway."

"I'm going to Keyland with Reven," said Elfwyn.

"I thought you wanted to find a cure for your curse," said Simon.

"It's more important to help Reven, though," said Elfwyn.

"Really?" said Simon. "I'd be inclined to think it was more important to get rid of the curse. However—"

"Thank you, good wizard," Reven said. "We must be going."

Jinx was surprised. People didn't usually interrupt wizards.

"Hmph," said Simon. "Jinx, try not to do anything stupid. Come back at once. And don't lose that thing."

He meant the aviot, of course. Jinx clenched his hand around it, in his pocket. The gold wings dug into his fingers and he resented it.

He would get rid of it at the first opportunity.

❧ ❧ ❧

"It's very good of you to do this for me, my lady," said Reven as they approached Butterwood Clearing.

"Oh, that's all right," said Elfwyn, thinking pink fluffy thoughts at him. "I just think my mother probably knows your real name, because she's the one who told me the story, about how your father killed your mother and your uncle killed your father and—oh, I'm sorry."

"No, no, it's nothing," Reven assured her cheerfully.

"No, I shouldn't have said that. It must be awful for you to talk about it."

"He *can't* talk about it," said Jinx. "That's the whole point."

Jinx could see that mention of these horrible events didn't really upset Reven at all.

"Oh, there's the old walnut tree," said Elfwyn. "I don't think the storm was so bad here, was it? We're getting close now." Gray clouds of worry. "I hope they don't mind me coming home."

"How could they not be delighted, my lady?"

"Very easily, in my experience," said Elfwyn.

4

What Berga Knew

Butterwood Clearing was big—nearly a mile wide, Jinx guessed. There were broad fields, pastures full of cows, and even orchards. Most of the clearings Jinx had seen were drab, dingy, and squalid, peopled with ragged folks balanced on the thin edge of starvation.

No wonder barbarians had invaded Butterwood Clearing, Jinx thought. Butterwood Clearing was, well . . . rich.

Something odd was happening.

People saw them. Particularly, they saw Elfwyn, in her red cape and hood. They came forward as if to greet her. But they stopped, and stood there, and didn't speak.

Jinx could see their feelings, and they weren't warm

ones. These people didn't like Elfwyn. Some of them hated her.

"Maybe we should leave," he muttered.

"Why?" said Elfwyn. "We came to see my mother."

"Because these people . . . aren't friendly," said Jinx.

"All Urwald folk are a bit shy," said Reven. "I'm sure they're kind enough at heart." He spoke louder. "Greetings, good people!"

The Butterwooders muttered. Red clouds of hostility formed. Jinx quickly reviewed the spells he knew, all four of them.

"What's all this?" A small man pushed his way through the crowd. People made way for him quickly.

"Hello, Helgur." Elfwyn's smile didn't go with her feelings, which Jinx could see were more of the say-nothing-and-try-to-hide-your-feet-behind-each-other variety.

"Who're you?" said Helgur.

"Elfwyn. Berga's daughter. We've met, remember?"

"Tell her to go away," said a man.

The Butterwood Clearing people muttered agreement.

"No secret is safe around her."

"She ferrets 'em out and tells them to everyone."

Helgur frowned at Elfwyn. "You have a curse on you. I've heard people talking."

"It's not her fault," said Jinx.

"This is my mother's husband, Helgur," said Elfwyn,

as if this was all perfectly normal. "Helgur, these are my friends Jinx and Reven."

Reven did a sort of bow, which involved shifting his shoulder ever so slightly to show that he was carrying an ax.

"Charmed," said Helgur. "My wife is in a delicate condition. She doesn't need any curses. And the feelings of the people in my clearing—"

"It's the lady Elfwyn's clearing, good sir," said Reven. "As I understand it, you are but an invader."

"That's the way we do things in the Urwald," said Helgur.

"I have a right to see my mother!" said Elfwyn.

"Please summon the lady's mother, good sir," said Reven. It came out like a command.

"Oh, here's Mother now," said Elfwyn, with a purple ripple of anxiety.

Jinx had never seen anybody in a less delicate condition in his life. The woman swung through the crowd like an ax. There was something vaguely Elfwyn-like about her grim, green determination, but she was all bunched-up and ready-to-spring where Elfwyn was sort of willowy and quick.

"What's this all about?" Berga demanded.

"Hello, Mother," said Elfwyn.

"I thought I sent you to your grandmother's."

Elfwyn tilted her chin defiantly. "Grandma's the one

who put the curse on me. You told me it was fairies!"

"Did she tell you that?"

"No, I figured it out for myself," said Elfwyn.

"And you believe what you figured out for yourself? Why? Who are these boys?"

"Yes. Because a wizard agreed with me. Reven and Jinx," said Elfwyn. "Friends of mine."

"What wizard?"

"Simon Magus," said Elfwyn.

"What were you doing associating with an awful wizard like that?"

"He helped us after we escaped from the Bonemaster. Mother, stop—"

"What were you doing with the Bonemaster?"

"He captured us," said Elfwyn. "Would you please stop—"

"And what exactly are you doing with these boys?"

"Traveling to the edge of the Urwald."

"What! The edge of the Urwald! And with boys! Why boys?"

"I told you, because they're my friends!"

"And why have you come back here?" said Berga.

"Because I wanted to ask you to tell us the story about the king of Keyland who was killed by his brother."

Reven winced. Jinx could see the next question coming, too.

"Why?"

"If I may answer that, my good lady—" Reven broke in.

But there was no stopping Elfwyn's curse. "Because Reven is the real king of Keyland." She turned to Reven. "I can't help it! She always does this. She uses my curse—she's done it ever since I was little."

"I quite understand," said Reven.

And Jinx saw that Reven wasn't annoyed—but he was calculating, in little rows of green and blue squares.

"Perhaps we should have this discussion back at the house," said Helgur, looking at the crowd.

"It's not your discussion," Berga snapped. "It's my discussion." She frowned. "All right, come up to the house, then."

She pushed through the crowd, trailing Elfwyn behind her. Reven and Jinx followed, and Helgur strode alongside.

They sat down at the kitchen table.

"Shouldn't we offer them something to eat?" said Helgur. When Berga frowned, he added, "It's an old barbarian custom."

Berga hmphed, and thumped a loaf of bread and a wedge of cheese down on the table. Nobody took any.

"Is he really the king of Keyland?" Berga demanded.

"The rightful king," said Elfwyn.

"Actually we don't know," said Jinx.

"We think he is," said Elfwyn.

"We had hoped you might tell us the tale of what happened in Keyland," said Reven, giving Berga his most charming smile.

"And then we'll go away," Elfwyn offered.

That seemed to clinch it.

"Very well," Berga huffed. "Once upon a time—"

"It wasn't that long ago, really, was it?" said Elfwyn.

"It's a story," said Berga. "Now, are you going to let me tell it like a story, or shall I not?"

"I'm going to let you tell it like a story," said Elfwyn.

"Very well. Once upon a time, in a kingdom far away, there lived a wicked king, a good queen, and their infant son. The wicked king fell in love with a lady as beautiful as the sky, and so he made sure that his wife pricked her finger on a poisoned needle. After she died, he married the beautiful lady. And they lived happily ever after for a few months.

"Then the king's wicked brother decided that *he* wanted to be king. So he summoned an evil fairy, and the evil fairy smothered the king in his sleep. Then he led the beautiful stepmother and the little prince into the forest, until they became lost, and they sat down under a tree together and died. And little birds came and covered the corpses with beautiful flowers. The end.

"Satisfied?"

"No," said Elfwyn. "What were their names?"

"Whose names?"

"Everybody's," said Elfwyn. "Nobody in your story has a name."

"They don't need names," said Berga. "When you're a king or a prince, everyone knows who you are."

"And there's no such thing as fairies," said Elfwyn. "So a fairy couldn't have killed the king."

"It's only a story."

"But it really happened, didn't it?" said Reven. "Whence came the tale, my lady?"

"I heard it from a traveler," said Berga.

"You mean a Wanderer?" said Jinx.

"No, if I had meant a Wanderer, I would have said a Wanderer. This was a traveler. A witch who had been living in the kingdom at the time."

"In Keyland, you mean?" said Reven.

"Yes, in Keyland. The witch may have told me more particulars, but they didn't fit properly into a story, and I don't remember them now."

"Do you at least remember the witch's name?" said Jinx, getting frustrated.

"Yes, of course. It was Witch Seymour."

"And might you know how to find this witch, good lady?" asked Reven.

"As a matter of fact, I do. I'll draw you a map."

She went to a cupboard by the wall and brought paper

and ink. Elfwyn had told Jinx that everyone in Butterwood Clearing could read and write, but he was surprised to see Elfwyn's mother just doing it, and having paper around the house and everything.

He wondered what magic made Butterwood Clearing so rich, and whether it was a spell that could ever be gotten to work on the other clearings.

⁓ ⁓ ⁓

Witch Seymour's house was two days' journey to the south. The trees were not at all happy to find Jinx guiding the Terror that way. The quickest way out of the Urwald lay to the east.

They camped that night on the path. Jinx started a fire, and Reven and Elfwyn went to gather more firewood. Jinx looked around for a place to hide the aviot Simon had given him. He didn't need Simon spying on him.

"We shouldn't have stopped here. We're too close to that pool," said Elfwyn.

There, where that thick oak branch joined with the trunk. That would be a safe place. Jinx took the tiny gold bird out of his pocket.

"What's wrong with that?" said Reven. "It's convenient for hauling water. And maybe bathing."

Jinx turned around, the aviot still in his hand. "No bathing!"

Reven looked amused. "Why not? I admit it's a little chilly, but—"

"There are probably nixies in the water," said Elfwyn.

"Really?" Reven dropped the firewood he was carrying. "I've never seen nixies."

"Stop!" Jinx stuck the aviot back in his pocket and hurried after Reven. "They're dangerous. My stepfather was killed by nixies! Nixies dragged him down deep into the water and nobody ever saw him again."

"I thought your stepfather was a troll. You cut his arm off, remember?"

As if he could forget. "The stepfather before that. George."

"Really?" Reven frowned. "Well, I won't get in the water. I'll just look."

Jinx sighed. Reven had a habit of charging in where Urwalders feared to tread.

The pool was very deep—just the kind nixies liked. It was probably connected by a tunnel to their underground caverns.

Reven crouched at the edge. "I don't think there even are any—oh wait, is that them? Way down in the depths?"

There were half a dozen of them, swimming around in hypnotic swooping patterns, weaving over and under each other.

"Yes," said Elfwyn. "Now you've seen them, Reven. Come away."

"In a minute, my lady," said Reven.

It happened very quickly.

A nixie shot to the surface, and popped her head up out of the water. She looked part cat, part frog, and part human. She smiled at Reven. He smiled back. She put her hands on his shoulders, as if just resting for a moment. Then she tugged, and Reven plunged headfirst into the water.

Ripples spread outward. Jinx could see Reven struggling, already impossibly far away, with all of the nixies clinging to him.

There was another splash.

"Stop!" Jinx yelled, too late. Elfwyn was swimming furiously down toward Reven and the nixies.

Jinx dithered, frantic. He could not swim. The nixies had Elfwyn now, were dragging her deeper.

He tried a levitation spell. It was hopeless. He couldn't levitate living people. "You can't if you think you can't," Simon always said.

Jinx took a deep breath and drew on the Urwald's life-force, feeling the power rise up through his feet from the roots of the trees all around him. He reached downward with the levitation spell, probing deep into the pool, and deeper still—Elfwyn and Reven were getting farther and farther away. He fought the huge weight of the water. The lifeforce of the nixies pulled against him. But the Urwald was stronger than that.

The whole squalling ball of nixies, Elfwyn, and Reven

inched slowly upward. It rose through the water, and then out of the pool, and hovered three feet above the surface, water cascading off the struggling nixies and people.

But the nixies weren't letting go. Jinx raised them higher still. The water was gone now and the nixies needed that to breathe. One of them let go of Reven's arm and fell into the pool. Then another fell. And another. Elfwyn elbowed one of them in the face, but it still clung to her, trying to grab her around the neck. Two others were strangling Reven, who had turned purple and was not breathing.

Jinx couldn't reach them. Simon would've been able to bring them all sideways to land; Jinx didn't know how.

A nixie had its hands around Elfwyn's throat now.

Jinx ran, leapt, and caught hold of a webbed foot. His momentum carried them all to the side. He hung down and groped with his foot for the edge of the pool. He hooked his foot around a helpful tree root and felt himself being drawn to the shore. Could the trees do that? Trees couldn't move.

Jinx, Elfwyn, Reven, and nixies tumbled to the forest floor. Jinx grabbed and hit the nixie strangling Elfwyn. The nixie snarled and let go of Elfwyn so it could claw Jinx. Jinx wrestled with it. It was rubbery and much stronger than it looked. It reached for his throat, and he put up his hands to block its long, treacherous fingers. Both his hands were trapped against his neck. The nixie was dragging and strangling him and he couldn't breathe.

Suddenly the horrible pressure stopped, and Elfwyn was pulling the nixie off of him, kicking it, flinging it in the water. And then Jinx saw glowing green eyes everywhere in the twilight.

"Monsters!" he croaked, just as the werewolves attacked.

He grabbed Elfwyn, but she pulled away from him and hurried to help Reven, who was still battling two nixies. Jinx and Elfwyn dragged Reven free, and the three of them ran.

Jinx and Elfwyn collapsed beside the fire, gasping. The snarl, yap, and squall of werewolves and nixies fighting was still going on a hundred yards away. Reven picked up his ax.

"You d-don't n-need that," said Elfwyn, shivering. Her voice was raspy from being strangled by the nixie.

"Those b-beasts will be after us next, I swan."

"No they won't," said Jinx. He drew on the flame inside him to make the campfire burn higher and hotter.

"T-truce of the Path," said Elfwyn, huddling closer to the fire and shooting Jinx a grateful glance.

Purple and pink uncertainty blopped around Reven's head. He lowered the ax.

"C-come to the fire before you f-freeze," said Elfwyn.

Reven did, but he kept looking over to where the yapping and squalling had now becomes splashes and snarls. "They're only animals. Surely they w-won't obey the Truce?"

"Yeah, they will," said Jinx. "Werewolves are thinking creatures. Unlike some people."

"They're still m-monsters," said Reven. "They would have eaten us, forsooth!"

"Probably," said Jinx. "But now we're on the Path."

"The Urwald is too dangerous for human habitation," Reven said.

"It is not," said Jinx. "If you're not a total idio—"

"You l-levitated us, Jinx," said Elfwyn.

Jinx hadn't really had time to think about this yet.

Magic on anything that had a lifeforce was much harder than magic on mere objects. Jinx remembered all the elaborate preparations Simon had had to go through to do a spell on Jinx himself. And yet Jinx had just levitated two people and six nixies.

Jinx and the Urwald. It had been the Urwald's power, with Jinx telling it how to work. And now he felt exhausted. It was as if the force of the Urwald had passed through him and wrung him out.

And he realized he was even more aware of the Urwald than he had been before.

"Someone's cutting down trees," he said.

"In the dark?" said Reven.

"No," said Jinx. "I mean every day. They cut down more every day. I can feel it."

"Less space for horrible monsters to hide in, then," said Reven.

"The trees are *dying*," said Jinx. "They're being killed."

"Well, it's progress," said Reven. "It has to happen."

"It does not!" Jinx looked over at Elfwyn for help, but she was asleep.

"Get rid of all the trees, and you'll get rid of all these monsters, forsooth." Reven tucked Elfwyn's blanket around her. Then he got out his own blanket and huddled into it. "You're sure about this Truce?"

"Utterly," said Jinx.

He was really annoyed. How could Reven be such a fool? And it wasn't just Jinx's own feeling—it came rumbling through the Urwald, running along the roots, humming through the tree trunks.

The Terror must go, said the trees.

He will, said Jinx. *I'm taking him to the edge.*

Too slowly. Too long. You wander here and there. When will he leave?

Soon, said Jinx. *We have to go talk to this Witch Seymour, and after that, we'll head straight to the edge.*

We made an agreement with you.

Yes, I know, said Jinx. *I take him out, and you don't hurt him.* A sudden thought occurred to him. *Those nixies and werewolves—*

We have no control over the Restless.

Of course they didn't, Jinx thought. The nixies had behaved like nixies, that was all. And the werewolves—well,

it was funny, now that he thought about it. The werewolves had attacked the nixies.

He got up and dragged a branch into the fire. And
noticed glowing eyes watching him from just off the path.

He lay awake the rest of the night. You do, in a situation like that.

5

Witch Seymour

"The map says we turn right here," said Elfwyn.

"Well, there are two rights," said Jinx. "So which one of them are we turning?"

Go to the Edge, said the trees. *The Terror must leave us.*

I'm working on it, said Jinx.

"Can't you ask your trees where she lives?" said Reven.

"They don't know," said Jinx. "Because witches don't live in clearings. The trees don't pay attention to where houses are, just to where trees aren't."

"What if we look for butter churn tracks?" said Reven.

But when they looked, they found the telltale round tracks in the mud on both paths.

"Well, my mother said it's a mile," said Elfwyn. "So we'll try one path for a mile and then we'll try the other."

"I wonder why your mother called her Witch Seymour," said Reven as they started down the path. "Aren't witches usually called Dame?"

"Yes," said Elfwyn. "Perhaps Mother doesn't like her, and that's her way of saying so. There are quite a few people she doesn't like."

They soon reached a little thatched cottage overhung with tall spruce trees, with chickens pecking around the doorstep.

There was no butter churn at the door. That was odd. Jinx thought that the witch might not be home.

They knocked.

At first there was no sound. Then they heard heavy footfalls crossing the floor. The door creaked open. A head stuck out.

"Yes?"

"Er," said Elfwyn. "We're looking for Witch Seymour."

"And you've found Witch Seymour. Who are you?"

"Elfwyn. And, um, these are my friends, Reven and Jinx. Are you *sure* you're Witch Seymour?"

The witch laughed, not very pleasantly. "Why, yes, I am sure. A great deal more sure than you are. But come in."

The door swung wide. The three of them looked at

each other, and then they wiped their feet vigorously on the doormat and went in.

"You're awfully damp," said the witch.

"We, um, fell into a pond last night," said Elfwyn.

"How lucky nixies didn't get you. Come stand by the fire, lest you catch your death."

The fire crackled pleasantly, and there was a small goat curled up on the hearth. It looked up and gave a mild bleat of greeting. Reven bent down to scratch its horn buds, trying to conceal the green-pink cloud of confusion around his head, Jinx thought.

"You're not quite what we were expecting," said Elfwyn.

"I didn't know there were male witches," said Jinx.

Witch Seymour made a *harumph* noise, which mostly came through his nose. "One dislikes the term 'male witch.' It de-emphasizes the essential. I am a witch."

"Er, why?" said Jinx.

"What do you mean, why? One's mother was a witch, and one learned witching from her, and now one is a witch, if it's quite all right with you."

"He meant no offense," said Reven. "But it is, perhaps, a bit unusual, sir, isn't it?"

"A bit," Witch Seymour conceded.

He was a stout man, bald on the top and with a great deal of black hair sticking out the sides of his head and face to make up for it.

"But let's assume you didn't come here to question one about one's career choice," said the witch. "And you're too big to eat, even if one went in for the gingerbread-and-ovens routine, which one doesn't. So to what does one owe the rather dubious honor?"

"My mother said maybe you could answer some questions for us," said Elfwyn. "About Keyland."

"And your mother might be?"

"Berga of Butterwood Clearing."

"Ah, Berga." The witch smirked. "Dear Berga. Then you're the girl with the interesting curse on her, aren't you?"

"Yes," said Elfwyn, embarrassed.

"Word does get around. Oh, and . . . you must be Dame Glammer's granddaughter, then."

Jinx could see that the witch was reluctantly impressed. Jinx had noticed this on their travels. As far as the witches were concerned, Dame Glammer was Somebody. And that meant Elfwyn was somebody, too, although with a small *s*.

"In that case, you'd better have some brew." Witch Seymour busied himself in the cupboards, getting cups and bundles of leaves.

"One had half been expecting you," said the witch, when they were sitting around the table with warm mugs of summer-smelling brew. "One heard rumors. Three strange children traveling with Simon Magus." He pointed to each of them in turn. "Nine-year-old boy, wizard's apprentice, lifts mighty fallen oak trees with one finger. Unexplained lad, not an Urwalder, terribly polite. Red-caped girl, sees deepest secrets of one's soul."

"That's not true," said Elfwyn.

"I'm thirteen," said Jinx. Well, he almost was. He didn't *look* nine, did he?

"I think you'll find rumor has its own truth," said Witch Seymour. "We are who people say we are."

"Who *who* says we are?" Elfwyn demanded.

"Rumor," said Witch Seymour. "Who rumor says. Do you know how fast rumor travels in the Urwald?"

"No," said Elfwyn.

Jinx hadn't thought it traveled at all. "The clearings never talk to each other."

"The clearings! No." Witch Seymour sniffed. "Little islands in the wilderness, the clearings. But the Wanderers do. And the Witchline does. Rumor travels fast. Wheeled on wagons and hopped about on butter churns."

"The Witchline?" said Reven.

"The butter churn brigade. And witches have a few other . . . methods . . . that one doesn't discuss with, pardon, outsiders."

"But you don't have a butter churn," said Elfwyn.

"One does not churn. One's center of gravity is too high." *If it's any of your business,* his expression added. "One hears things, however. The Witchline has been humming for weeks about that alarming Simon Magus, hither-and-yonning with a bunch of strange children, bothering everybody about the Bonemaster."

"It's not *bothering* people," said Jinx. "The magicians need to do something about the Bonemaster. Simon put wards to hold him in Bonesocket—"

"Oh, Simon. Spare me Simon." The witch rolled his eyes. "You think anybody's going to put themselves out helping Simon fight the Bonemaster? So that Simon can set up as Bonemaster in his place?"

"Simon doesn't want to do that!" said Jinx. "The Bonemaster killed a whole lot of people, in case you didn't know."

"I did know." The witch was frowning, but the clouds around his head said Jinx was amusing him. "Killed a lot of people with the help of his apprentice. And do you know who his apprentice was?"

Oh. That.

"Who?" said Elfwyn.

"Simon," said the witch, with grim satisfaction.

"Really?" said Reven.

"I don't think he *helped* him," said Jinx. "He was just—" He stopped. All he really knew was that there was a wall inside Simon's thoughts, beyond which Jinx couldn't read, and that Simon's time with the Bonemaster was behind the wall. "There," he finished lamely.

"Oh, yes, he was just . . . there," said Witch Seymour. "And you know the funny thing? One didn't hear very much about the Bonemaster before Simon was *there*. One knew who he was, of course, but he was just a wizard among other wizards, wanting power like they all do, but not especially having any. And then suddenly the Bonemaster was the biggest, most powerful, most dangerous wizard in the Urwald. And as far as one knows, the only difference was, he had got himself an apprentice named Simon."

Jinx could see the surprise and dismay floating around Elfwyn's and Reven's heads. They didn't know Simon like Jinx did. Simon wasn't, Simon wouldn't—

"Simon isn't like the Bonemaster," said Jinx. "He doesn't go around killing people for power."

"Perhaps we know different Simons," said the witch. "I find people behave quite differently toward different people, don't you? You're his apprentice, I take it. Poor you."

"*Not* poor me," said Jinx. "Simon took me in when I didn't have anywhere to go. So, lucky me."

"Oh? One now learns, at any rate, that Simon is kind to children. It shows there's some good in the worst of us. Now let's hear from the young man with the foreign accent," said the witch, nodding at Reven. "Bragwood?"

"I grew up in King Rufus's court in Bragwood, good, er, witch," said Reven. "But I'm headed . . ." He stopped.

"To Keyland?" said the witch. He turned to Elfwyn. "Now I shall be brutally unfair. Why Keyland?"

"Because Reven is the king of Keyland," said Elfwyn.

"Ha." Witch Seymour looked down at the goat, which was nibbling on the cuff of his trousers. "Didn't one say when one got up this morning, Whitlock, that today was going to be an interesting day?" He turned back to Elfwyn. "Keyland already has a king, you know."

"Yes," said Elfwyn. "We were hoping you could tell us how he came to be king."

"Ah. Now the situation becomes clearer, Whitlock, eh?" The witch rubbed the goat's head with the back of a finger. "But first one wants to know what you already know. Ah, I won't ask you, dear." He held up a hand to stop her. "Let's hear it from the King of Nowhere, shall we?"

"Certainly, sir," said Reven. "There's not much that I can tell you. I was born in—" he stopped. "And then I—" he stopped again. "Bragwood. With my stepmother. And I was raised there."

As Reven spoke, Jinx watched the orange and red lines of his curse weave and bounce around him, interrupting his speech.

"And by means of fairy tales and other devices, she managed to make it known to me that I was—" said Reven. A cloud of sorrow, shot through with anger. "And then King Rufus killed her."

By rolling her downhill in a barrel stuck about with nails, Jinx remembered. He winced.

"Hm. That is, indeed, not much. Curse, eh?" said the witch.

Reven reached down and petted the goat. He couldn't even say that it was a curse.

"Any stepmother might tell stories about lost kings," said the witch. "It doesn't mean you are one."

"It was more than stories," said Reven.

"Was the curse on her too?"

Reven couldn't answer that either.

"If that curse wasn't put on you by Dame Morwen herself, I miss my guess," said Witch Seymour. "Ah, she was an artist, was Morwen. Well, one can hardly resist the chance to ingratiate oneself to a possible king, can one, Whitlock? I shall tell you what I know."

He took a sip of brew, wiped his mustache with the back of his hand, stuck his hands into his vest pockets, leaned back in his chair, and began.

"Fifteen years ago, in Keria, the capital of Keyland, a boy was born to King Kyle and his young bride, Queen Kalinda. We shall say, for the sake of argument"—he nodded at Reven—"you. All very proper, an heir to the throne, as required. Then—"

"What was the boy's name?" said Elfwyn.

"Raymond," said Witch Seymour, frowning at the interruption. "Prince Raymond. I suppose they ran out of *K*s. About six months later, the queen died. And this was unusual. Had she died sooner, it might have been child-bed fever. But why wait six months, and then die? People thought it very improper. Poison was spoken of. Not, of course, publicly. That could have led to beheadings and dancing in red-hot shoes and all that sort of thing."

"For the poisoners?" said Jinx. "Did they know who they were?"

"No, for the people who spoke of it, of course. Key-land is that kind of place. Naturally one assumed the king had done it. He promptly married one of Queen Kalinda's attendants, a Lady Esmeralda, who was, you'll forgive me, much better-looking than your alleged mother, young man."

"You saw my mother?" said Reven.

"Once or twice, once or twice. Well, there was muttering, naturally, why wouldn't there be, especially among the family of the late queen. So when the king's brother, Duke Bluetooth of Bayland—"

"Was he really named Bluetooth?" Jinx interrupted.

"Yes," said the witch, with a purple puff of annoyance. "Do you want to hear this or not?"

"Sorry," said Jinx.

"Where was I?"

"The Duke of Bayland," Elfwyn said.

"Yes. Duke Bluetooth. Yes, well, he seized the throne. Killed his brother. Did it himself, very properly, no assassins or poison or anything like that. He ran him through very nicely with a sword, as brothers ought, and he meant to do the same for the queen and the baby prince, only somehow or other in the confusion—" The witch stopped, took a sip of brew, and looked around at all of them.

"Yes?" said Elfwyn.

"What happened?" said Reven.

Jinx didn't say anything, because he was still annoyed at being shushed.

Witch Seymour smacked his lips over the brew. "That just happens to be the little bit that nobody knows. The lovely young queen grabbed up her baby stepson and fled from her brother-in-law. Some say he caught up with them and slew them both, and wiped his bloody sword on his sky-blue velvet pantaloons. I myself do not believe that. If they had been crimson, he might have, but sky-blue? Ridiculous. Others say she fled into the forest—that's the Urwald to us—and was immediately devoured by werewolves. Or possibly vampires, I forget. Myself, I have always wondered if she might have known her way around the Urwald better than that. She had the look, to me, of an Urwald girl."

"Lots of Urwald girls get devoured by werewolves," said Jinx.

"Your friend doesn't seem to think that's what happened."

"No," said Reven. "That's not what happened." He took a deep breath. The lines of his curse were red, and he had to struggle to say anything. "You can cross the Urwald if you stick to the path."

"Oh yes. Trust an Urwald girl for that," said the witch. "So, off you go to Keyland. Taking Simon's apprentice with you because Simon's decided to dabble in foreign affairs. And then what do you do? Do you go to the palace and explain to King Bluetooth that you're back now and he'll have to step aside? A problem: you can't explain anything, because of your curse. Another problem: he's still got that sword. What's the plan, eh?"

It was a good point.

"I'm going with him," said Elfwyn. "To explain to people who he is."

"And which people did you intend to explain to?" said Witch Seymour. "Because one can't recommend explaining to King Bluetooth. Not from what one's seen of him."

"We hadn't really planned," said Elfwyn.

"You don't say."

"What would you advise, sir?" said Reven.

"Speaking to Dame Franca. If she's still alive."

"Who's Dame Franca?"

"Well, if you *are* Prince Raymond, she was your nurse-maid."

"Does she live in Keyland?" said Elfwyn.

"She did, the last one heard. She can probably tell you if our boy is really Prince Raymond. Don't go calling her 'Dame' Franca, mind. Call her 'Missus.' No point in getting her killed."

"I'm afraid I don't follow," said Reven.

"Beheaded. Invited to foxtrot in red-hot iron footwear. Parboiled. Et cetera."

"For being called Dame?"

"For being a witch. Why do you think one left Keyland?"

"Oh," said Reven.

"Talk to her, but be careful. We don't necessarily know whose side she's on, do we, Whitlock? If she's still alive, and still in Keyland, chances are she's on King Bluetooth's side, beheadings notwithstanding, and will turn you over to him for his soup of the day."

"I see."

"Don't do anything without thinking about it three times first, young man. That's the best advice I can give you. No good waiting till after you're chained to a gridiron, roasting over a slow fire, and *then* wondering if you might have been better off making a plan."

"Yes," said Reven. "I see. Thank you."

They stayed the night at Witch Seymour's house. Jinx didn't entirely like the witch—especially not when he said such unpleasant things about Simon—but the man was an almost bottomless well of information, about Keyland and everything else. They talked long into the night—Jinx, Reven, Elfwyn, the witch, and the goat. Actually the goat didn't speak, but Witch Seymour frequently asked its opinion anyway.

Jinx ended up telling the witch all about how he had come to live at Simon's house.

"Father, killed by werewolves. Mother, taken by elves," Witch Seymour summarized. "Ever think of going to Elfland yourself?"

"No," said Jinx. "You can't go to Elfland."

"Of course you can. There are numerous stories about it, aren't there, Whitlock? Getting there's quite simple. The difficulty seems to arise merely in the matter of coming back. Elves aren't alive, you know, and they're not exactly dead either, and it makes things complicated, transition-wise. But you get to Elfland through the Glass Mountains, if the trolls let you, and, well, then you take it from there."

"No I don't," said Jinx. "In all the stories, if people do manage to get out again, they come back and find a hundred years have passed in the Urwald."

"There are minor inconveniences, yes."

Jinx had no plans to go to Elfland. But he wondered,

once again, why there was something he couldn't quite remember about elves, something snagging the edge of his thoughts.

Well, never mind. He had enough to worry about, getting Reven out of the Urwald.

6

The Edgeland

They walked along the path toward Keyland, and the trees talked about the constant hacking and chopping at the edge of the Urwald. Oh, and they wanted Reven out.

"That wasn't true, what Witch Seymour said about Simon, was it?" asked Elfwyn.

"Um, which part?" Jinx was distracted by the trees.

"About him being the Bonemaster's apprentice."

"Kind of," said Jinx.

"And you knew that? Why didn't you tell us?"

"I forgot."

"All that time the Bonemaster was holding us prisoner and threatening to kill us, you *forgot*?"

"I didn't know then," said Jinx. "Anyway it was kind of an accident, Simon being his apprentice. He didn't know he was evil."

"He couldn't tell from all those skulls and bones and things all over the place?" said Reven.

"Well they're not really all over—"

"Simon doesn't have that kind of thing around his house, anyway," said Elfwyn. "And he uses ordinary cups to drink out of, not, you know—" she made a skull shape with her hands.

"There was a skull in his workroom, though," said Reven.

"Oh, that's just Calvin," said Elfwyn.

Jinx was surprised that Elfwyn knew Calvin's name.

The closer they got to the edge of the Urwald, the more Jinx felt the pain and terror of the trees. The cutting was going on relentlessly, from first light to sundown.

"The good Witch Seymour seems to think Simon helped the Bonemaster rise to power," said Reven.

"Well, duh," said Jinx. The treecutting was really quite painful. "Because the Bonemaster was using Simon's life *for* power, remember? That doesn't mean it was okay with Simon."

"You keep twitching," said Elfwyn.

"Well they're chopping u— trees," said Jinx. He'd almost said *us*, which was crazy, because he wasn't a tree.

62

"Perhaps you could try not to think about it," said Reven.

"I can't not think about it! If someone was hacking at you with an ax, do you think you could not think about it?"

"Nobody is—" Reven began.

Jinx grabbed Reven's hand and slapped it against a silver maple growing beside the path. "There! Feel that! Can't you feel what's happening?"

"No," said Reven.

Elfwyn put her hands against the maple trunk.

"Well, *you* should be able to," said Jinx.

She frowned. "I can feel something kind of—cold. Like, it's alive. Only alive being cold instead of warm."

"Really?" Reven put his hand back on the trunk. "I can't feel anything. It just feels like a tree trunk."

Reven was hopeless. Jinx turned to Elfwyn. "You can't hear anything, though?"

"No. Are you sure you—"

"Yes," said Jinx.

"It's not that I don't believe you—"

"Good," said Jinx.

Reven shook his head. "I can't feel anything."

⌣ ⌣ ⌣

The endless mumbling and muttering of the Urwald's voice had an end after all. There was a blank space in the Urwald's mind, an edge.

"Here's the Wanderers' Bridge," said Elfwyn. "Cripes, it's bright up ahead."

Jinx came around a bend in the path and saw the open sky, aglow with golden sunset clouds.

"The Urwald really does end," said Elfwyn. "I mean, I knew it did, but I sort of didn't quite believe it." She ran to the side of the wooden bridge and leaned over the railing. "Look at this!"

Jinx looked down, and immediately wished he hadn't. Water rushed by in a brown torrent eighty feet below. He felt ill.

"Oh, sorry. I forgot about you and heights," said Elfwyn.

Reven walked across the bridge like it was nothing. "The chasm must be why they stopped lumbering here."

Jinx looked across the bridge and saw what Reven meant.

The clearing on the other side went on and on—an enormous field of tree stumps, weathered silver-blue.

"Looks like they went on cutting north and south from here," said Reven.

"South." Jinx gritted his teeth, looked straight ahead, and walked across the exact center of the bridge. He got to the other side and breathed again. "They're cutting twenty miles south of here now."

The stump field extended forever to the north, and forever to the south. To the east, it stopped after a mile or so. Beyond it were fields and farms and, black against the sky, the distant shape of the city.

"You can see the horizon out here," said Reven. "You can breathe." His thoughts were like sunshine bursting through a cloud, or like finding something important that you thought was lost forever.

Elfwyn had come across the bridge too. "Oh, how awful. Who cut down all the trees?"

"Keylanders," said Jinx. "Anyway. Bye, right?"

He needed to go back and help Simon deal with the Bonemaster.

"Are we going to Keria tonight?" said Elfwyn. "It's kind of late, don't you think?"

"I think we won't." Reven turned back to the bridge.

"Hey!" Jinx ran to block the way. "Where do you think you're going?"

"Back into the Urwald," said Reven. "We'll camp there for the night. A person can't just walk into a country and take it over, forsooth. I need to think."

"You can think out here," said Jinx. "Which incidentally is still the Urwald."

Reven looked around at the field of stumps. "You think so, good Jinx? It doesn't look like it."

"It's just a part that's been murdered, that's all," said Jinx.

"It's a kind of Edgeland, isn't it?" said Elfwyn. "Or

anyway, that's what I think."

"It can't be the Urwald, because there are no trees and no monsters," said Reven. He stepped around Jinx and crossed the bridge.

Elfwyn went back across too. Jinx steeled himself, and followed.

"I'll go find some firewood," said Elfwyn.

Jinx grabbed Reven by the arm. "The Urwald wants you out. You can't come back."

Reven smiled an annoying smile. "According to who?"

"According to me."

"You and what army?" said Reven, still smiling.

"Me and the Urwald."

Reven looked up at the towering trees above them, then across the chasm to the field of stumps. He raised an eyebrow.

And Jinx hit him. He hadn't known he was going to do it, but he did, right in Reven's stupid face, which was some satisfaction, even though a second later Jinx was lying flat on the ground with a very sore mouth. He scrambled to his feet, hit Reven again, and got knocked down again. Jinx became very busy getting hit by Reven, and hitting Reven back as many times as possible.

"What are you doing? Stop it!" Elfwyn cried, and the hitting ceased abruptly. "How dare you hit Jinx? He's younger than you, and littler, and—"

"Hey," Jinx interrupted, before this description of him could get any worse. "I hit him first!"

"That's true, my lady," said Reven fairly. "He did."

"Well, don't do it again, either of you," said Elfwyn. "Fighting won't solve anything."

"You don't know that for a fact," said Jinx.

"Hmph," said Elfwyn, and began building a fire.

Jinx had a split lip, and one eye was starting to swell shut. He was glad Elfwyn didn't fuss about this. He hated being fussed over. But he was pretty sure if he'd been Reven, she would've fussed.

Reven looked down with concern. "Sorry about that." He reached out a hand.

"Shut up." Jinx got up, ignoring Reven's hand. "I *did* hit you first."

"Yes, but you let me see you were going to. You shouldn't do that. And you should hit through, not at. Like this." Reven took Jinx's arm and guided it.

Jinx pulled away. "You couldn't have seen." *He* hadn't even know he was going to.

"You were putting your face like this and moving like this," said Reven, demonstrating. "You shouldn't ever do that. Don't let your enemy see that you're going to hit him until you do it, and then hit him so he stays down."

"And until then, just smile and act friendly?" said Jinx.

"Of course," said Reven. "That's being civilized."

"This is the Urwald. We're not civilized."

"You're telling me," said Reven.

"Could you come light this fire, please?" Elfwyn called.

Jinx glanced over and lit it with a thought. Then he looked back at Reven. "We have magic, though."

"Are you two done being better than each other?" said Elfwyn. "Because you could help me get dinner."

"Yeah, in a second." Jinx looked at Reven, and thought about asking him to show him how to do that hitting-through-not-at thing after all. But he decided not to give Reven the satisfaction. Right now, anyway. He'd ask him later.

Darkness drew in, and they all huddled around the fire. The Urwald muttered and murmured. The Listener had promised to take the Terror out of the Urwald. But the Terror was still here.

～～～

Several days had passed, and Reven still had not left the Urwald. Well, he'd *left*—they all had, to explore the countryside—but he kept coming back, every night.

The Urwald was growing uneasy. So was Jinx. He needed to get back home. He was worried about Simon and the Bonemaster.

"You could at least camp out where there aren't any trees," Jinx said. "That Edgeland place."

"We'd be too visible," said Elfwyn.

Walking through the field of stumps upset Jinx. He missed the Urwald's vast green lifeforce. Keyland seemed to him to have far too much open space. The farther they walked the more uncomfortable he felt.

There were villages and farms and things. It was so different from the Urwald that Jinx couldn't help being fascinated. How did people live like this, exposed to the sun and to—well, everything? Each other, even?

The houses were square and timbered, like the houses in Butterwood Clearing. Chickens and goats roamed in the dooryards. Gardens, fields, and orchards went on for miles. There was space for them. Jinx wondered if the extra open space was what made Elfwyn's home clearing rich.

Keyland had interesting new things to eat, too—peach preserves, and blackberry pie.

Reven talked to people. Jinx hung back and noticed how *many* people there were, and how they all seemed to move and speak too quickly.

Reven didn't talk about being king. He couldn't, because of his curse. He was just—very friendly. People gathered around, and Reven let them do most of the talking. Elfwyn and Jinx stayed off to the side—Elfwyn to avoid having to tell the truth unexpectedly, and Jinx because he didn't like the whole business anyway.

But now it was evening, and they were back at their camp, eating gingerbread that they had bought in one of the villages. The Urwald was muttering.

You promised to take the Terror to the Edge, Listener.

We're at the Edge, said Jinx. *He won't leave. What do you want me to do? He's stronger than me.*

Stronger than you? Is he? What sort of strength? What is strength, to the Restless? Strength is power. You have great power, Listener. The Terror has great power also. This was the trees arguing with each other.

You have great power, you mean, said Jinx. *I don't. Why don't you conjure up a wind and blow him out of here?*

A wind is difficult. A wind is seldom possible. A wind must begin somewhere, it must flow from somewhere, it must be guided and strengthened.

"Jinx, can you show me how to light the fire?" said Elfwyn. She and Reven had made a heap of sticks in the fire ring.

Jinx looked at it, and it lit.

"But I want to do it," she said.

Jinx put the fire out. Elfwyn stared at the wood hard, then scowled at it. She grunted. Jinx laughed. She glared at him.

"You kind of have to take fire from somewhere first. Here." He lit the wood. "Now you have to suck it into you. Not really suck it," he added quickly. "But with your mind, kind of."

Elfwyn frowned at the fire. The flames went out.

"Mayhap the wood was a little damp," said Reven.

"It wasn't," said Jinx. "Now you have it inside you. Put it back, but not all of it."

She frowned at the charred wood, and flames leapt from it.

Jinx couldn't help feeling jealous. It had taken him ages to learn to start fires. But anyway, he said, "You're kind of good at magic."

Elfwyn beamed.

Reven looked at Elfwyn in surprise, and Jinx saw the calculating squares change for a moment to bright happiness at Elfwyn's smile.

"You notice we haven't seen a single monster since we've been here?" said Elfwyn. "I think they don't like to come this close to the edge. Monsters like the deep Urwald."

"They need the trees," said Jinx.

"Yes," said Reven. "*Monsters* need trees."

"Look," said Elfwyn. "Who's that on the bridge?"

7

The Fireside and the Palace

Jinx wasn't sure anyone was there at all until he moved closer and saw pink threads of fear in the darkness, pushed aside by green waves of curiosity.

"Who's there?" he said.

"'Tis us." It was a woman's voice. "Humble Keylanders." A cluster of people stood on the bridge.

"Come over, good folk," said Reven.

"Are you sure it's safe?" she said.

"Of course it's not safe," said Jinx. "It's the Urwald."

Reven went over to greet them. He bowed over the woman's hand. "Welcome."

"You can't welcome people to the Urwald," Jinx told

him. "It's not your—"

"Welcome to our fireside," said Reven.

He made a wide, inviting gesture, and the knot of people came trooping off the bridge and gathered around the fire.

"We just came to see if it was true." The woman looked up at Reven.

"If what was true?" said Elfwyn.

"Are you really the king?" a teenage boy asked Reven.

A shimmer of nervousness appeared around Elfwyn.

"There've always been rumors about the lost prince," the woman said. "But now folks are saying he's back."

"Are you him?" the boy demanded of Reven. "Are you the king?"

"The king is the king," said Reven, red lines glowing as he got close to the edge of his curse.

"Who are you, then?" said the woman.

"Reven, from Bragwood."

The people smiled at each other and nodded, and Jinx saw a warm glow of excitement pass through the crowd. Elfwyn pulled up her red hood—hiding, he thought. It was as if she both did and didn't want people to ask her who Reven was.

"Why are you in the Urwald, er, sir?" a boy asked.

"I traveled through it from Bragwood," said Reven, smiling.

"The Urwald is dangerous," said the boy.

"Yup," said Jinx, eager to encourage that kind of think-ing. He wanted all these strangers out.

"It's full of dreadful magicians and terrible beasts!"

"Exactly," said Jinx.

"And talking trees!" a girl added. Jinx was startled, and wondered where on earth she'd gotten that from.

"What are you going to do now, er, Reven?" said a woman.

"I wish to speak to a good lady named Franca," said Reven.

This seemed to please the people. "It was Mistress Franca what was his nursemaid," someone whispered.

"Do you know where I might find her?" Reven asked.

Nervousness. Purple little ripples of fear. Shaking of heads.

There was a loud clatter on the bridge, and three horses trotted into the pool of firelight. They were ridden by two elegantly dressed men and a lady. A girl, really—about Reven's age. But the way she was dressed made you think "lady."

Instantly all the Keylanders dropped to their knees and bowed their heads. Reven, Elfwyn, and Jinx were the only ones left standing.

Jinx had never seen real live horses before. He found them altogether too large. He backed up closer to Elfwyn.

"What's this, hey?" One of the men rode his horse

close to the fire, and Jinx was afraid the people on the ground would be trampled. "Little moonlight gathering in the forest, hey? Conspiracies and plots!"

He was dressed in blue velvet, with a sweeping plumed hat. He had a cruel nose.

"Really, Sir Thrip. How can they gather moonlight?" The lady brought her horse up too.

This was way too much horse for Jinx. Horses seemed to be all hoof and snort. He grabbed Elfwyn's arm in case she was scared.

"What lovely horses," Elfwyn said.

"It talks!" said Sir Thrip, looking down at Elfwyn in feigned surprise. "A speaking woodrat!"

Reven stepped in front of Elfwyn. "Do not insult the lady, sir."

"What's this one?" said Sir Thrip. "Not Urwish, eh? What sort of accent is that?"

"Bragwood, I think you'll find," said a lazy, laconic voice—the man on the third horse didn't bother to ride closer. He looked around. "So this is the Urwald, is it? Frightfully tree-y, what?"

"It *is* a forest, Lord Badgertoe," said the lady.

"Too much wood," said Lord Badgertoe. "Ought to just burn it. Always said so. Gets in the way, the Urwald."

"Who're you?" said Sir Thrip, poking a stirruped foot at Reven.

"Reven of Bragwood."

Jinx was interested by the little black flash of worry in Sir Thrip's thoughts.

"And I think you should apologize to the lady for calling her a woodrat," Reven added.

"Nothing but woodrats in the Urwald," said Lord Badgertoe ponderously. "Don't even bow before their betters."

The people on the ground still hadn't looked up.

"Woodrats and monsters," said Lord Badgertoe. "Dragons and trolls and ghouls."

"Yup, we've got all those," said Jinx.

"Werewolves," Lord Badgertoe said. "Werewolves and werebears and were-what?"

"Werechipmunks," said Jinx.

"Oh!" The lady on the horse laughed. "Werechipmunks."

Reven shot Jinx a look. "Werechipmunks are no joke, my lady. They are small and harmless-looking, but surprisingly dangerous."

"It looks to me like the whole business is a joke," said Sir Thrip, smiling nastily. "Some foolish little people will believe any sort of rumor they hear. But when wise men investigate, what do they find? A boy and a couple of woodrats."

"I'm frightfully bored," said Lord Badgertoe.

"Very well," said Sir Thrip. "Let us depart. And anyone with a head on his shoulders—who wants to keep it there—will do the same." He looked down at Reven. "As for you, young what's-your-name, you'll stay in the Urwald if you know what's good for you."

He clucked to his horse, which wheeled around with entirely too many hoofs in the air, and trotted away. Lord Badgertoe's horse followed sedately after.

Without saying anything, the people who had been kneeling on the ground got to their feet and began to shuffle across the bridge.

Only the young lady remained. She looked down from her horse and frowned. "Who are you, really?"

She spoke to Reven. It was as if Jinx and Elfwyn weren't there.

"Reven of Bragwood, my lady." Reven bowed.

"And I am Lady Nilda." She reached down and took Reven's hand (Elfwyn fumed) and examined it. "Such courtly manners—but calluses on your hands. Reven of Bragwood is a name we've heard. I wonder if it's true, what we've heard."

"That depends on what you've heard, forsooth," said Reven.

"And you want to see Mistress Franca." She still hadn't let go of his hand.

"How did you know that?" Jinx demanded. "You weren't here when he said it."

Lady Nilda looked at Jinx as if trying to decide whether

he was worth answering. "I waited on the other side of the bridge and listened."

"Spied, you mean," said Elfwyn.

"Perhaps I can help you meet Lady Franca," Lady Nilda told Reven. "Will you tell *her* who you are, I wonder?"

Reven kissed her hand (which Jinx thought was a bit much) and said nothing.

"Interesting," said the girl. "Come to the palace. Third postern gate, midnight tonight."

She let go of Reven's hand, turned her horse, and trotted away into the darkness.

~ ✿ ~

"It's probably a trap," Jinx said.

But he went along to keep an eye on Elfwyn. He was worried about the way she kept thinking pink fluffy thoughts at Reven.

They followed a wide road toward the city, passing through sleeping villages that all looked as rich as Butterwood Clearing. Here and there were small stands of moonlit trees, but not enough to keep Jinx from feeling exposed and uncertain.

The city smelled of smoke and bad drains. They made their way through winding cobblestone streets, skirted some men singing loudly on a street corner, and came into a wide square that reminded Jinx of the market in Samara. The palace filled one side of the square: arches and towers, merlons and machicolations.

They had to turn down an alley to find the third postern gate, which was actually a small wooden door.

"Shouldn't there be a guard or something?" said Jinx.

"Ssh," said Elfwyn.

Reven tapped at the door.

The door opened.

"Come in," said Lady Nilda. "And keep quiet. I shall take you to Dame Franca."

Reven stepped inside. Elfwyn and Jinx followed.

The lady led them through wide green marble halls. Reven looked around with great interest, and Jinx had an impression Reven was thinking this wouldn't be a bad place to live. Jinx thought it looked cold and uninviting. He thought houses should be mostly kitchen.

At least there were no cats.

Lady Nilda led them into a small chamber lit by a crackling fire.

Dame Franca was a mound of flower-printed skirt and shawl in a chair, very wrinkled and old, but her eyes went snap-snap, taking everything in.

The eyes settled on Reven. "And who might you be, young man?"

"Reven, good dame." He knelt down at her feet and looked up into her face. Jinx could see the orange edges of his curse.

"Hm," said the witch. "Well, that's interesting."

"What's interesting?" said Elfwyn. "Do you recognize him?"

"He looks like a silly young man who wants to do far too much and doesn't have the least idea how to begin."

"But . . . do you know his real name?"

"What do *you* think his name is, girl?"

"Raymond. Prince Raymond."

There was a silence, into which Reven dropped, "Elfwyn can't lie."

Jinx was furious at this betrayal of Elfwyn. "She can too lie, if she wants."

"Indeed not. You know about her curse, good Jinx." Reven turned to Dame Franca. "You can ask her if you like."

Dame Franca narrowed her eyes at him. "So, Elfwyn, this is Prince Raymond?"

"Yes," said Elfwyn.

"And you have a curse on you that you must tell the truth?"

"No," said Elfwyn.

Elfwyn was managing her curse, Jinx thought. The witch hadn't described the curse *exactly* right when she'd asked the question.

"Elfwyn has to tell the truth if she's asked a question," said Reven.

Jinx grabbed Reven by the shoulder, pulling him over backward. "Shut up! You've got no business telling people about her curse!"

"Children, children." Dame Franca smiled in a way that made Jinx's neck itch. "Perhaps we should test him. I'm not certain whether this young man is Raymond."

"Well, I am!" said Elfwyn.

"And why is that?"

"I just am. I'm sure."

"Oh ho, *you're* sure, are you! So it's that kind of truth you tell!"

"What do you mean?" said Reven. "She has to tell the truth."

"Some truth," said Dame Franca. "The same truth as everybody's truth. The truth *she* knows."

Jinx had half noticed this before. If Elfwyn was wrong about something, she'd tell the wrong truth.

"A curse where you really had to tell the truth, whether you knew it or not, now that would be a curse worth having," said the witch.

She summoned Lady Nilda, who'd been standing by the door, and whispered something in her ear. Lady Nilda nodded and swept out of the room.

"Didn't the prince have—I don't know, a birthmark or something?" said Elfwyn. "Or a scar? Or—anything?"

"No," said the witch. "Prince Raymond was a very

ordinary baby. Nothing to mark him off from the rest. Until he got that curse put on him, of course."

"The one that keeps him from saying who he is," said Jinx.

"Now you're giving away Reven's curse," said Elfwyn, turning on him.

"It's not the same," said Jinx. "Your curse can hurt you. People can use it. Reven's using you."

"Reven's curse can hurt him too!" said Elfwyn.

"Not like yours can." How could she be so *stupid* about Reven? "He's going to use you as long as you let him!"

"I'm helping him," said Elfwyn. "That's not the same thing as being used!"

"And I appreciate it, good lady," Reven put in. He smiled at her. Elfwyn glowed.

"He doesn't feel the same way about you that you feel about him," said Jinx.

The silence that followed this remark was ice cold, and Elfwyn's bright-red pool of hurt spread out into it.

"You—" Elfwyn started.

"Really—" said Reven.

"I don't know what you're talking about," said Elfwyn.

"All those pink fluffy thoughts." Jinx dug himself in deeper. "Reven's not thinking pink fluffy thoughts at you. He's—"

Elfwyn turned and ran out of the room. The door slammed shut behind her.

"Was that necessary?" said Reven.

Before Jinx could answer, the door burst open again.

The two men who'd been with Lady Nilda in the forest swept in. Lazy Lord Badgertoe, moving faster than Jinx would have thought possible, grabbed Jinx by the collar and lifted him right off the floor. Jinx flailed and kicked, choking, and then got slammed up against the marble wall. There he was allowed to breathe again, but when he tried to struggle free, Lord Badgertoe kicked him.

Dame Franca got to her feet. "The tall one says he's Prince Raymond, my lord." She smiled tightly. "Why don't you find out?"

"Oh, we'll find out." Lord Badgertoe laughed, a sound like empty barrels falling down stairs. "We always do."

Dame Franca hobbled out of the room, and the door shut behind her.

8

The King of Nowhere

Sir Thrip had wrestled Reven into a corner. "Who are you?" he spat.

"Reven of Bragwood," Reven said. He had one eye swollen shut, and a gash on his forehead.

"I thought you said you were Prince Raymond, hey." Sir Thrip, fingers twitching madly, drew his sword. The sword jumped and jerked in his hand, dancing less than an inch from Reven's throat. "Tell me who you really are."

"Reven."

"Kill the other one," said Sir Thrip.

Something sharp bit into Jinx's neck. He felt blood trickling down into his collar. He reached for the fire inside him, and discovered to his horror that it wasn't there.

"Don't!" said Reven. "I'll tell you who I am."

"You can't," said Jinx, fighting down panic. Why couldn't he do magic? Where was his power?

"I can! I'm—"

Jinx watched Reven struggle to speak. The blood running down Jinx's neck was puddling behind his collarbone. He struggled to stay calm. He knew he could do magic, he knew the fire must be there—

"Yes?" said Sir Thrip.

"I'm—" Reven spluttered.

"Where do you come from?"

"Bragwood."

"The truth. Who is your father? Who is your mother?"

Reven opened his mouth and closed it, like a startled goldfish.

"You'll tell us who you are by the count of five, or your friend dies. One. Two."

There! Jinx's magic was just barely there, a tiny flicker inside him. He tried to set Lord Badgertoe's clothes on fire. Power and concentration. He hardly had any power, so he concentrated as hard as he could. A tiny brown dot appeared on Lord Badgertoe's sleeve, and then widened, painfully slowly.

"I'm—" said Reven again.

"Three."

A thin thread of smoke rose from the brown spot as Reven struggled to speak. The spot became an ashy gray circle. Still no flames.

"Four . . ."

"I'm—" said Reven.

Finally a tongue of flame licked up from Lord Badgertoe's velvet sleeve.

"Five. Five, five, FIVE!" Sir Thrip turned to Lord Badgertoe. "What do you think?"

"It's definitely him," said Lord Badgertoe. "Prince Raymond." The flame crawled from his shirt cuff up to his shoulder.

"Yes, obviously. But do we let him live?"

"That was the whole point in the first place, wasn't it?" said Lord Badgertoe.

"Great Keys, man, you're on fire! Burning like a pretty little candle!"

Lord Badgertoe looked down and yelped. He swatted furiously at his sleeve. Jinx pushed past him and rushed for the door. Then he stopped. There was Reven, still held prisoner, Sir Thrip's sword leaping and wriggling at his throat. Lord Badgertoe tore off his velvet doublet, threw it on the floor, and stamped on it. Jinx had no more magic left to use. Before he could decide what to do, Lord Badgertoe lunged forward and tackled him. Jinx hit the stone floor hard, and for a moment everything went black.

". . . red-hot iron shoes," he heard when he came around again. It was Lord Badgertoe talking.

"No." Reven's voice. "There will be no red-hot iron shoes."

"But he's obviously some sort of magician."

"Nonsense," said Reven. "He's my friend."

Jinx scrambled to his feet. But Sir Thrip and Lord Badgertoe barely glanced at him. They had lowered their swords and were talking to Reven, who was making no effort to get away.

"As you are a friend to us," said Lord Badgertoe.

Reven fixed him with a look that positively dripped disdain. "Indeed?"

"A safety net," said Sir Thrip. "You were our escape hatch. If King Bluetooth got out of hand, all we had to do was remind him that we could feed his guts to geese whenever we chose, and bring back his nephew."

"We hardly expected you to bring yourself back, though," said Lord Badgertoe. "It complicates things."

"Complicates things? Not necessarily," said Sir Thrip. "I've grown weary of our old king. It's time for a fresh face. And Bluetooth's pretty hard to manage."

"You might find me hard to manage too," said Reven. Rather unwisely, in Jinx's opinion, but then wisdom wasn't really what you expected from Reven.

"If we found you hard to manage, we'd take steps," said Sir Thrip.

Reven turned his gaze on Sir Thrip. Sir Thrip took a step backward.

"Then you'd have no one," said Reven.

Lord Badgertoe and Sir Thrip looked at each other.

"Notice the air of nobility," said Sir Thrip. "Born to command."

"With a certain amount of guidance," said Lord Badgertoe. "No one commands without guidance."

"He's a natural leader. Quite unlike this woodrat." Sir Thrip nodded at Jinx. "Royal blood always shows."

"Certainly it does with such assistance as yours," said Reven, dabbing at the cut on his forehead. "Now, if you'll excuse me, I am going to look for a friend of mine. Come along, Jinx."

He started toward the door, and Jinx, annoyed at being summoned like a dog, nonetheless started to follow. Sir Thrip seized him. Jinx felt a knife point jab into his back.

"Jinx is coming with me, good sir," said Reven, even more icily.

"He's a magician," said Sir Thrip. "Magicians dance in red-hot iron shoes, hey. It's the law."

"The law has changed," said Reven.

"You can't change the law," Sir Thrip said. "You're not king."

"Not yet." Reven shoved Sir Thrip aside, knife and all, and grabbed Jinx. "Let's go."

Out in the cold night air, Jinx's head cleared. "Why did they just let us leave?"

"Because they need me," said Reven. "Where do you think the Lady Elfwyn went?"

"Back to the Urwald," said Jinx.

"Perhaps we can catch her. It's terribly dangerous for her to go there alone."

"It's safe enough," said Jinx. "For Urwalders."

Reven shot him a disbelieving look.

"She can handle stuff," said Jinx. "You remember her and those wolves? And the werebear?" It was his personal opinion that Elfwyn was safer with monsters than with Reven. "You've got no right to use her curse."

"She offered, very kindly, to tell people who I am since I have no way of telling them myself."

"But telling people about her curse, and asking her questions in front of people—that's not fair."

"Before you leap to the lady's defense, why not find out if the lady wants defending?"

Jinx didn't answer that, because he couldn't think of anything sufficiently cutting to say. "I still don't see why they let us leave."

"If they accept that I am—" the blank seemed to fit naturally into Reven's conversation now—"then they can hardly expect me to take orders from them."

"But . . ." Jinx stopped walking. They were in the palace square. No one was around except a small yellow dog snuffling for scraps between the cobbles. "They want to use you. You heard them. They want you so they can overthrow this guy." He jerked his head at the palace. "If you won't cooperate—"

"Then they're stuck," said Reven. "They have no revolution without me."

Jinx shook his head. He didn't understand.

"They need someone to put in King Bluetooth's place," said Reven, in a very quiet voice.

"But they can put just anybody in his place!"

"Keep your voice down, please. No, they can't."

"Why not?"

"Because." Reven's eyes glittered in the darkness. "People believe in kings."

"I don't," said Jinx. "I don't think there's anything special about—well, you. Okay, so I suppose you are this Raymond person. So what? He was a baby. How can a baby be better than some other baby?"

"If you can't keep your voice down," said Reven, "then we'd better get away from the palace."

They walked on, through an iron gate and down a dark street.

"There will be no more dancing in red-hot shoes," said Reven after a moment. "They will have to accept that."

"What will *you* do to magicians?"

"Employ them," said Reven. "There will be no boiling of people alive and no . . . rolling people down hills in barrels stuck about with nails."

There was a gray cloud of pain when he said this, and Jinx knew he was thinking about his stepmother.

"I wish for no cruelty of any kind," said Reven.

"I don't see how you'll get to be king without being cruel," said Jinx.

"I may have to fight," said Reven. "But I won't kill unnecessarily."

"What about the trees?" Jinx demanded. They had come to a stop in a narrow street that led down to the river.

"What about them?"

"Are you going to stop the treecutting? If you're king?"

Reven looked down the street, which was lined with small stone houses. He looked back at Jinx. "You see how it is here. People are poor."

"Not especially," said Jinx. "Not as poor as Urwald people. You didn't answer my question. Which I suppose means actually you did."

"Why should Urwald people be poor when they're surrounded by valuable timber?"

"Maybe we don't care if we're poor," said Jinx.

"*You're* not poor. You live with a wealthy wizard who gives you everything you need."

"But—"

"Half the Urwalders are shivering in leaky huts. At least half. Don't you think they'd prefer—"

"If they sold the trees there wouldn't be an Urwald anymore. Besides, you're not *buying* trees from them, you're just cutting them down. Stealing them. Nobody has the right—"

"*I'm* not doing anything." Reven's eyes glittered again. "I'm not king. It seems to me those trees are just places for monsters to hide."

Reven's willful stupidity was making Jinx's stomach hurt. "The trees are *people*."

Reven shrugged. "You say you can talk to them. But nobody else can. Don't you think that's a bit strange?"

"Nobody else listens! And it's not just the trees. The Urwald is a—a thing. A whole living thing that we're all part of."

"If you say so. What it isn't, good Jinx, is a nation. And that means it's waiting to be taken over by anyone clever enough to try. Surely even you can see that."

"And what about Elfwyn?"

"While I hesitate to say 'mind your own business'—"

"Mind your own business," said Elfwyn, stepping out of the shadows.

"You shouldn't spy on people!" Jinx was relieved to see her anyway.

"Speaking of spying," said Elfwyn. "*You* shouldn't—" She stopped.

There was a sound of hoofbeats. Elfwyn grabbed Jinx and Reven and hauled them into the shadow of a house.

Two men on horseback clomped down the street. There was just enough moonlight to see their green palace-guard uniforms.

"They can't get far," a guard said. "Foreign spies. Three of 'em."

"Hope we find 'em first." The horsemen passed by. "The king's offered a bag of gold to anyone who captures them alive. They'll dance in red-hot iron shoes for sure."

Their voices faded away.

"But they just let us go!" said Jinx.

"Lord Badgertoe and Sir Thrip did," said Reven. "But someone must have told the king."

They hurried through the sleeping city, down winding, stair-stepped streets to the river. They ran until they were out of breath, then they stopped under an enormous, spreading oak. Jinx climbed up onto one of the branches and wrapped himself in the tree's aliveness. Reven told Elfwyn what had happened after she left, while tactfully avoiding the subject of why she'd left.

Jinx resolutely refused to fill in the parts Reven couldn't say because of his curse, but neither Elfwyn nor Reven even noticed he was doing it. Jinx leaned up against the tree trunk and felt neglected and put-upon.

Abruptly the scene around him changed. He saw a whole forest of trees, spread out along both sides of the riverbank. But when he leaned forward for a closer look, the forest vanished.

Weird.

"That Dame Franca creature was on the king's side after all," said Elfwyn. "Just like Witch Seymour said she might be."

"Indeed not, my lady. She didn't summon the king. She summoned Sir Thrip and Lord Badgertoe."

"Well, that's just as bad. They attacked you. Why didn't Jinx do magic?"

"He did set Lord Badgertoe's sleeve on fire," said Reven. "As I mentioned."

Elfwyn looked up at Jinx. "Why didn't you set all their clothes on fire? You could have. Remember back at Bonesocket? You set the *air* on fire."

"I was using the Bonemaster's power when I did that," said Jinx.

"But don't you have any of your own?"

"Not a whole lot, since you mention it," said Jinx.

"I thought wizards had their own power," said Elfwyn.

"Yeah, well, here's an interesting thing: I'm not a wizard."

"Then you shouldn't try to do magic at all," said

94

Elfwyn. "Because in this country you could get executed for it."

"No problem," said Jinx. "I'm going home anyway."

"You can't!" said Elfwyn. "We have to stay and help Reven."

"I don't have to," said Jinx. "And neither do you. You *said* you wanted to learn magic, and to find out how to lose your curse."

"I have to do this first." Elfwyn stood up so that her eyes were almost level with Jinx's—the branch he was sitting on was low. "If I don't stay, there'll be nobody to say who Reven is."

"So? Big deal. It's nothing to us whether he becomes king or not. It won't stop people from cutting down the Urwald."

"They can't cut down the Urwald," said Elfwyn. "It's too big."

"They're cutting down *trees*." Jinx stood up on the tree branch and glared down at her. "Real living trees. You're an Urwalder. Don't you care?"

He could feel the oak tree's power coming up through his feet. It wasn't as much power as that of the Urwald itself, not even close, but this was a grand old tree and it had a lot of lifeforce.

"And how are you going to stop them by going home?" said Elfwyn. "It's better if you stay here and—"

"What, try to change Reven's mind? He hardly *has* a mind," said Jinx, getting really angry. "He's using both of us, and I'm sick of it, even if you aren't."

Reven's eyebrows drew together like swords and there was a green flash of real anger, with no calculating squares at all. He took a step toward Jinx.

Jinx drew on the tree's power and set the ground in front of Reven on fire. The ground was a mush of dried grass, broken sticks, and dead leaves, and it burned nicely. Reven hopped back, alarmed.

"Put that out, Jinx!" said Elfwyn.

Jinx didn't feel like putting it out. He turned the fire a dark angry purple to let Reven know how he felt, and he let the flames climb higher and higher.

"When the guards see that—" said Reven.

"Which they can hardly help doing—" added Elfwyn.

"They'll be down here, and arrest you," said Reven. "Which is fine with me."

"They'll arrest all of us," said Elfwyn.

"No, because we're leaving," said Reven, taking her hand.

"Someone's coming!" said Elfwyn.

Jinx sucked the fire into himself. He jumped down from the tree branch.

The three of them scrambled down the riverbank and crouched among the high reeds. Jinx felt cold water soaking his knees.

There were loud clanks, men walking with swords and shields. Beams of lantern light danced across the ground as footsteps came toward them.

Elfwyn's elbow dug into Jinx's ribs and she mouthed *concealment spell* at him.

Oh. Right.

Jinx drew on the fire he had inside him now and turned it into the strongest concealment spell he could manage. He grabbed hold of Elfwyn's arm and then Reven's. He concentrated hard. *We're not here, we're not here.*

The trouble was, he didn't have nearly as much power as he would've had in the Urwald. He didn't know if his spell was working.

The light from one of the guards' lanterns illuminated Elfwyn's face. She had a smear of mud running down from under her eye to her chin.

The guards looked at her, and through her. Then they walked past. They squatted at the water's edge, looking about for footprints or something; Jinx didn't know. Finally their leader called to them and they turned and tromped back up to the tree.

And stayed there. Jinx could sense the distant clouds of their thoughts, muddling along redly and brownly.

Elfwyn jerked her head to the side and mouthed *let's go*.

Carefully, slowly, Jinx took a step along the path beside the river, then another. Elfwyn and Reven started moving too, as silently as possible. Every time one of them accidentally made a noise Jinx's heart jumped, and they all froze and listened.

They could hear the men talking beneath the tree.

"Supposed to be some sort of trouble from abroad," said one of them. "Spies from Bragwood, *I* heard."

"Just an excuse to attack Bragwood," said another man. "Looking for one, ain't they?"

"Those flames were purple."

"So you think Bragwooders can make purple flames?"

"They can if they're hiring magicians."

"Them, employ magicians? Hah. Now I've heard *we—*"

"Be careful what you say."

The voices were fading now, as Jinx and his companions moved farther away, but he heard one of the men say something about

"—red-hot iron shoes—"

Out of earshot, they hurried along the path.

9

A Rather Disturbing Spell

The path beside the river met a wagon track, and they walked along it in the darkness. Jinx sensed the Urwald's lifeforce ahead of him. Nobody was cutting trees now, but Jinx still found he knew where it was happening as easily as he knew where his own feet were.

"We can't go back to our camp," said Elfwyn. "Those awful lord-sir-whatsit-things know where it is."

"I'm not worried about them," said Reven.

"I am," said Jinx. "Because when someone sticks a knife in my neck, I get worried. I'm funny like that."

"So which way—" Elfwyn began.

"South," said Jinx. "You're both coming to see the

treecutting with your own eyes. Then you can tell me that there's nothing wrong with it."

"I never said there was nothing wrong with it," said Elfwyn. "I just said—"

"You said the Urwald was too big to cut down."

"Well, it is."

Jinx remembered how he had seen the Urwald when he had flown above it—a sea of green treetops going on forever. But not really forever. Here, they were now beyond the edge.

"Can we stop?" Reven asked after a while. "Or do we have to walk all night?"

Jinx was getting tired too. "We can stop."

Elfwyn waited until Reven had gone off to look for firewood. Then she turned on Jinx. "You shouldn't read people's minds without their permission. And by the way you're completely wrong. But you still shouldn't do it."

"I can't help it! And anyway it's not reading minds. It's just seeing colors." He had to get her to understand about Reven. "You're thinking pink fluffy thoughts at him, and he's thinking these blue and green squares that are—"

"What color are *your* thoughts, Jinx?" Elfwyn demanded.

"They're not any—"

"Of course they are! Who ever heard of a person with no color to their thoughts!" Elfwyn's voice shook. "You only see other people's thoughts through the color of yours, did you ever think of that!"

"You don't understand what I'm talking about at all," said Jinx, and went to help Reven.

～ ～ ～

The others fell asleep, but Jinx lay on his back staring up at the stars. He just couldn't get used to the idea that there were so many of them, a vast dome of sparkling lights, pink and blue and gold.

He was worried about leaving Reven, who he was beginning to realize was more dangerous outside the Urwald than in it. Reven was becoming Raymond, the King of Nowhere, a king with some very wrongheaded ideas about the Urwald.

Jinx ought to stay and keep an eye on him. But Simon expected Jinx back soon. If he didn't go back, Simon was likely to come looking for him, and probably not in a very good mood. That could be unpleasant. Besides, Jinx was worried about the Bonemaster.

Jinx got up quietly and crept away from the fire. He leaned his back against a sycamore tree, closed his eyes, and thought. He jammed his hands into his pockets, and touched the aviot that Simon had given him.

Oh. Yes. That might work.

But where could he put it that Reven wouldn't find it?

Jinx approached cautiously—Reven was a light sleeper.

Drawing on the fire for power, Jinx levitated one of Reven's boots. Then he silently grabbed it out of the air and retreated to the sycamore.

He used his knife to pry the heel off the boot. He cut a tiny hole, slipped the gold bird inside, and jammed the heel back on.

At least he would be able to keep an eye on Reven.

It began to rain. The road was muddy and slippery, and soon after sunrise the treecutting started again. Jinx could see the dark mass of the Urwald rising a mile or so to the east, and that was close enough for the pain of the treecutting to reach him.

Elfwyn and Reven were walking ahead of Jinx, but not so far ahead that he couldn't hear them talking.

"This ability of Jinx's to read minds," Reven said. "Did he regain it when he got his life back?"

Jinx winced.

But Elfwyn surprised him. "Jinx can't read minds."

"What can he do, then?" Jinx could tell from Reven's voice—and from Elfwyn's pink fluffy thoughts—that he was smiling sweetly at her. "You know what I mean."

"He can do magic," said Elfwyn. "You've seen him."

She's doing it again, Jinx thought. She's managing her curse.

A puff of frustration from Reven. But his voice still had

the smile. "Can Jinx see what I'm thinking?"

"No."

"Then what can he see?" said Reven.

"The sky," said Elfwyn. "The—"

"What can he see when he looks at what I'm thinking?"

It was too direct, and Elfwyn had no defense. "Colors, I think," she said miserably.

"Why don't you ask me?" Jinx demanded.

Reven turned around and smiled. "I beg your pardon. I had the impression you didn't like to discuss it."

The road skirted the edge of the forest, two deep tracks worn by wagon wheels. Twice, wagons creaked past them laden with the corpses of slaughtered trees.

They smelled the carnage before they saw it. The air was thick with the blood of murdered trees. Jinx could hear the screaming, too—louder and louder the closer they got.

They came over a rise and saw the horror stretched below them.

It was vast. It went on for miles. The smell of sap was overpowering.

"Jinx, slow down!" Elfwyn called.

Jinx hadn't realized he'd started running. He ran on. Down below, at the edge of the Urwald, a mass of men was at work, axes swinging. He could hear Elfwyn and Reven catching up to him. He was in a red haze of pain.

"Jinx, what are you doing?" said Elfwyn. "You can't

stop them! They've got axes!"

"And I've got magic." Jinx was out of breath and it hurt to talk.

They were close enough now that he could hear the axes chopping into the trees' flesh. The sound hurt. Everything hurt. The pain of the dying trees almost blinded him. But he could feel strength, too—the lifeforce power of the Urwald filled him as soon as he came within its reach. It spoke.

The Listener is here, said the trees.

I'm here, said Jinx. What was he supposed to do, though? The lumberjacks hadn't even turned around. There were about twenty of them, big tough-looking men with strong arms from swinging axes.

He's brought the Terror back with him, said the trees.

And then *Stop them, Listener.*

Jinx climbed onto a tree stump.

"What are you doing?" said Reven. "Remember what Witch Seymour said—"

Jinx cupped his hands. "Hey! You! Idiots! Listen up!"

One lumberjack who had stopped to rest turned around. He grinned and nudged the man standing next to him. One by one the men turned around, axes in hands, and advanced on Jinx.

"You forgot what Witch Seymour said," said Elfwyn.

"Stop right there," said Jinx.

The men did, grinning. They hefted their axes.

Jinx was much too angry to be afraid. "Who are you?" he demanded.

The biggest lumberjack, who was wearing a red tunic and green breeches, said, "Siegfried. Who're you, brat?"

"I'm Jinx. You're to stop cutting trees at once. It's not allowed. You don't have permission."

"Permission from who?" said Siegfried.

"From the Urwald." Jinx could tell from Siegfried's accent that he was a Keylander. "From us."

"Oh!" Siegfried turned and smirked at the man next to him. "We don't have permission from them!"

Jinx felt anger building up from his feet to his head. Elfwyn was right—his feelings did have colors. Right now he was at the center of a bright red flame of fury. "Stop laughing!"

"It's better they should laugh at us than kill us," said Reven under his breath.

"Shut up," Jinx told him. He had no time for Reven. Reven was an idiot. The lumberjacks were idiots. And Elfwyn, she was the biggest idiot of all, because she was an Urwalder like him and yet she couldn't see what was happening.

"Put down your axes," said Jinx. "And leave them here. Take your wagons, and go away, and don't come back."

"Ooh, we don't even get to keep our axes," said a

lumberjack. The other men snickered.

"Shut up, Eric," said Siegfried. He wasn't laughing anymore. "We'll give this little brat our axes all right."

He took a step toward Jinx and raised his ax.

At the same instant Reven stepped in front of Jinx and raised his. "Stay back!"

Jinx was so surprised he almost forgot to be angry. Reven was prepared to face down twenty armed men by himself—he really was an idiot. No, not completely by himself, because Elfwyn stepped up beside Reven, and drew—a knife! A knife that looked really useful for slicing cheese with.

"Get out of the way," Jinx said to them. "I'm handling this."

"And you're doing so well," Elfwyn said. She brandished her knife menacingly at the men.

One of the men shoved Elfwyn roughly out of the way.

And Jinx lost his temper.

The red flame of anger burst, filling the air with bright red-green light and a loud roaring noise. Jinx felt the Urwald's power surging up through his feet and he threw it outward as hard as he could. He didn't know what kind of spell he was doing. The power was handling all that. Jinx was just the wick that burned with it. The air burned. The sky went dark. Everything went black. There was shouting. Sounds of feet running. A soft thud—that was Jinx, hitting the ground.

He sat up, painfully. The sky was light again. The flame and anger were gone. Jinx blinked around at the wide field of stumps.

"What happened?" he said.

"Supposing you tell us." Reven's voice was tight and cold, and there was a silver-blue glimmer of fear.

Jinx turned to Elfwyn. "What happened?"

A red shimmer. Elfwyn was afraid of Jinx too. "You did a spell."

"Siegfried . . ." Jinx got to his feet, shakily. "Is he dead?"

"Yes," said Reven.

"No," said Elfwyn.

Well, Elfwyn must be telling the truth. Jinx looked all around. The men had retreated into a cluster a stone's throw away. They held their axes in front of them but they, too, were gathered under a purple cloud of fear.

Three feet in front of Jinx, a small ash seedling had sprouted from the ground.

"Ash trees grow very fast," said Jinx. The tree hadn't been there a few minutes ago.

"How—how did you do it?" Elfwyn demanded.

"Do what?"

"You turned a man into a plant," said Reven.

"Siegfried, actually." Elfwyn's voice trembled on the

edge of panic. "You turned Siegfried into a tree."

"Just a seedling," said Jinx. "An ash seedling." He didn't know how he had done it. He kind of thought that the Urwald had done it. Mostly.

He felt dizzy. He couldn't stop looking at the tree that had been Siegfried. Jinx had turned a man into a tree. It was an act worthy of the Bonemaster.

"Can't you turn him back?" said Elfwyn.

"No," said Jinx.

"Won't?" said Reven.

"Can't," said Jinx. He tried. He could feel the power, but he had no idea how to turn a tree into a man.

"Um, look." Elfwyn pointed.

The lumberjacks were moving forward, their axes at the ready, and this time none of them were laughing.

10

Dangerous Jinx

"What are you going to do now?" Reven murmured, raising his own ax. "Turn them all into greenery?"

Jinx still felt the Urwald power flowing through him. He didn't think he could turn them all into trees. His magical skills were really very limited. Concealment spell? Wouldn't work. Door spell? There was nothing to lock. Levitation? Oh—

Jinx drew on all the power he could, and levitated the axes.

It was a struggle. The lumberjacks clung to the escaping axes with both hands, and for a minute there, Jinx and the Urwald were lifting tons of dangling lumberjack as the axes fought to rise and the lumberjacks swung with their feet a yard or two off the ground. Then one by one, as they realized what was happening, the men let go and dropped to the ground, falling and rolling. They scrambled to their feet, cast frightened looks at Jinx, and fled. One or two of them glanced nervously back at their axes, which rose until they were floating twenty feet in the air.

Jinx looked down at the ash seedling in despair. Unfortunately, the moment he broke concentration to do this, he lost control of the levitation spell. The axes came thudding and thunking down all around.

"Gah!" said Jinx.

"Cripes," said Elfwyn.

"Odbodkins!" Reven glared at Jinx. "Are you trying to kill us?"

"I forgot about them," said Jinx.

"You forgot that you had hung a score of axes over our heads?"

Jinx looked at the little forest of axes, their blades half buried in the dirt.

"Those almost hit us!" said Elfwyn.

She edged closer to Reven. She and Reven seemed to have moved to the other side of an invisible divide and to be gazing distastefully at Jinx across it.

Jinx suddenly felt shaky. The axes could easily have killed all three of them.

"You wouldn't have cared if you had hit us, I swan," said Reven. "As long as it saved your trees."

"Of course I would have cared," said Jinx. "It was an accident, all right? I forgot the axes were up there."

"Forsooth, I'm beginning to think you're insane," said Reven. "How many people will you kill to protect your trees?"

Jinx got annoyed. "As many as it takes."

"You really are a werechipmunk," said Reven. And Elfwyn didn't say anything to contradict him. Her thoughts were red and shimmery and afraid of Jinx.

She wanted to get away from him. They both did.

Well, Jinx had done what he wanted, right? He'd escorted Reven out of the Urwald. And then he'd brought Reven back and made him see the treecutting. As for Elfwyn . . .

He started to ask her if she was staying with Reven, then didn't bother. Obviously she was.

"Yeah," said Jinx. "I'm a werechipmunk. And you're willing to sacrifice anybody and anything to become king of your stupid little country. You'll even make friends with those Lord-Sir-Whatsits that made Dame Morwen dance in red-hot iron shoes!"

"Dame Morwen cursed Reven," said Elfwyn.

"Good for her," said Jinx. "Listen, Reven or Raymond or whatever. Don't come back to the Urwald."

And he turned his back on them, left them surrounded

by twenty axes and the ash seedling, and walked straight into the Urwald.

The trees murmured and mumbled all around him. But for once that didn't make him feel better.

～ ～ ～

Jinx wandered through the forest, not caring where he was going, just determined to get deeper in and farther away. The problem was that he was running away from what he'd done, and it wasn't working. Somehow what he'd done seemed to come with him.

The trees couldn't really understand his distress over turning Siegfried into a tree. After all, they *were* trees.

But he'll never go home to his family, Jinx said. *I mean I utterly turned him into a tree, okay? It's like he's dead.*

Not dead, no, said the trees. *Growing. Sunlight. Worms.*

Yeah, yeah, worms, said Jinx. *Wonderful. I'm sure he's thrilled.*

Anyway Jinx was pretty sure it had been the trees' idea, though it wasn't like he hadn't done his part. He'd been very angry and he supposed he'd wanted to kill Siegfried.

He remembered the trees had once told him that he'd misuse their power. He reminded them of this.

Humans misuse power, said the trees. *Magicians do. Wizards do. It is the way of wizards.*

What I think happened, said Jinx, *is that you misused me.*

After that he didn't talk to the trees for a long time.

Day became night. It grew bitterly cold. Jinx had dropped his blanket when he'd run to stop the treecutters. And he didn't want to light a fire so far from the Path, where the ground was thick with saplings and fallen wood. So he walked to keep from freezing. Once he stopped and shivered inside a concealment spell while a werebear went past.

Toward morning, Jinx reached a path. He followed it, heading north and east and wishing he had something to eat. He was getting dizzy and stumbling a lot.

He leaned against a tree. He tried to remember the hungry times from when he was little, and the stories he'd heard. What had people eaten?

Suddenly he saw a teenage girl with deep brown skin and a bright blue dress. She crouched at the base of an oak tree and picked at the bark.

"Uh, hello," said Jinx.

The girl didn't look up. She put something into her mouth.

"Are you eating bark?" said Jinx.

The girl ignored him. Dizzily, Jinx unleaned from the tree—but as soon as he moved, she vanished.

Well, that was odd. Even by Urwald standards.

Jinx went over to the oak tree. It seemed bigger than it had been a moment ago. The girl had left no footprints in the frost. A ghost?

He touched the tree. Instantly the girl reappeared. She peeled some lichen off the bark and put it in her mouth. Jinx put out a hand to touch the girl and wasn't particularly surprised that his hand went right through her.

Jinx took his hand off the oak. The tree immediately grew thicker and the girl disappeared.

He looked at the lichen, doubtful. Some lichen was poisonous. He supposed the trees were trying to tell him that this lichen was not, but did the trees know or care whether she'd been poisoned?

He picked some of the stuff. He put it in his mouth and chewed. It was like eating wood. He didn't drop dead.

It didn't really do much for him.

It did clear his head a little, though. Or at least he thought so, until he looked up the path and saw the girl again. She was older now—almost grown up. And she looked completely there, although Jinx knew she was not. She reached toward a tree branch that hung over the path—and the branch bowed down and touched her outstretched hand.

What the—?

Listeners, said the trees. *Listener.*

You're trying to make me think I'm crazy, said Jinx shortly, and walked on.

The trees murmured to themselves. *The Listener isn't listening.*

114

It was the shortest day of the year—and Jinx's thirteenth birthday. What a way to spend a birthday. He was cold, hungry, and practically a murderer. Things could hardly get worse.

Of course they could.

Jinx heard clawed feet scrabbling along the path behind him. He wheeled around to see a wolf charging him. Suddenly it reared up on its hind legs and grinned at him—a werewolf. Jinx could see handlike paws, surprisingly intelligent golden eyes, and . . . fangs. Jinx clutched his knife.

"Truce of the Path," said the werewolf.

Jinx took his hand off his knife, reluctantly. Simon had told him never to trust to the Truce unless he had to. He wished he couldn't see the werewolf's hunger. It was only slightly reassuring that this werewolf was wearing spectacles.

The werewolf held out a hand. "I'm Malthus."

Swallowing hard, Jinx took the werewolf's hand and shook it. Almost-human fingers stuck out of matted fur and ended in broken yellow claws. Jinx managed to suppress a shudder as the talons slid over his skin.

"Jinx. Uh, nice to meet you," Jinx lied.

"I've been watching you for some time," said Malthus.

This is not exactly the most reassuring thing to hear when you're many miles from home and alone on the Path.

"Why?" said Jinx.

"Reasons of my own," said Malthus. "Shall we walk on?"

They walked on.

"Do you know you're a Listener?" said the werewolf.

"Of course," said Jinx.

Malthus tapped a claw against his lower lip, a thinking kind of gesture. "But you don't know what it means."

Jinx started to say that he did, too, but decided arguing with a werewolf wasn't a great idea. He shrugged.

"If you want to survive," said Malthus, "you'll figure it out sooner rather than later. The Urwald can't wait much longer, you know."

"I have a pretty good idea what Listener means, thanks. What do you mean by the Urwald?" It was a question that had been troubling Jinx lately.

"Us," said the werewolf promptly.

"Us—?"

"Werewolves."

"I see," said Jinx. The trees had told him that the Urwald meant the forest and all the Restless—but when it came down to it, they mostly seemed to think it meant the trees.

"And the trees and various other creatures," Malthus added.

"I think I may be hallucinating you," said Jinx. "I'm really hungry."

"Do not mention hunger, please," said the werewolf.

"I am expending considerable effort on not eating you. Do you ever wonder what we gain by keeping the Truce?"

Jinx started to say that everybody gained the use of the Path, but Malthus probably meant what *werewolves* gained, and you hardly ever saw werewolves on paths. In fact, Jinx had never seen one on a path before. In fact—

"I've seen you before," said Jinx. "You had a notebook."

A blue blop of pleased surprise from Malthus. "You remember that."

"And there was someone else there." The memory was like a dream trying to slip away as he woke. "Elves. Two elves."

"They cast a spell to make you forget," said the werewolf. "Do you remember anything else?"

"No." It was frustrating, because the memory seemed impossibly distant, and yet he had a feeling it hadn't happened all that long ago.

"You overcame an elf's spell," said Malthus. "At least partially. How unusual, and how encouraging. Think about flames, and wicks, and balance. I must leave you now. I'm really getting *quite* hungry."

The werewolf shook hands again—it wasn't any less creepy the second time—and then went down on all fours and ran off into the forest.

When night fell Jinx could walk no farther. He hardly had the strength to gather firewood—he just hauled one dead branch onto the path, lit it, and lay down to sleep. The tree roots murmured and mumbled beneath him. Jinx lay as close as he could to the fire and shivered until he went to sleep.

He dreamed he was walking along an icy path, with high glass cliffs on either side of him. A cold wind blew and there were no trees anywhere. He looked down at his feet and found that they had been replaced with glass ones, and that an icy transparency was creeping up his body.

Someone shook him, hard. "Hey! Are you alive?"

This seemed to Jinx a very difficult question and he couldn't think how to answer it. He opened his eyes to see how much of him had turned to glass. It seemed none of him had.

"Bring blankets." A woman's voice. "Get some fire-wood."

Then people were pulling Jinx upright, wrapping blankets around him, and the smoke from a new fire was stinging his eyes. He heard the murmur of the Wanderer language. In the predawn light he could make out the shapes of the Wanderers arranging themselves around the fire—seven people, eight donkeys, and a small donkey cart. Jinx recognized them—they'd camped in Simon's clearing many times.

And he guessed they'd saved his life. He meant to say thank you, but what came out was, "Do you have anything to eat?"

"Oh good, he's talking. Get him some bread," said the woman.

"A long time ago, Keyland used to be part of the Urwald," said Jinx.

"He's babbling." A boy's voice. "He's crazy. Oh, it's that wizard's boy."

Jinx wasn't babbling—he'd only just realized what the lone oak by the river had meant when it showed him forest all around it. The boy—whose name, Jinx remembered, was Tolliver—shoved a chunk of bread into Jinx's hands. Jinx ate it.

Jinx rode in the donkey cart, which he didn't like much—it jolted, and it made him feel silly. But Quenild, the chief Wanderer, insisted that he was too weak to walk.

So he bumped and jostled along all day, wrapped in blankets and burrowed in among sacks of woolen cloth and small kegs of sugarplum syrup. Tolliver walked beside him.

"So did you learn to do any magic yet?" Tolliver said.

"Of course."

"Let's see some."

Jinx thought of doing something really spectacular, but then he remembered Siegfried. Using the Urwald's power was dangerous. He used the fire inside him, and levitated a sack of cloth a few feet in the air.

Tolliver looked reluctantly impressed. "You're still short, though."

Jinx dropped the sack back into the cart. The donkey stopped, turned around, flicked its ears, and shot Jinx an annoyed look.

"Now you've upset Biscuit." Tolliver sang a little song in Wanderer language, something about carrots and warm straw, and Biscuit snorted and started walking again.

"Seriously? You sing to your donkey?" Jinx felt he had some lost ground to make up, because Tolliver was right—he *was* short.

Tolliver reddened. "What were you doing freezing on the path, anyway? Did the wizard kick you out?"

"Of course not. I'm traveling." Jinx remembered Tolliver had once accused him of never having been anywhere. "I just came from Keyland."

"You should've brought blankets with you. And food. That's what people do when they travel." Tolliver jumped up and touched a branch hanging over the path. "At least people with brains."

"There are lumberjacks cutting down trees back there." Jinx extracted an arm from the blankets and waved vaguely southeastward.

"Seen 'em."

"Doesn't it bother you?" said Jinx.

"Nope," said Tolliver. But Jinx could see that it actually did.

"If all the trees get cut down, and there's no Urwald

120

anymore, what will the Wanderers do?"

"Same thing we do now," said Tolliver. "You think we just work the Urwald? Man, there's Wanderers everywhere. Anyway, the Urwald's too big to cut down."

"That's what you think," said Jinx. "The Urwald used to go all the way to Keria. And probably a lot farther. So miles of it have been cut down already."

Tolliver looked skeptical. "When?"

"Oh, I don't know." The oak by the river hadn't told him. All it had done was show him a forest that was gone now. "Ages ago, probably. Before we were born."

"So why worry? The Urwald'll be here after we're dead. Or at least some of it will."

"That's not good enough." Jinx tried another tack. "Look, how big is the Urwald?"

"Weeks," said Tolliver. "Months." He pointed south. "Six weeks that way." He pointed north. "A month that way." He pointed west. "A month that way or"—he pointed northwest—"two months that way."

"And you guys go, what, everywhere in it?"

"Pretty much," said Tolliver.

"What if you kind of told people what was happening? The trees getting cut down and stuff? Maybe they would get together and do something about it."

"Nope," said Tolliver. "They wouldn't." He jumped at another branch, but missed it.

"How do you know?" said Jinx.

"'Cause they're Urwalders," said Tolliver.

"What's that supposed to mean?"

"Urwalders don't get together, they don't unite, and they don't do anything," said Tolliver. "That's just the facts."

~ ✎ ✎

They camped on the path that evening, and the next day Jinx was allowed to walk. Around noon they reached the Blacksmiths' Clearing. The houses here, too, looked a bit nicer than the ones in most clearings. Maybe the Urwalders who lived closer to the edge were richer than people in the deep Urwald.

Jinx was hoping he'd be able to talk to the people here about the treecutting. Maybe he could prove Tolliver was wrong about Urwalders.

Although he rather suspected he couldn't.

The smell of charcoal smoke from the forge filled the clearing. The Wanderers set up camp while their leader, Quenild, went to the largest house to confer with the inhabitants.

Jinx was helping to feed the donkeys when Quenild came back, looking grave.

"They don't want us here," she said.

"What do you mean they don't want us?" said Tolliver. "How are they going to sell their stuff without us to carry it?"

The other Wanderers, meanwhile, were looking at Jinx.

Jinx got the message. "Do you mean they don't want me?"

"We're leaving," said Quenild.

"Hold on," said Jinx. "Why don't they want me here?"

"Some sort of rumors going around about you," said Quenild. "Flashes of lightning, turning men into stones—a bunch of nonsense. Pack up."

"No, I'll go," said Jinx. "I mean, they don't mind you staying here if I leave, do they?"

"Simon has always been hospitable to us," said Quenild.

Jinx could see she wanted to be talked into staying. "Well, um, you have been too. Hospitable." They'd saved his life, actually, but he was embarrassed to say that in front of Tolliver. "But I need to go anyway. I have to get home."

Jinx could see the little blue cloud of relief. The Wanderers needed the Blacksmiths' Clearing. It was an important stop on their route.

"At least take some food with you," said Quenild. "And a blanket."

❦ ❦ ❦

Over the next few days Jinx learned that the people in the Blacksmiths' Clearing were not alone in their opinion. How many people he was supposed to have killed and just how he'd done it varied from clearing to clearing, but the result was the same—slammed, barred doors and orders shouted through the cracks to go away and leave them alone.

Fortunately the Wanderers had been generous, and it wasn't till the third day that Jinx started to run out of food. It also began to snow heavily that day. Jinx was close to Witch Seymour's house, so he went there.

⌐ ⌐ ⌐

Magicians took hospitality very seriously, and they didn't spook as easily as clearing people did. Witch Seymour answered the door with Whitlock the goat at his heels.

"Ah, Simon's apprentice. Alone, I see. And not yet twenty feet tall nor breathing fire, all rumor to the contrary. Do come in."

Jinx stomped snow off his boots. The fire was crackling and the little cottage smelled pleasantly of soup and baked potatoes.

"Come thaw out by the fire. What's become of your companions? Have you killed and eaten them?"

"Of course not." Jinx knew the witch was joking, but after being kicked out of five clearings Jinx was losing his sense of humor. "They stayed in Keyland."

"And you decided to rampage back through the Urwald, burning houses and devouring children as you went? Brew?"

"Yes please," said Jinx. "To the brew, I mean."

The witch put some leaves into a cup, poured a ladleful of boiling water over them, and set it in front of Jinx.

Jinx breathed in a smell of late-October rain. "Is that what they're saying on the Witchline?"

"The Witchline isn't quite that gullible." Witch Seymour sat down in a chair by the fire, and Whitlock curled up at his feet. "But one does hear things here and there. What *did* you do?"

Jinx took a sip of the brew and burned his tongue. "I went to Keyland with Reven. And then Elfwyn decided to stay there with him."

"And then?"

Jinx shrugged and didn't meet the witch's penetrating gaze. He'd wanted someone to talk to about what had happened. Witch Seymour wasn't the right sort of someone at all. Probably the only things you should tell Witch Seymour were things that you wanted repeated down the Witchline from one edge of the Urwald to the other.

He blew on the top of his cup and watched the leaves float around in a circle, widdershins.

On the other hand, maybe Witch Seymour could help him understand what had happened back at the treecutting.

"What's the difference between witches' magic and wizards' magic?" said Jinx.

"Oho, he won't answer questions, but he expects to have them answered, Whitlock," said the witch, leaning down to scratch the goat's horn buds. "Wizards are arrogant, one hears."

Jinx folded his arms, annoyed. "Well, but I mean, most witches are women, right? And most wizards are men. So what makes you a witch and not a wizard? It's got to be the kind of magic you do, right?"

"It's got to be," said Witch Seymour. "Soup?"

"Yeah. Thanks."

"We're magicians, you and I," said Witch Seymour, handing Jinx a bowl of soup. "And magicians stay out of other magicians' business. That's how we keep the peace."

"What peace?" said Jinx. "That's how you—"

"We."

"—we, then, let the Bonemaster do whatever he wants. And that's how we let those Keylanders cut down trees!"

"Keylanders?"

Jinx suddenly realized that there *was* something he wanted repeated down the Witchline. "There are people cutting trees. Haven't you heard rumors about that?"

"No," said the witch. "Do tell."

Jinx told, leaving out only the part about turning Siegfried into a tree.

"So one gathers they're cutting quite a *few* trees."

"Miles of them," said Jinx.

"And you weren't able to stop them."

"Of course not." It was only as Jinx said this that he realized that there hadn't been any treecutting since he'd turned Siegfried into a tree. The Urwald hadn't

126

mentioned any pain at all.

The lumberjacks had run away, and left their axes. But surely they had come back for them later? Or found new ones?

"And this boy who thinks he's Prince Raymond, he's in favor of cutting trees?"

"Utterly," said Jinx. "He wants to turn the trees into money. I think he wants to reward people who help him become king by giving them money from the trees."

"More likely he intends to give them the land the trees grow on."

Jinx looked at the witch to see if he was joking again. "How can you give someone land?"

"I assure you it's very much the custom in Keyland for people to own land. No doubt young Reven intends to assign large swaths of the Urwald to his most loyal followers."

It took a moment for the full horror of what the witch was saying to sink in. "Like, not just the clearings?"

"Not just the clearings."

"Everything?"

"Exactly so."

"And then they would cut down all the trees and turn them into money."

"And burn out the stumps and farm the land, one imagines."

"We have to stop them!" said Jinx.

"That certainly seems desirable," said the witch, rubbing Whitlock's left ear. "But how does one stop them, eh?"

"One doesn't," said Jinx. "All of us stop them."

"Oh, you think so?"

"How many of us are there?"

"What a question," said Witch Seymour. "One doesn't even know how many clearings there are. And then, of course, how many wizards."

"What about witches?" said Jinx.

"One hundred and three, not counting dabblers and dilettantes. One hundred and three really dedicated to the business. No, I'm sorry—" The witch frowned, and counted on his fingers. "One hundred and two. Dame Wygglof died last summer—old age."

It occurred to Jinx that probably only magicians died of old age in the Urwald. Simon's father was the oldest nonmagician Jinx had ever met.

"What if—" Jinx had been thinking about this. "What if we were a country, like Keyland is? Then we could tell people not to cut our trees down, right?"

"It wouldn't work," said Witch Seymour. "Would it, Whitlock? You can't make a nation of the Urwald. Urwalders are individualists."

"Maybe the magicians are," said Jinx. "But I think the clearing people are mostly just poor."

"They're still individualists," said Witch Seymour.

"What's that mean, anyway? Isn't everyone?"

"Not like Urwalders. Urwalders won't take orders," said Witch Seymour. "Urwalders do not believe in kings. Do they, Whitlock?"

"Is that how you make a country?" said Jinx. "By declaring somebody king?"

"Oh yes," said Witch Seymour.

But Jinx could see that actually the witch didn't know, any more than Jinx did.

"Well, we have to do something," said Jinx. "We all have to get together and do something."

"Most of us, you'll find, won't even speak to each other," said Witch Seymour.

Jinx wouldn't ordinarily have gone to Cold Oats Clearing, but it was going to be another cold night and he was running out of food. And he figured Egon would take him in, since Egon thought Jinx was his grandson.

The path up to the clearing was still obliterated by fallen trees. Jinx climbed over them one by one. Eventually he left the path and picked his way around the tree corpses as best he could, trusting the Urwald to remind him of where the clearing was.

It was odd no one had cleared the trees from the path.

He couldn't smell smoke. You'd think people would have fires going.

He could see daylight through the trees now. The clearing was ahead. There was no sound and still no smell of woodsmoke.

But there was something else, an acrid, sour smell that reminded him of when his hut back in Gooseberry Clearing had burned down when he was little.

Then he came out into the clearing and saw.

11

The Bones of
Cold Oats Clearing

Cold Oats Clearing lay in ruins. Some of the houses had been blasted apart. Others had been burned. Things were scattered around that would have been collected if there'd been anyone to collect them—blankets, dishes, a lone pink sock.

Jinx stood for a moment, listening. Silence, except for the raucous cry of a raven.

Cautiously, Jinx moved toward the nearest ruin.

He saw a confusion of footprints in the snow. A big, booted set came toward the house. A smaller set, widely spaced, as if someone had been running, led toward the forest.

Jinx followed the booted footprints from one ruin to another. The houses looked worse than they had after the storm—roofs gone, walls charred and broken. The burnt smell was everywhere. From some of the houses, people had run into the forest. From most, they had not.

Here and there, small, frozen drops of something purple stained the snow. Jinx felt power coming from the drops. A magician had been here.

He came to the house that had belonged to Egon, Simon's father. No footprints had escaped from it to the forest. There were just those big bootprints—coming to the house and going away—and a small splash of potion and—oh. This.

Two long, cold bones were stuck diagonally into the snow, crisscross.

Just then Jinx heard something crunching toward him through the snow.

He seized one of the bones as a weapon, ducked behind a broken wall, and waited.

The crunching came closer.

"It's no good hiding. I can see your footprints."

Oh, right. Drat. He should have done a concealment spell. Anyway, it was only Simon.

Simon in a mood. Red-green—grief, maybe, even though he'd said he hated these people, and orange anger around the edges. Simon's anger was almost always orange.

"Some of them got away," said Jinx.

Simon grabbed Jinx by the front of his coat and threw him against the wall. Jinx was completely unprepared for that. However, he did what he could and kicked Simon in the kneecap. Simon yelped a swear word and grabbed his knee. Jinx slithered away and ran out of the ruins and back to the edge of the woods. If he was going to fight a crazed Simon, Jinx needed to be close to his power source.

"You ought to calm down," said Jinx, when Simon came toward him again.

"Shut up, you murdering little—"

"What, you think I killed them?" Jinx was astonished. "It was the Bonemaster!"

"And how do you know that, eh? You were with him!"

"Are you insane? What, you think I'm in league with the Bonemaster or something? This is me, Jinx!"

This was the weirdest thing that had ever happened to Jinx. It was as if the sky had turned green and rain fell up instead of down. Simon was attacking him.

If this really was Simon.

"Who are you?" Jinx demanded.

"You know who I am."

Jinx was really terrified. This looked like Simon, and it sounded like Simon, and it had jagged orange anger like Simon, but it had to be some kind of shape-shifter. Or the Bonemaster. Or—

Whatever it was, and it sure looked like Simon, it drew back its hand preparatory to casting a spell. Panicking, Jinx pulled on the Urwald's power as hard as he could and struck out at the thing that was attacking him.

There was a deep green flash and a loud bang, and everything went black. Jinx fell to his knees.

He stayed there for a moment, stunned. He wasn't sure if the Simon-thing's spell had hit him. He wasn't sure what he'd done. Melted snow soaked through the knees of his trousers. He got to his feet and looked all around. No ash seedling. But Simon, or whoever it was, was gone.

And Jinx was suddenly sure it really had been Simon. Because the thoughts had looked like Simon's, and a shape-shifter wouldn't have known to copy Simon's thoughts, would it. Nobody could see that stuff except Jinx.

The footprints from Simon's boots stopped eight feet from where Jinx was standing. Just stopped.

The horror of it was somewhere out at the edge of Jinx's consciousness, trying to get his attention. He walked all around the place where the footprints ended. What had he done?

"Up here, if you're wondering."

Jinx looked up. He saw nothing but sky.

"Over here."

Jinx wondered if Simon was floating over the Urwald, as Jinx had done after he'd gotten smashed falling off the cliff. Then he saw a tiny scrap of purple high in the boughs of a pine tree.

"Are you going to get me down from here, or what?"

"Um, did I put you up there?"

"Yes."

"Oh. Good."

"Good?!"

"I mean, good I didn't turn you into a tree."

"Get me down from here *now*."

"Oh. Right." Jinx thought. "How do I do that?"

"How do you—how should I know how you flippin' do it? Undo whatever you just did!"

Jinx felt for the Urwald's power and let it flow up through his feet. He felt immensely powerful. He had no idea what he'd done to put Simon up in the tree. He tried hard to reach Simon with the power and levitate him as he'd done the nixies.

Nothing happened.

"It's no good," Jinx said. "It doesn't work because I don't feel how I did when I put you up there."

"And how's that?" Simon demanded.

Jinx didn't really want to admit it, but—"Scared."

"Think about what I'll do to you if you don't get me down, and you'll be plenty scared."

"It doesn't work, because I know you won't really do it."

"Want to bet?"

"Can't you just climb down?"

"Look at these branches. You tell me."

"Wait." Jinx had an idea. "Stay right there!"

He ran back to the ruins of Egon's house and found a plank from the smashed kitchen table—the table where he and Elfwyn and Reven had eaten stew. He brought it back and laid it in the snow near the foot of the tree.

"Now, hold on, I'm going to levitate this," he said.

He drew on the Urwald's power again and raised the plank up, and up and up. He kept his eyes on it, since it was much harder to do magic out of sight, and he tried hard not to blink.

"Now, get on it," said Jinx.

"Get on it? Are you crazy? You think I trust your levitation skills?"

"You shouldn't say stuff like that, it undermines my confidence," said Jinx.

Simon said some more cusswords.

"If you won't trust me, you're just going to be stuck up there," said Jinx. "Look, you can levitate it too, okay? We both will."

"I know I can't levitate my own weight at this height," said Simon.

"You can't if you think you can't," said Jinx. Without meaning to, he blinked, and the plank dropped several feet. He levitated it again.

"That was certainly confidence inspiring," said Simon. "I blinked."

"It doesn't matter if you blink as long as you keep concentrating," said Simon. "Concentrate harder."

Jinx tried to. "You'd better get on pretty soon or I won't be able to concentrate anymore."

Simon reached out, grabbed the plank, and, keeping a tight grip on the pine branch with one hand, sat on the plank. It stayed floating right where it was.

"Right." Simon let go of the branch, keeping his hand ready to grab it again. "Let's go down."

Jinx concentrated. The plank rose higher. Simon swore. "Down, idiot! Not up!"

"I don't know how to do down! And don't call me an idiot."

"How can you not know down? Down is part of the flippin' spell."

"I just drop stuff," said Jinx. "I don't know how to start out with down."

"Down is just the reverse of up. Here."

Jinx felt a little lurch as Simon took control of the spell. Simon wasn't using the Urwald's power, exactly, but he was using Jinx's spell. It became Simon's spell.

Jinx felt his way into Simon's spell—he realized suddenly that this was the way he should learn magic, by looking around the inside of a spell, not by trying to understand Simon's explanations. Jinx could see now how "down" worked. He took the spell away from Simon.

Now that he had the hang of it, Jinx lowered Simon faster and faster, so that at the last part Simon's boots hit the ground hard and skidded. Simon fell off the plank into the snow.

He got up, brushed snow off his robe, and grabbed Jinx by the chin. "Look at me."

"You did this already," said Jinx, looking back. "I'm not in the Bonemaster's power. What are you suspecting me for? I didn't think *you'd* done it."

"Me? Why would I wipe out Cold Oats Clearing?"

"Because you loathed them," said Jinx.

"I don't go around killing people."

"What about Calvin?"

"Fine, so you're not in the Bonemaster's power. What am I supposed to think, when I hear all kinds of rumors about you, and then I come and find you here and everyone's been murdered?"

"For one thing," said Jinx, "you could believe me instead of stuff you hear about me from other people."

"All *you* said was that some of them got away," said Simon. "The Bonemaster might've said the same. And after all that time you spent in Bonesocket, how do I know what he's done to you?"

"He can't control me, can he?" Jinx was suddenly

doubtful. "There's no such thing as a mind-control spell. That's what you told Sophie."

"Well. Sophie." Simon dismissed her with a wave. "You can't go around telling her everything. She over-reacts."

"So there is such a thing as a mind-control spell?"

"There might be. How would I know?"

"You're supposed to know a lot about magic," said Jinx.

"Don't take that tone with me," said Simon. "At least I know more than three spells."

"But I have a lot more power than you," said Jinx.

He hadn't meant to say it. It had just slipped out. But surely Simon had sensed it, anyway, just now when Jinx had taken over the spell.

"You're using the Urwald," said Simon. "How do you do it?"

"I don't know," said Jinx.

"Hm," said Simon. He looked around the clearing. "What happened here?"

"You're asking me?"

"Obviously."

"I guess—" Jinx thought about what he had seen. "It looks like the Bonemaster came and, um, turned people into bones. He probably took most of the bones with him. Because he, um—likes bones, I guess?"

"He does," said Simon.

"And it looks like some of the people got away, but I guess, um, I guess your dad probably didn't."

"Hm," said Simon.

"Is that purple potion something the Bonemaster uses for deathforce magic?" Jinx asked.

"Yes. We'd better look around and see if there's anybody we can help."

So they searched, in a wide circle, scrambling over fallen trees and sliding in the snow. But the footprints faded out among the forest leaves.

"There's no knowing how long they've been gone," said Simon. "And I have to go and hunt the Bonemaster."

"How did you know to come here?" said Jinx. "Did you know he'd escaped?"

"Yes, but I was looking for you," said Simon. "After I found he'd broken through the wards, I went home and looked in the Farseeing Window. But instead of you, I see that idiot boy who wants to be a king."

"I figured I should keep an eye on Reven. He might be dangerous."

"Supposing you explain to me what all these rumors are about you."

"Oh. I kind of turned a guy into a tree."

Jinx had been wanting for a week to talk to someone about this, and it was a relief to finally tell it. He didn't leave anything out, the Urwald's power or the way he'd lost his temper or anything. Because there was this about Simon: He wasn't ever going to slam and bar his door and yell at Jinx to go away.

"Can you change him back?" said Simon.

"No," said Jinx.

"Well, I suppose it worked."

"What?"

"You were trying to get them to stop chopping down trees. It worked, right?"

"Yeah," said Jinx. "That doesn't make it all right, though."

"Possibly not," said Simon. "But there's nothing we can do about it." He frowned. "Just how long have you had this Urwald power?"

"Since, I guess since that time I first did the concealment spell, when I sprained my ankle and a werewolf was coming after me."

"And you never thought to mention it till now?"

"Well, you didn't ask." Jinx figured Simon knew perfectly well that Jinx had been deliberately concealing it.

"And you could have used this power to help me with the wards around Bonesocket, and you didn't?"

"I didn't—" The enormity of what Simon had said hit Jinx. He looked around the ruined clearing. "I hate myself."

"Waste of time," said Simon.

"But if I had—"

"Anything that starts with 'if I had' is always a waste of time. The question is, what are you going to do now?"

"I don't want to use it anymore," said Jinx. "It uses me."

"All power is like that," said Simon.

"But the Urwald has . . . opinions. It could make me hurt someone it wanted hurt. . . ." Jinx stopped. Hurting Siegfried had been bad. But supposing he'd hurt Simon? That would have been horrible.

He suddenly didn't want to use the Urwald's power anymore, at all, ever.

"The trick with any power source is to be in control," said Simon.

"I can't be in control of the Urwald! The power's changing me. I'm as bad as the Bonemaster!" said Jinx.

Simon gazed at the burnt, blasted clearing. "Really? In what way?"

"Siegfried," said Jinx.

"Nonsense," said Simon. "He's not dead, and you'll figure out a way to turn him back eventually. Besides, you didn't do it on purpose, and you didn't do it for yourself. Nothing like the Bonemaster."

"Oh, great, so I'm not as evil as the Bonemaster."

"Yes. That was my point. And by the way, this tendency to wallow in self-pity is not your best quality," said Simon.

"What is, then?" said Jinx, curious.

"You get things done."

"I get things *done*? That's *it*?"

"What, you'd rather be admired than useful?" said Simon. "Plenty of people are neither."

"Yeah, but—"

"Now, do we need to stand around here soaking our feet in the snow, or can we go home?"

"We can go home," said Jinx.

And they did.

12

The Eldritch Tome

"You can't go after the Bonemaster without me," said Jinx.

They were in Simon's workroom, and Simon was stacking up books that he wanted Jinx to study.

"No? Am I not old enough?" Simon flipped a book open, frowned at it, and added it the stack.

"I thought we were both going to go after him."

"Think again," said Simon. "It's always been my plan to send you to Samara. Anyway, I thought you wanted to go."

"I did. Before. But there's stuff here I have to do. And you need my help."

"Yes. Here's the help I need," said Simon. "I need you to go to Samara, enroll at the Temple—"

"But you need my help to catch the Bonemaster!"

"—and use the library there to find out everything you can about the Qunthk bottle spell."

"What's Qunthk?"

"The language the spell is in."

"But you already have a book about the bottle spell."

"Yes. The Crimson Grimoire. But it doesn't tell enough. It doesn't explain what he's done to his own life . . . that strange bottle you said you saw in his cellar last summer."

"It wasn't a cellar," said Jinx. "It was more of a horrible underground-passage kind of crypt thing. And I *did* see it."

"That's what I said. If we don't figure out what he's done, we can't defeat him. There will be other Qunthk books at the Temple. There's one in particular—"

"Why didn't you look for it when you were there?"

"Because, if it's any of your business, I was more interested in other things at the time."

"What other things?" said Jinx.

"Finding the healing magic, for one thing."

"What's the healing magic?"

"I don't know, because I didn't find it," said Simon.

"Should I try to find it?"

"No, you should try to learn about the bottle spell!

And learn everything else about magic that you can. Learn KnIP."

KnIP—Knowledge is Power. Sophie had told Jinx that KnIP was Samaran magic. "But magic's illegal in Samara!"

"Very. Don't get caught. Now, let's assume I can count on you for that. You're to—"

"Won't they recognize me?" said Jinx. "They all saw me last year."

"That wasn't even close to all of them," said Simon. "And I doubt they'll remember you. They don't look at people much."

"They remembered you," said Jinx.

"Didn't they just." Simon added several more books to the pile and frowned at Jinx. "Hm. Well, you've grown, haven't you?"

"Probably not," said Jinx. "I think I'm shrinking."

"No one will have really looked at you," said Simon. "They recognized me because I was there for years. And you won't see much of the scribes in the hall, anyway."

"What about that Preceptress lady?"

"Oh, you'll probably see her here and there making speeches. Just sit near the back and don't let her get a good look at you."

This didn't sound like much of a plan to Jinx. "If I came with you to look for the Bonemaster—"

"I said no," Simon snapped.

"But—"

"Look. Where do you think he's likely to be?"

"I don't know." Jinx imagined the Bonemaster running through the Urwald from one clearing to another, killing everyone. But wizards wanted power. If the Bonemaster killed all the people in all the clearings, then who would he have power over? "Maybe he'll be back at Bonesocket?"

"That would be my guess also. And where is Bone-socket?"

"In the Canyon of—oh."

"I assume you can't use your tree power in there among the rocks, or you would have done a better job of escaping from him than you did."

"I escaped from him!"

"In several pieces, yes. Very impressive. No, you're going to Samara, and I'm going to Bonesocket."

"If I can't use the trees' power in the canyon," said Jinx, thinking aloud, "then I couldn't have helped you strengthen the wards anyway."

"There are ways to move power," said Simon.

"Then why can't I—"

"Because," said Simon. "You are going to be in Samara, learning KnIP."

"You're thinking that you're going to kill him," Jinx said. "You can't kill him! He's tied your death to his."

"And? How many Cold Oats Clearings am I worth?"

"But . . ." Jinx was getting seriously upset. He didn't want Simon to die.

"I'll try to imprison him if I can. If I can't, I'll kill him. You, meanwhile," said Simon, "are going to be in another world, out of his reach."

"Maybe I'll follow you," said Jinx.

"Maybe you won't."

"If *I* killed him, would the curse still—"

"You're not going to kill him. He has undoubtedly bound your death to his as well. He would have taken care of that while you were his prisoner last summer."

"Oh," said Jinx.

He had a feeling that the Bonemaster was his responsibility, more than Simon's, but he wasn't sure why. It was all mixed up somehow with his almost-memory of elves.

"If there's a way to undo a deathbinding curse, you'll find it in the Temple libraries," said Simon. "Probably in a Qunthk book. There's a source some of the other Qunthk books refer to. It's called"—Simon made a sound as if he had a fishbone stuck in his throat.

"It's called *what*?"

"In Urwish, it's called the Eldritch Tome."

"The Eldritch Tome? And it's in the Temple library?"

"I don't know. But if it is, find it."

"What if it isn't?"

"Then you won't find it. But you're to stay there until you're sent for."

"How can I be sent for if you're dead?" Jinx demanded.

"The Bonemaster doesn't want to kill me. I'm worth nothing to him dead. He wants the bottle with my captive life back." Simon selected a very thick book bound in dragonskin, and added it to the stack. "And he's not going to get that. I expect to survive."

Jinx looked at the pile of books and felt hopeless. "You know what I think?"

"I can scarcely wait to find out."

"I think the Bonemaster, well, like, wiped out Cold Oats Clearing because he *wanted* you to come after him," said Jinx.

"That strikes me as extremely likely."

"So you'll be walking right into a trap."

"A trap for him, or for me?" said Simon.

"For you!"

Simon handed Jinx the book. "Put that on the pile."

The pile had grown too high for Jinx to reach the top. "What's in all these books?"

"Things you have to know to be admitted to the Temple."

"You mean they might not let me in?"

"They'll let you in. There's a test, that's all."

"What if I fail it?"

"You'd better not."

Jinx levitated the book to the top of the pile. The whole stack teetered for a moment, and then it collapsed, sending books cascading everywhere. Jinx ducked a flying volume. All the cats fled the room.

"Your job is to study these books, pass the test, get into the Temple, find the Eldritch Tome, and learn about the bottle spell. And learn KnIP." Simon turned to go. "Oh, and pick those books up."

Furious, Jinx levitated all the books with a whoosh and dumped them on the workbench.

~ ~ ~

Before Simon left, he taught Jinx two small spells. One was the word for opening the hiding place inside the thirteenth step in the south tower staircase. The word was *khththllkh*, and Jinx had to practice several times before he said it right.

Simon reached in and took out a green bottle. They both watched the tiny figure of Simon pacing around in a circle at the bottom of the bottle. This was Simon's lifeforce. The Bonemaster had bottled it years ago, when Simon was his apprentice.

Putting Simon's lifeforce back into Simon would require a talented wizard. Jinx was supposed to become that wizard. Someday.

"If—" said Jinx.

"Then you're to smash the bottle," said Simon.

"But can't I—"

"Not yet, you can't," said Simon. "You haven't learned enough."

"I could at least try," said Jinx.

"No, you couldn't. There are too many ways to mess it up if you don't know what you're doing."

Simon put the bottle back under the step. Jinx said *khththllkh* backward to lock the hiding place.

The other new spell was the one for watching Reven.

It involved putting another aviot on the stone sill, gazing into the Farseeing Window, and concentrating on Reven's aviot, the one Jinx had planted on him.

It wasn't that hard, as spells went, and Jinx got it right by feeling his way inside it. Reven appeared in the window, walking beside a river in the snow, hand in hand with Elfwyn.

"But where are they?" said Jinx.

"It appears to be Keyland," said Simon.

"Well, yeah, but what part?" It had been three weeks since Jinx had turned Siegfried into a tree. He knew Reven had left the Urwald, and not returned. The trees would have told Jinx if the Terror had come back. But what was he doing? Had he allied himself with Sir Thrip and Lord Badgertoe? Had he got followers? Had he taken all those abandoned axes as weapons for his revolution?

"The window doesn't really tell you much, does it?" said Jinx.

"Only what it wants to."

"The thing about Reven is he knows how to . . . work people." Jinx stared at Elfwyn and Reven, still trudging along in the snow. "Elfwyn said she wanted to learn magic and get her curse taken off her, but instead she's following Reven around and—" Jinx couldn't think how to explain the situation without admitting that he could see thoughts. "Following him."

"That's her choice," said Simon.

"But she's being really stupid about Reven!"

"You'll find, as you get older, that there's an area of life in which there are boundless opportunities for stupidity," said Simon.

"But I told her what he's like!"

"I'm sure *that* went over well. Are we through here?"

"I guess," said Jinx.

Simon handed Jinx the aviot, and Jinx stuck it in his pocket.

13

Through the Door

"I expect to reach Bonesocket by dawn," said Simon. "The Bonemaster could die any time after that, and if he's tied your death to his, I'm not sure what will happen. I want you out of the Urwald by midnight tonight. You'll stay in my house in Samara. Don't come back for any reason. Not even for an instant."

"What about the animals?" said Jinx.

"Ermentraud will look after them." Ermentraud was a woodcutter's wife who was their closest neighbor.

Simon dumped a handful of Samaran money on the kitchen table—a couple of gold birds, a bunch of silver snakes, and some copper crescent-moon shapes. "You'll need to buy some Samaran clothes. You can get your food in the marketplace, but stay away from the Temple until the term starts. You're supposed to have just come from Angara."

Jinx stuck his finger into a coiled silver snake. "Why?"

"Because nobody really knows much about Angara. It's a little backwater country a few hundred miles north of Samara. And they speak Herwa there, which you more or less know. And if you seem strange—which you will—people will put it down to your being Angaran and not very bright."

He handed Jinx a slim volume called *Sojourn Among Savages*. "Here's a book about Angara. Study it when you're done studying the other stuff."

"I'm never going to be done studying the other stuff," said Jinx, looking at the piles of books.

"Just don't take any of those books out of the Samaran house. Don't take them to the Temple with you."

"Why not?"

"Because books are viewed with great suspicion in Samara."

"Then why—"

"A lot of things aren't going to make sense," said Simon. "Just keep quiet and wait until they do. Be polite and don't call attention to yourself. Bow to any scholar above you in rank, which will be all of them. And—"

"I don't want to bow," said Jinx.

"Do it anyway. You're playing a role. Nobody must find out you're from the Urwald. They don't know there's any way to get to the Urwald, and you're not going to tell them. Oh, and absolutely do not do any magic. At all. Magic is highly illegal and you can be put to death for it."

"And you're sending me there to learn magic."

"Yes," said Simon.

"Wonderful," said Jinx.

"And watch your mouth. In fact, I can't send you there if you can't watch your mouth."

Anything Jinx might say to this would be taken as evidence that he couldn't watch his mouth. He glared at Simon.

"Good," said Simon. "And take this."

Jinx took it—a letter to Simon's wife. There had been lots of early versions of the letter that had gotten crumpled up and thrown into the air, where they burst into silver flames and then rained down as glittering pink ashes. This final version was sealed seventeen times with enchanted red wax.

"Give it to Sophie immediately," said Simon. "And don't read it, or—"

"You'll turn me into a toad." Jinx was looking forward to seeing Sophie again. She'd always been kind to him. Simon was kind too, Jinx supposed—but Sophie was actually nice about it. She never said "drop the attitude" or "because I said so."

Besides, he could ask her stuff. Though he supposed he could try asking Simon. "Have you ever talked to a werewolf?"

Simon gave him an odd look. "Of course not."

"I did," said Jinx.

"Nonsense. You wouldn't be standing here with all your pieces still attached if you had."

"But I did," Jinx insisted. "After, um, Siegfried . . . when I was wandering around, I met a werewolf. He told me I had to figure out what a Listener is."

"Were you hungry and tired?"

"Well, yeah, but—"

"You hallucinated a talking werewolf. And Listeners are just an old legend."

Jinx tried again. "What about elves?"

"What about them? They're dangerous. You'd better not try talking to them either," said Simon. "Here's twenty aviots to pay for your tuition at the Temple."

The gold was cold and very heavy in Jinx's hand. "It costs that much?"

"Yes," said Simon. "So don't screw up."

Jinx thought of something Reven had said. Simon *was* rich. Most magicians were merely comfortable.

"Why do you have so much money? And, like, this

house and stuff?" Jinx asked.

"I inherited it."

"But your dad, um, only just died."

"And wouldn't have left me anything if he'd had it," said Simon. "It was left to me, if you must know, by the great wizard Egbert Magus."

"Who was he?"

"A magician who took me in after I left the Bonemaster. On his good days, he tried to teach me everything he knew."

"What about his bad days?"

"On his bad days, he generally thought he was an onion."

"That's awful," said Jinx.

"No, it's not. What was awful was when he thought he was a potato masher."

"Oh."

"He always said to me, 'Mildred, one day this will all be yours.'" Simon made a wide gesture, encompassing books, cats, and the door to Samara.

"Er, he called you Mildred?"

"Often as not."

"Maybe he really meant to leave everything to Mildred," said Jinx.

"If she ever shows up, we'll talk," said Simon. "But I think she may have been a dog he once had."

"Oh," said Jinx. "Um, was that why you went to Samara to find the healing magic? For Egbert?"

"Yes."

Jinx was relieved to hear this. He'd been afraid, for a minute there, that Egbert had become Calvin. "So you didn't, like—"

But no, there was a familiar blue glow when Simon spoke of Egbert the Onion. It seemed he had been genuinely fond of him.

"Didn't what?"

"Didn't find the healing magic," Jinx amended.

"Of course not. They keep it well hidden."

"Why?"

"Oh yes," said Simon. "Why. Wait till you get to Samara. Then you'll see."

"I'm coming back pretty soon, though, right?" Jinx had frantic thoughts of Reven and the Bonemaster.

"You're staying there as long as it takes."

"To find the Eldritch thing?"

"You're to bring me the Eldritch Tome immediately."

"But taking the book—isn't that stealing?"

"Wait till you've been there a little while. Then tell me whether you think taking a book from the Temple is stealing."

"But . . . what if you don't come back?" said Jinx.

"Sophie'll look after you."

"I don't need to be looked after!" said Jinx. "I didn't mean that."

"Then you'll look after her. Anyway, you can stay on in Samara. Become one of those Temple things, like Sophie."

"I can't do that," said Jinx. There was too much that needed doing here—too many threats. Lumberjacks, Reven, the Bonemaster. Once again he had that odd feeling that the Bonemaster was *his* responsibility.

"Just make sure you're out of the Urwald by midnight," said Simon. "And don't worry about me. I'll come back."

After Simon left, Jinx began to have second thoughts. He should have insisted on going with him, deathbinding spell or no. It was true that the Urwald's power was making Jinx do frightening, unpredictable things, but he wouldn't mind doing a few unpredictable things to the Bonemaster.

On the one hand, Jinx wondered if he ought to follow Simon and insist on helping him. On the other hand, he had a pretty good idea of how much Simon would appreciate that. On the third—well, moving on to feet, then—it didn't matter whether Simon appreciated it or not. Jinx didn't want Simon to get killed. It wasn't like Jinx could necessarily do anything to *prevent* it, of course, but—

There came a familiar pounding on the door. Jinx groaned inwardly and went to open it.

"Hello, chipmunk!"

Dame Glammer stood there in the deep blue evening, just as she had when Jinx had first seen her many years ago—snow swirling around her butter churn.

"Come in," said Jinx, standing aside. He didn't want her here, he really didn't, but magicians had to be hospitable. It was a rule.

She took off her wraps and dumped them on him. "Simon here? I'll be staying the night. Where's my granddaughter?"

"Don't you know?" said Jinx. "Hasn't the Witchline told you?"

"Ah, you've been traveling." She chucked him under the chin, which Jinx hated. "And become such a clever little chipmunk! Know all about the Witchline now, do you?"

Jinx went over and busied himself at the fire, to avoid being chinchucked anymore. "Do you want some—kind of soup stuff?"

Cooking was something he was even worse at than spells. Throwing everything into a pot and boiling it didn't seem to do the trick, somehow.

Dame Glammer sniffed at the pot and wrinkled her enormous nose. "No, I'll whip something up, chipmunk. You go back to your stacks and stacks and stacks of books. Where's Simon?"

"Around. I'll make up the spare room for you," said Jinx. He didn't want to tell her Simon wasn't here. He found her frightening.

He went to look for blankets. He didn't like the idea of being alone in the house with her. But it was all right, he told himself. Dame Glammer was an old friend of Simon's. And just because she was also an old friend of the Bonemaster's didn't mean—well.

Jinx really wished she wasn't there.

But when he came back out to the kitchen, she'd made some sort of thing with onions and potatoes happen, and an omelet, and there was a smell of apples baking in the oven.

Which did make up, a little, for having to be cackled at.

Jinx pushed some books out of the way, dislodged a cat, and set the table.

"Simon! Dinner time!" the witch called merrily as she scooped fried potatoes and onions onto Jinx's plate. "No, he's not here, is he, chipmunk? He'd never have let me so much as peel an onion if he was."

That was true. Simon couldn't stand to see other people cook, because they did it all wrong.

"Now, I wonder where he's gone," said Dame Glammer, as a cat hopped into her lap and another curled around her ankles. "Can he have gone after the Bonemaster?"

"I don't know," said Jinx. The omelet was pretty decent, and the potato stuff was really good.

"And did my granddaughter stay in Keyland with that very ambitious young chickabiddy? She's as much of a fool as her mother was. Doesn't she want to be a witch?"

Jinx rather thought Elfwyn wanted to be a wizard. But

anyway, he could agree she was a fool. "She wants to get rid of her truth-telling curse."

"Does she?" Dame Glammer cackled.

Annoyed, Jinx added, "And she knows where she got it from, too."

But that just made Dame Glammer cackle more. "And she still thinks she can get rid of it? Well, I don't know how staying in Keyland will help."

"*Can* she get rid of it?" said Jinx. "Will you take it off her?"

Dame Glammer grinned. "Why don't you stick to your own concerns, chipmunk? What an awful lot of books you have. Are they magic?"

"No," said Jinx. They were not, not a single one of them. "You know what the Bonemaster *did*, right? You must have heard about it on the Witchline."

Dame Glammer frowned, an unusual expression for her. "Magicians don't interfere with each other."

Jinx clenched his fists. "We can't let him just go around killing people. We have to stop him. We have to all get together and stop him. And Reven—"

He tried to explain to her that the Urwald was being threatened, from within and without, by the Bonemaster and lumberjacks and Reven. But it was just like it had been talking to everyone else.

"Urwalders don't get together," she said. "We like

space, dearie. We like to mind our own business, and have others mind theirs."

She sniffed. "I think those apples are done. Why don't you go get them, chipmunk?"

The baked apples were bubbling with cinnamon. Jinx burned his fingers on them. He dug his spoon into apple mush. "Do you know anything about elves?"

"They're neither dead nor alive, and they're best left alone."

"Why? What can they do to you?" said Jinx.

"Carry you off to the Eldritch Depths. Turn you into a little crystal chipmunk, and put you in their glass gardens."

"Would they ever, like, talk to someone?"

"No chipmunk had better talk to them, if he knows what's good for him. Simon doesn't want you turned into a garden ornament, does he? Where *is* Simon, chipmunk?"

"Around," said Jinx. "So, like, what about werewolves?"

"What about them, dearie? Why do you want to talk to elves and werewolves?" She cackled. "You have enough troubles. More than you know, chipmunk. You don't need to go looking for more."

She was no help. Well, soon Jinx would see Sophie again. Sophie was a scholar, she'd studied the Urwald and its ways, and she always took Jinx seriously.

She could answer his questions if anybody could.

It was almost midnight. Dame Glammer was snoring loudly in one of the north tower rooms. Jinx didn't much like leaving her alone in the house, but at least Simon's bottled life was safe in the south wing. The front door would let in the people it knew—Simon's witch friends, and Elfwyn if she chose to come. And Reven, Jinx realized. But this door that led to the workroom and the secret entrance to Samara was more selective. It knew only Jinx, Simon, and Sophie.

Jinx looked around Simon's workroom. He'd put all Simon's stuff away on the shelves. The only thing left on the workbench was Calvin.

Jinx picked Calvin up. He was yellowed and old-looking. How long did it take for a skull to get that way? Simon had never admitted to killing Calvin, but he'd never denied it either. But Simon wasn't really old enough to have—

Calvin blinked furiously. What was that about? Oh. Jinx picked a dead fly out of one of Calvin's eye sockets. The skull grinned its thanks.

Jinx had only recently learned to recognize power sources. He saw now that Calvin was one.

Jinx thought of Cold Oats Clearing, and the bare, cold bones standing criss-cross. He remembered the purple potion in the snow. . . . Deathforce magic. Had Calvin been killed the same way?

At least Simon didn't *use* Calvin's power. As far as Jinx knew.

Jinx set Calvin down gently on the workbench. It occurred to him suddenly that he wouldn't have much power when he got to Samara. He remembered his terror in Keyland when he'd discovered that he had none.

"There are ways to move power," Simon had said. Maybe if Jinx just made sure there was enough fire inside him, he'd be able to do magic in Samara.

He went back out to the kitchen, and drew fire from the stove into himself. Then he levitated his huge stack of books and, pushing them ahead of him, went through the magically hidden door at the end of the corridor and into Simon's house in Samara.

~ ~ ~

Usually Jinx liked to read, but this wasn't reading, it was cramming, trying to get endless facts into his head and make them stick there—the history, geography, and laws of Samara, and of all the countries around Samara, and several books about math. Jinx was aware that math existed, but he didn't care. So he put those aside to concentrate on everything else.

He read *Sojourn Among Savages*. It had been written by a Samaran named Iznak who had spent two weeks in Angara, and most of what he wrote was pretty much what Simon had said—that people from Angara weren't very bright. Mainly this was because they did things differently from the way Samarans did them.

Once, in the night, Jinx heard a scratching on the Samaran door of the house. Nervous, he went to open it. Nobody. The moonlit street was empty.

He kept hoping Simon would come back. Simon had said he'd leave a signal when it was safe to return to the Urwald.

"An egg," he'd said. "Right here." He'd pointed to the low table in the front room of the Samaran house.

"An egg?" said Jinx.

"On second thought, no. An egg is too useful. Someone might take it."

"Who?" said Jinx.

"I'll move this table over by that wall. That's the signal. When the table's by the wall, you can come back to the Urwald. Not before."

"But you said you wanted the Eldritch Tome right away."

"If you can get it, leave it here. Hide it under the sofa cushions."

"Shouldn't I just put it in the book room?"

"Absolutely not in the book room. Under no circumstances."

"Why not?"

"Because," said Simon. "I said so."

166

Jinx had to struggle every day not to go back to the Urwald and look for Simon. Simon could be out searching for the Bonemaster, anywhere at all in the vast unmapped expanse of the Urwald.

Samara was hot. The sun glared down. Jinx walked around the outside of the Temple—past the gates that opened onto the market square, with the pillars and portico emblazoned with the words

KNOWLEDGE IS POWER

and past more halls and towers and outcroppings, to a small, unspectacular-looking gate. There was a bald, sallow man in a white robe blocking it.

"Here to be examined?" the man asked, in Samaran.

"Yes. I want to study—stuff," said Jinx.

"Novice lectors must pay twenty aviots."

"I know that," said Jinx.

The man held out his hand. "You can pay me. I'm the Gatekeeper."

"What if I don't pass the test?"

"That's your lookout," said the gatekeeper. "Mine is keeping out anybody that doesn't have twenty aviots."

This struck Jinx as extremely unfair.

But he had to find the Eldritch Tome. Without it, the

Bonemaster couldn't be defeated. He had to learn KnIP. And he had to find Sophie and get her to answer his questions about werewolves and elves. And Listeners. Jinx scooped the golden birds out of his inside pocket and, reluctantly, dropped them into the gatekeeper's cupped hands.

"Name? Age? Homeland?"

"Jinx. Thirteen. I'm, uh, from Angara."

The gatekeeper opened the gate for Jinx, and stood aside.

14

The Test

There were about forty people waiting to be tested. Jinx joined them, feeling very alone.

"Yinks?"

A scholar with dark-brown skin, and spectacles perched on the end of his nose, sat at a table. He peered around expectantly. Jinx went over to him.

"You are Yinks?" The man smiled. "I am Omar."

"Jinx, please," Jinx tried.

Omar smiled again. "Yes. Yinks. Now then, Yinks. Are you ready to be tested?"

"I guess. Yeah." And hurry up! Jinx could feel every single fact he'd memorized rushing to escape.

"Very good. Who was the seventeenth empress of the Perhatan City-State?"

"Olabisi the Unavoidably Delayed."

People nearby were tilting their heads to hear the questions. Omar glanced sideways at them, and Jinx saw quite clearly that the man changed the questions every time. That was odd—Jinx wasn't used to seeing thoughts as distinctly as he saw Omar's.

"And how, in that ancient empire, might one obtain permission to practice law?"

"By sacrificing a sacred camel to the law gods," said Jinx.

The next question caught him by surprise.

"What are the intelligent beings of the Urwald?"

"Uh," said Jinx.

Now here was the thing. He could see in Omar's mind that he wanted three answers. Jinx didn't have the foggiest idea, however, which three creatures Omar wanted. Trolls? No, probably not. Vampires?

"Humans, werewolves, and elves," said Jinx.

And saw immediately from Omar's thoughts that he had gotten the question wrong.

Omar kept smiling. "Divide 171 by 3, multiply by 40, and divide by 12."

Ouch. This was not Jinx's kind of thing at all. But—there was the number, sitting right in front of Omar's brain.

"One hundred and ninety," he said, relieved.

Omar moved on to testing Jinx in languages. This was easy. Jinx talked to Omar in Samaran, Herwa, and Urwish. He would have kept going with more languages, but Omar stopped him.

"Excellent." Omar switched back to Samaran. "You pass. Welcome to the Temple of Knowledge. You are now a Lector. Your Urwish accent isn't very good, I'm afraid, but you have quite an advanced vocabulary."

"Uh. Thanks," said Jinx, taking the silver badge that Omar handed him. That was it? Wasn't Omar going to ask him about the Cheese Wars, or what caused the revolt of the Gnatcatchers of Upper Gribslime? Jinx suddenly felt he remembered everything and that Omar was unfair not to ask him.

Omar looked down at his list. "Satya!"

Satya was a girl with golden skin, and black hair that swished around her shoulders when she walked. Jinx listened to her answering questions. She didn't even need to stop and think. But she wasn't nearly as good at languages as Jinx was.

Jinx examined the badge in his hand. It was stamped with an image of a locked book.

"Want me to put that on for you?"

The girl named Satya took the badge from Jinx's hand and pinned it to his collar.

"You're Yinks?" she said.

"Actually it's pronounced Jinx."

The girl frowned with concentration. "ZH-inks."

"That's very close," said Jinx.

"You're from Angara?"

Apparently that was the sort of news that got around fast about a person. "Yes."

"Right in Agnopolis, or out in the country?"

"Um, yeah. Agnopolis."

"Cool," said Satya. "I spent six months in Agnopolis brushing up on my Herwa. Go Grapemen, eh?" She stuck her fist out.

Gack! Jinx tried hard to hide his alarm. He stuck his fist out too and said, "Yes. Go. Exactly."

She smiled, and Jinx saw that she knew he'd never been anywhere near Agnopolis in his life. Oddly, this seemed to please her.

"You did real well on the test," she said.

"Not as well as you," said Jinx.

She shrugged. "The only thing you got wrong was that question about the Urwald, and really, Urwald questions are tough."

"Yeah. Well. What *are* the three intelligent beings of the Urwald?"

"Witches, wizards, and humans," said Satya.

"But—" Jinx stopped himself from saying witches and wizards *were* humans. "Oh, well. Now I know."

"Anyway, don't worry," said Satya. "The guy before you only got two questions right, and they let him in. I kind of think the most important question is 'Have you got twenty aviots?'"

Just then a woman in gatekeeper's robes called "Yinks!"

Jinx went over to her. She was peering down a list.

"From Angara, are you?"

"Yes," said Jinx, defensively.

"Might as well put you in with Wendell. *He* won't object." The woman handed him a key. "That's for your room."

~ ~ ~

Jinx found room 411 on the fourth floor at the end of a long corridor. He knocked.

The door banged open, and a boy stepped out into the hall. "Come in! I'm Wendell." He looked around. "Help you carry your bags?"

"I don't have any bags," said Jinx.

"Well, come in! My room is your room. Obviously. I mean, well, you're the new roommate, right?" The boy looked down at Jinx and scratched his head uncertainly.

Wendell had yellow hair that stuck up like a brush, and a confused but amiable expression. And he was older than Jinx. About fifteen, Jinx guessed—about Reven's age.

Jinx stepped into the room. One side looked very lived in, with books and papers scattered around and stray socks under the bed. The other had a bed, and nothing else.

"That's your side," said Wendell. "Well, unless you want this side. I can always move."

"You were here first," said Jinx.

"No, really, if you'd rather have this side, I can move. I don't mind at all."

"I wouldn't," Jinx assured him quickly, because Wendell was already gathering up his socks preparatory to making the move. "This side's great."

"Okay." Wendell dropped the socks back on the floor. "Well, make yourself at home. Obviously. What's your name?"

"Jinx."

"Jinks," Wendell repeated.

"You said it right."

"Oh, well. Urwish, right? Languages are the only thing I don't totally suck at," said Wendell, with an embarrassed smile. He sat down on the bed. "I'm pretty lousy at everything else. But people expect that of you when you're from Angara."

"Glup," said Jinx.

15

The Mistletoe Alliance

"So where are *you* from?" said Wendell.

"Um—"

"Oh, right! You must be the other guy from Angara. Someone said there was one."

"Go Grapemen," said Jinx.

"Really? Everyone's entitled to their opinion, I guess." Wendell had been leaning back on his elbows, but he rolled to his feet. "You want me to show you around?"

"Sure."

From outside, the Temple of Knowledge had been huge. But inside, there was just a square, four stories high, containing bedrooms, a dining hall, classrooms—

"Where's the library?" said Jinx.

"Right down here." Wendell led the way down a hall that ended in double doors. He swept the doors open with a flourish.

The library wasn't small, exactly. It contained, altogether, maybe twice as many books as Simon owned.

Well, it wouldn't take long to find the Eldritch Tome, if it was here. Jinx walked along one wall, reading titles.

"Er—where are the books about magic?"

"There aren't any," said Wendell.

"But—I came here to study magic." He remembered what Sophie had said about studying magic at the Temple. "Magic in theory, I mean."

"Oh, you'll do that when you go out into the main Temple," said Wendell, gesturing vaguely eastward. "Here in the Hutch, we just study the basics. The Seven Truths, the Thirteen Fallacies, and the Nine Virtues."

"The Hutch?"

"The Lectors' Square. It's where they keep the lectors who haven't made scholar. If you make scholar, they let you into the main Temple. There's tons of books and stuff there." Wendell shrugged. "We're not allowed in there, of course."

"But I have a friend in there that I have to see!"

"You could probably go around and ask for him at the visitors' entrance."

Jinx had to see Sophie soon. If he couldn't get into the libraries, then he needed her to steal the Eldritch Tome. Of course, she might refuse. Sophie took a dim view of all things magical. But surely when she understood how important it was . . .

Besides, he needed Sophie to explain to him about werewolves, elves, and Listeners.

"How long does it take to make scholar?"

"Varies," said Wendell. "But only one in ten make it."

"One in *ten*?"

"Well, yeah, but you'll make it. I can tell you're smart. Most of my roommates have been smart. In fact, all of my roommates have gotten through." Wendell smiled like he didn't mind this, and there was an orange puff of hurt that said he minded it very much.

"All your roommates? How long have you been here?" said Jinx.

"Four years."

"Four years? And you haven't—" Jinx stopped himself, because the orange puff of hurt was starting to grow. "Er, are the Nine Virtues or whatever pretty hard to learn, then?"

"For me they are," said Wendell. "Because I kind of suck at that stuff. You have to argue your point of view, you know? And I'm not very good at that."

Suddenly Wendell kicked a bookcase. "I hate it here!"

A book plopped out onto the floor. Wendell knelt down and dusted it off carefully, and checked it all over to make sure it hadn't come to any harm.

"Why do you stay, then?" said Jinx.

"I've got no choice. My grandfather wanted me to be a scholar, and he left all this money for it. So far my family's spent eighty aviots and I'm no closer to making scholar than I ever was. I'm stuck here till the money runs out."

"Just leave," said Jinx. "What's stopping you?"

"My grandfather's *dead.*"

"So?" Jinx realized that had come out wrong. "I mean, that's too bad, but—"

"You don't know much about Chemeans, do you?"

Oops. Uh-oh. Jinx ran through *Sojourn Among Savages* in his head. The Chemeans were a tribe in northern Angara. There was something in there about—"Er, they dig their dead up and sit them down to dinner?"

Wendell smiled. "We only do that once a year. And it's not, I mean—well, it's this big holiday, and we carry them around in a procession. It's quite—well, weird, actually."

"You don't eat dinner with them?"

"Well, the dead don't actually eat, just we do. I mean we don't eat the—we eat regular food, obviously."

Jinx found this deeply disturbing. But he tried hard not to show it, because Wendell was watching him closely for just that kind of reaction, and the big orange blob of hurt was waiting to grow.

"Um, so, like, they eat too?" said Jinx.

"No, of course not. They're dead. But they sit up at the table, or, well, we tie them to the chairs, kind of. But, see, once you're dead, you're a god, you know? I *have* to do what my grandfather said. There's no way out."

Jinx was nonplussed. "I guess if that's what you believe—"

"It's not," said Wendell. "But the rest of my family believes it, enough to keep throwing away aviots till there's nothing left. So I have to keep trying. What's the word? Persevere."

Jinx thought of something Elfwyn had once said. "A girl I know says—"

"You know a girl?"

Jinx laughed. "Well, yeah."

"I wish I knew a girl. Sorry, go on. She says?"

"There are plenty of girls here," said Jinx. It was a thing he had noticed.

"Yeah, but you can't actually *know* people here," said Wendell. "You'll see what I mean. Everyone's too busy trying to get ahead. Anyway, this girl, she said?"

"She said sometimes you're happier if you don't persevere."

"Oh, she's right about that." Wendell sighed. "But like I told you, I've got no choice. Come on, it's almost dinner."

"Hang on," said Jinx. He wanted to find a really thick book about Angara.

~ ~ ~

Jinx cursed Simon in his head. Jinx had only a one in ten chance of even getting *into* the Temple? And, meanwhile, he couldn't learn anything about magic at all. Why had Simon neglected to mention this? Was he just getting rid of Jinx? Sticking him in Samara while Simon went off to get himself killed by the Bonemaster?

What Jinx ought to do right now was walk out of this silly lector jail, walk straight through Samara and back to the Urwald.

But first, he had to get the Eldritch Tome.

He was going to have to ask Sophie to get it for him. The problem was, he hadn't had a chance to find her yet. They never let him alone for a minute. There were classes all the time.

It was like Wendell had said—a lot of talking about the Fallacies, Truths, and Virtues. Jinx couldn't see what this had to do with real life—real life was stuff like having to worry about whether some guy was going to invade your country when the people who lived in it didn't even know it was a country, and wondering if you had imagined talking to werewolves and elves, and if not, what should you do about it. During a discussion of the Fourth Fallacy ("You can believe what you see with your own eyes") he asked:

"What makes a country—well, a country?"

Omar smiled at him. "Precisely!"

Jinx waited for Omar to say more, but Omar did not. "Well, what does, then?"

"How did Samara begin?" said Omar.

Jinx remembered this from the stuff he'd crammed into his head at Simon's house. "Three women poured out water from jugs, and the water from one of the jugs became the Crocodile River, and—"

A girl named Bridget snickered. Several other lectors sneered.

Omar smiled. "Seriously, Yinks."

Jinx *was* being serious. He'd read it in a book.

"The warring river tribes signed a treaty to join together and fight the encroaching brigands from the inner desert tribes," Satya supplied.

Jinx turned to her. "How?"

Satya frowned. "What do you mean, how?"

"How did anybody get them to agree to work together?" Jinx thought about the Urwald clearings that didn't trust each other, and the magicians that didn't want to get involved.

"They did it because they had to, of course," said Satya.

"But what made them realize it?" said Jinx.

The other lectors were looking at Jinx like he was stupid. But he had to know.

"Because things were bad," said Bridget scornfully. "People were attacking them, duh."

Omar clucked his tongue disapprovingly at her. She shrugged.

"Why don't you tell us how Angara became a nation, Yinks?" said Omar.

Jinx froze. He didn't remember this. He wasn't sure the books he'd read had mentioned it at all. No, wait, there had been something about people being formed from rocks. Jinx started to say it and then realized it might just be a legend. And Bridget was already waiting to sneer.

Wendell cleared his throat nervously, and Omar looked at him in surprise.

"It was King Welmut," said Wendell. "Well, he wasn't king then, obviously, but he arrived and all the Chemeans and Murkians and stuff were just . . . well, hanging around, obviously, and he said all the land was his and started killing everybody so they made him king, and well, like . . . that was Angara, you know. . . ."

"'Obviously,'" said Bridget. It had taken Wendell a long time to get all this out, and people were rolling their eyes and squirming with impatience.

So there were at least two ways to become a country, then. But which was more like the Urwald—Samara's way, or Angara's?

Both, Jinx thought. If all the clearings unite, it'll be

like Samara. And if the Bonemaster gets us all under his control, or Reven conquers us, it'll be like Angara.

"How do you get other countries to . . . well, admit that you've got a country?" said Jinx. "Like, I mean, not just treat you like you're a part of their country?"

"You fight a war, duh," said Bridget.

Jinx tried to imagine Urwalders fighting a war. It didn't work. For one thing, everything he'd read about wars suggested they had a lot of people on each side. You'd never get Urwalders to all fight on one side. Each clearing would be its own side.

"So what's the next question?" said Omar.

"How do you get people to unite?" said Jinx. "I mean work together, when they really don't even like each other much?"

"Ah." Omar folded his hands and rested his chin on them. "That, Yinks, is one of the great questions."

Jinx wished Omar would supply an answer or two.

"You know, Yinks, it has often been said that a person must leave his own country in order to truly understand it."

Yeah, great. But how were you supposed to understand your own country when there was no one you could ask?

There was one thing he did know about his country. It wasn't going to unite under any king. Jinx remembered how the Keylanders had gathered eagerly around Reven, and looked at him with shining eyes. Witch Seymour was

183

right; Urwalders would never do that.

"I thought we were supposed to be discussing the Fourth Fallacy," Bridget said.

~ ~ ~

There was a heavy iron door between the Lector's Square and the main Temple. Jinx tried it—it was locked. Without thinking, he did a door-opening spell, but it was no good. The door was locked with a plain old lock, not magic.

A gatekeeper materialized at his side. "What are you doing?"

"Nothing," said Jinx, putting his hands behind his back.

"Are you under *orders* to try to get into the Temple?"

Pretty much. "Orders?" Jinx tried to laugh. "No. Why? From who? I was just curious."

The gatekeeper glowed suspicion. "Curiosity isn't wanted. Run along."

The next day a scholar summoned Jinx into an empty classroom.

"I am Proctor Ling," she said.

"I'm Jinx."

"Yes, I know that. I am told by Docent Omar that you show an unusually quick understanding of the Truths, Virtues, and Fallacies."

"Thanks," said Jinx. He didn't say that he couldn't make head nor tail of the Truths, Virtues, and Fallacies.

He had already figured out that that was the point of them.

"Tell me, Zinx, why are you here?"

"I want to be a scholar."

She pushed her spectacles down to the end of her nose and stared at him over them. "Why don't you tell me why you're *really* here?"

Jinx was startled. Had someone recognized him?

"To learn stuff! I want to know—everything, really."

At that, her thoughts acquired a silver glow of suspicion. "Why?"

"I don't know." Jinx was getting nervous. "To help the people back where I come from."

"And that's"—she glanced down at a paper in her hand—"Angara?"

"Go Grapemen," said Jinx.

"Hm. Perhaps. But scholars stay *here*, you know."

He tried hard to look innocent. "Well, yeah, but I can still go back and, like, tell people stuff. We're pretty backward in Angara."

"Knowledge is power." She watched his face carefully.

"Right," said Jinx. "Exactly. Like it says on the front of the Temple."

"And that doesn't mean anything to you?"

"Sure it does," said Jinx. "It's a saying." *Also a kind of illegal magic.*

"Tell me, Zinx, have you ever heard of the"—she

squinched her mouth around the words as if they tasted unpleasant—"Mistletoe Alliance?"

"The what? No."

"You speak excellent Samaran."

"Thank you," said Jinx. "What's the Mistletoe Alliance?"

"A gang of desperate criminals trying to steal the knowledge that is guarded in the Temple."

"Oh." It seemed a bit unfair that she was suspecting him of exactly the wrong thing. "I never even heard of them. Why are they called that? I mean mistletoe doesn't grow here, does it?"

"It doesn't grow anywhere," she said. "It doesn't exist."

"Oh," said Jinx, remembering helping Simon gather it in the forest.

"In mythology, mistletoe is the key to life and death, the magical balance between the two."

Jinx wanted to ask her what that meant, but he had a feeling now would be a really bad time to show an interest in magic. "So, um, is that why lectors aren't allowed into the libraries?"

"Precisely," said Ling. "Knowledge must be kept safe. And for all we know, you could be one of their agents. You say you're not Samaran, but you speak the language like a native."

"I started learning it when I was little," said Jinx.

"Hm. Well, we will be watching you."

Jinx decided it was all right to get a little irritated.

"You can watch me all you want, because I have nothing to do with them."

"Then you have nothing to fear," said Ling.

Jinx decided not to ask what people who *were* in the Mistletoe Alliance had to fear.

~ ~ ~

When they finally got a free minute, Wendell showed Jinx the way to the visitors' entrance. They had to go around the outside wall of the Temple and in through a separate gate. There was an arched doorway, with a counter blocking the way.

The woman behind it wore white gatekeeper robes.

"Name?" she asked.

"Er, mine?"

"No, that does not matter. The scholar you wish to speak to."

"Sophie." Jinx had now learned Sophie's whole name, in the Samaran system. "Sophie Maya Simon."

In Samara you started out with your mother's or father's first name as a last name, and if you got married you added your husband's or wife's first name after that.

"There's nobody here by that name."

"But you didn't even look in your book," said Jinx.

"I don't need to look in my book, young man, to know that there is nobody here by that name," said the woman coldly.

"*Could* you look, please?" said Jinx.

"No, I could not," said the gatekeeper. "Because I do not need to look, because there is nobody here by that name."

"She's a professor here," said Jinx. "Maybe she just goes by Sophie Maya."

"I think I would know the name of a professor."

"Are there any Sophies at all?" said Jinx, desperate.

"No."

"But there has to be one!"

"Who are *you*?" The woman looked threatening.

"You said that didn't matter," said Jinx.

"Anyone who comes in here, wearing a lector's badge and acting rude, I want to know the name of."

"Let's go," said Wendell.

And Jinx had to agree—he didn't want the gatekeeper to report him to somebody and get him kicked out of the Hutch.

It was strange, though. There had been no sign of anything but anger floating around the woman's head—a sort of nebulous white anger that went through life looking for things to fix its attention on. She didn't seem to be lying. It seemed there really *was* no Sophie in her book.

16

Crocodile Bottom

"I don't get it," said Jinx, when they were outside. "She *has* to be here."

"Who is Sophie, anyway?" Wendell asked.

"A friend." Jinx opened his mouth, and then closed it—he couldn't tell Wendell any of the things that would explain why Sophie was important to him. "She's—I've known her since I was little. She, uh, visited us in Angara."

"Oh." Clearly none of this sounded desperate to Wendell. "Well, she'll probably turn up. She's probably right here inside the Temple. That gatekeeper seemed like one of those people who just say no all the time because they can." He brightened suddenly. "Hey, you want to go into the city?"

"We're allowed?" It seemed to Jinx that life in the Hutch largely consisted of not being allowed to do things.

"Sure. This isn't really a prison," said Wendell. "Well, not for most people, anyway, it is for me obviously, but we're allowed out."

What Jinx really wanted was to find Sophie. But he would like to get out. Days in the Hutch were packed with classes and exams. There was hardly time for anything else but eating and sleeping.

"We'll just skip the after-dinner lecture," said Wendell.

"We're allowed to do that?"

"Sure. Well, you probably don't want to," said Wendell.

"I do. I really do."

They went around to the Market Square. The gates to the Temple there were closed, and guarded by three stony-faced gatekeepers.

"That's weird," said Jinx, as he and Wendell stood looking up at the words

KNOWLEDGE IS POWER

"Did there used to be gatekeepers there?" Last year he'd walked right through the open gates and no one had stopped him.

"No. There was some kind of fuss a while back and they put more gatekeepers on."

Jinx knew about the fuss—he'd caused it.

"Are the gatekeepers there all night?"

"Why? Are you thinking of breaking in?" said Wendell.

Jinx laughed uncomfortably. How was he going to find Sophie, and the book?

"Let's go to Crocodile Bottom," said Wendell. "It's a *real* place."

"Not like the Temple?" said Jinx.

"Not at all like the Temple."

It was evening, and the square was nearly empty. Jinx and Wendell crossed it and turned down a street to the north. They walked past inns with tables out on the street where people were eating and drinking.

"This is Temple Close," said Wendell. "Hardly anyone ever gets attacked here."

"That's good," said Jinx.

"You're really worried about your friend, huh?"

"Yeah," said Jinx. "Why would her name not be in that lady's book? How many professors are there, anyway?"

"I don't know. You could ask Omar. Are you sure she didn't just leave?"

"I guess she could have. Do professors leave a lot?"

"I think pretty much never," said Wendell. "I mean once you're in the Temple, you're in it for life."

"Not me," said Jinx, without thinking.

"Really?" said Wendell. "Why are you working so hard to get in, then?"

"There's just stuff I want to learn," said Jinx.

"What kind of stuff?"

"Oh, stuff. Everything."

"I see." There was that orange blob of hurt again, which sometimes got on Jinx's nerves. "Probably stuff I'm not smart enough to understand."

"You are smart," said Jinx, annoyed. "You just have to talk the way the teachers want, that's all. All the Fallacies are true, and all the Truths are false, but you have to be able to make an argument the other way around. That's what they want."

"Well, that doesn't make any sense to me," said Wendell.

The streets became narrower and twistier. There were more people around, and though they were dirtier and more ragged than the people in Temple Close, they laughed more. And there were lots of dogs. They sniffed at Jinx's feet and wagged their tails. Jinx scratched their ears and decided he liked dogs better than cats.

"If I could do anything I wanted, I'd live in Crocodile Bottom," said Wendell. "I got a job down here once, guiding some merchants for a few days. They were staying at the Twisted Branch, and they *sort of* spoke Samaran, but people wouldn't listen. I took them all the places they needed to go—it was great. And they paid me eighteen silver serpents, and when I got back to the

Temple nobody even noticed I'd been gone."

"Why don't you just leave, then?" said Jinx.

"Grandpa," said Wendell tersely.

The air started to feel different. And then Jinx saw why. There was a tree, growing beside a tumbledown house. A real tree, with branches.

"There are trees down here!"

"Yeah," said Wendell. "There're even more around the Twisted Branch. It's down here—down Strait Street. I asked Satya to come down here with me one time, but she said she hates to go out in the city at night."

Jinx groaned inwardly. Ever since he'd introduced Wendell to Satya, the conversation always came around to her sooner or later.

"Actually she said she hates to go out in the city at all," said Wendell. "You think she likes me?"

"Sure," said Jinx. "Why wouldn't she?"

"Well, why would she?"

"Because you're perfectly likeable," said Jinx.

"Lots of people don't like me."

This, unfortunately, was true. Most of the lectors scorned Wendell. They knew he'd never make scholar.

"Anyway, we're talking about *girls*," said Wendell. "*Girls* is different."

"Yeah, I don't know," said Jinx. Actually he did—there hadn't been any signs of pink fluffy thoughts from Satya.

"Here we are," said Wendell.

They came into a courtyard full of trees. There was an inn behind it—much bigger and louder than the inns in Temple Close. But Jinx's attention was caught by the people in the courtyard.

"Flipdancers," said Wendell.

The flipdancers made Jinx forget about Sophie, the Temple, and everything.

They leapt into the air, turned backflips and somersaults, sprung up and landed on each other's shoulders, and then flew off again, turning over and over in the air and landing lightly on their feet. It had to be magic.

When the flipdancers bounced to a stop, a tiny creature with a tail came through the crowd, shaking a tin box in its paw.

"What's that?" said Jinx.

"A monkey. He wants coins, if you've got any. Hey, get away, you." Wendell swatted at the monkey's hands as it tried to reach into his pocket.

Jinx laughed and gave the monkey a silver serpent. It was a lot, but it was Simon's money, and the flipdancers had been great. He turned to watch the monkey scramble away. The crowd was breaking up, and—

Now, that was odd. There was a girl hurrying down the street, and Jinx couldn't be sure in the darkness, but she looked an awful lot like Satya.

"Did you follow the story?" said Wendell. "See, that

backflip that girl did at the end means betrayal, and the kind of swish they do with their right foot means marriage—so, like, she thought she was going to marry this guy, and he ran off—"

"What?" said Jinx. He was still watching the girl in the street, and she hadn't tossed her hair like Satya did.

"Flipdancing always tells a story," said Wendell. "Only there's always a double meaning, like in this case it was really about Samara going back on their agreement not to make war against Vesalia."

A woman nearby scowled at Wendell and hurried away.

"How do you know that?" said Jinx.

"Figured it out," said Wendell, with a shrug.

"You figured out what flipdancing means and you can't figure out the Truths and Fallacies?" said Jinx.

"Well, sure," said Wendell. "Flipdancing is real."

Jinx looked down the road. The girl was nearly out of sight now, and she still hadn't shaken her hair. It probably wasn't Satya. "What's down there?"

"Where?" Wendell looked where Jinx pointed. "The river. Crocodiles, pressmen, crooks. It's kind of cool, actually."

"What are pressmen?"

"They knock you on the head, throw you in a bag, and ship you off to the army. You wake up in the middle of whatever war Samara's fighting at the moment."

"Samara's in a war?"

"Sure, all the time." Wendell looked at him oddly. "You must have had to pass through the checkpoints on the road from Angara. We'd better get back, you know. It's getting kind of late."

Jinx looked down the road toward the river. If that really was Satya he'd seen— "They don't grab girls, do they?"

"No," said Wendell. "But they'd sure grab us if they caught us."

Jinx and Wendell started home. Jinx gave up worrying about Satya. "That monkey was cool."

"Oh yes," said Wendell. "He's just like the ones that pass the hat at the puppet shows back home in Agnopolis."

❧ ❧ ❧

Omar seemed like the most approachable of the teachers. Maybe he would tell Jinx where Sophie was. Jinx stopped him in the hall after class.

"Yes?" Omar smiled down at him. "By the way, that was an excellent explication of the Third Truth."

"Thanks." The Third Truth was *No one has ever been wrong since the world began.* "Was I right?"

"It doesn't matter whether you're right," said Omar reprovingly. "What matters is how well you defend your statements."

But Jinx could see quite clearly in Omar's thoughts that he'd been right: No one is ever wrong from their own point of view. It suddenly occurred to Jinx why Omar's thoughts were so easy to see.

"Excuse me," said Jinx. "Do you ever feel, like, sad or mad or anything like that?"

It was rather a personal question, but Omar was not perturbed at all. "Sometimes, perhaps, but as little as possible. I strive for complete equilibrium. Do you know why?"

"Why?"

"Because I wish to have a purely rational mind."

"Oh. Um, so does that mean, like, that you have thoughts *instead* of feelings?"

"An interesting way to put it." Omar smiled. "I shall have to think about that."

That's why I can see your thoughts so clearly, Jinx wanted to say. But the remark would not have made him and Omar better friends, so he kept it to himself.

"What's the Mistletoe Alliance?" Jinx asked.

Omar smiled at him. "An interesting example of citizen rebellion. It raises some fascinating questions. What is knowledge?"

"Um, I don't know," said Jinx. "Stuff people know. But, well—they steal knowledge, right? How can you steal knowledge?"

"Exactly so!" said Omar.

This was not very helpful. "How *do* they?"

"In various ways. One is to steal books," said Omar. "Of course, they often return them."

"So they borrow them," said Jinx.

"Not quite borrowing," said Omar, "because they steal the knowledge out of them."

"You mean the books are blank when they give them back?" Jinx asked, confused.

"I mean that they allow many people to read them. After this has been done, the books are often left tied up in bundles on the portico of the Temple, as if to mock those within. Or this was done in the past, rather, before guards were posted. It's fascinating, really."

"It doesn't sound very wrong to me," said Jinx. "I mean it doesn't sound like a crime."

"And why doesn't it seem wrong to you?"

"Well, because it doesn't hurt anyone," said Jinx. "The books come back, and more people have read them, and, well—that's what books are for, isn't it?"

"That's a theory, certainly," said Omar, smiling. "And really, young man, it's a theory you would perhaps do best not to share with anyone else."

Especially since Jinx was planning to steal the Eldritch Tome if he could find it. "Um, I was wondering . . . do you know a professor named Sophie?"

Omar frowned. "Named . . . ? No. No, I'm afraid I'm not acquainted with anyone of that name. Now if you'll excuse me, this has been a very interesting discussion, but I have some lecture notes to prepare."

And because Omar's mind was so easy to read, Jinx could plainly see a picture of Sophie's face floating right there in the middle of Omar's thoughts.

17

Simon Takes a Turn for the Worse

No one would tell Jinx where Sophie was, or even admit she existed. He needed advice. Maybe Simon was back by now. He might have moved the table over to the wall, signaling it was safe for Jinx to return.

It was difficult to get rid of Wendell, who was always eager to go out into the city. In the city Wendell was almost a different person—at least, he was a much more confident, less nervous and diffident person.

Jinx followed the winding streets through the part of town called the Eastern Crescent, till he got to the blue-violet door to Simon's house.

The front room was thick with dust. Were there

footprints in it? Jinx couldn't tell. Anyway, the table was right where it had been. Simon hadn't come back.

Jinx went through the book room to the enchanted door that led to the Urwald. Once he passed through it he'd be in the Urwald—and subject to the Bonemaster's deathbinding curse.

Suppose Simon had killed the Bonemaster, and triggered the curse? Then Simon was dead. What about Jinx? Would he drop dead when he opened the door? Or would he survive because he hadn't been in the Urwald when the Bonemaster died?

Jinx opened the door. So far, so good. He took a breath, which might be his last, and stepped into the stone hallway of Simon's Urwald house. He was still alive.

He lit a candle. Cats punched their heads against his knees and yowled. The workroom was exactly as Jinx had left it. He went out to the kitchen. There was no sign of Simon anywhere. He had never come back.

Jinx went up the winding staircase to the Farseeing Window. He willed it to show him Simon, but it showed him nothing but the dark Urwald night.

Jinx felt a longing to talk to someone. Elfwyn, for example. The window used to always show him Elfwyn, before he'd ever met her. It didn't now.

He put an aviot on the sill, and concentrated on the bespelled coin in Reven's boot.

Shapes moved in the darkness of the window. Gradually Jinx made out a boiling mass of fighting men and women, some armed with axes, some with swords, and some with sticks. Then the moon came out from behind a cloud, and he could see Eric the Lumberjack lying on the ground, not moving. Somewhere in that seething battle must be Reven, but Jinx couldn't pick him out. He couldn't see Elfwyn. He really hoped she wasn't there. But she probably was. Thinking pink fluffy thoughts amid the mayhem.

He put the aviot in his pocket, ending the spell. Then he stood looking into the window for a while, hoping it might show him what had happened to Simon. It didn't.

Maybe Simon had been captured by the Bonemaster. Or maybe Simon was, well, dead, in which case there wasn't anything for Jinx to do but try to figure out how to do the bottle spell.

The bottle! Why hadn't Jinx thought of that before? Clutching the candle and tripping over cats, he rushed downstairs, through the kitchen, and up the stairs that led to Simon's room. He knelt before the thirteenth step, said "*Khththllkh,*" and drew out the bottle containing Simon's life.

He examined it in the candlelight. The tiny Simon was sitting on the floor of the bottle, his arms around his knees, staring straight ahead. Was he dead? No, Jinx could see him breathing. But why was he just sitting there? He did sit down sometimes, it was true, but mostly he paced around. Jinx gave the bottle a shake.

The figure didn't glare at him as the real Simon would have. But then it had never seemed to notice what went on outside the bottle. Jinx pinged the bottle with his fingernail, but the figure didn't look up.

One of the cats rubbed its head against the bottle. Jinx shoved the cat away, and, clutching the bottle, ran down the steps to Simon's workroom. He tore feverishly through the bookshelf till he found the Crimson Grimoire, the only book Simon had about the bottle spell.

He turned the pages. Jinx found Qunthk impossible to understand. Usually languages just talked to him if he paid attention. Qunthk didn't. It was the same language as the *khththllkh* spell, but that was about all he could tell. How had Simon ever learned it, anyway?

Frustrated, Jinx tossed the book aside and gave the bottle a shake. The tiny Simon inside it fell over.

Simon made no effort to get up. He just lay there. Still breathing.

"Sorry," said Jinx. He wondered whether he should shake the bottle some more to try to get Simon upright again.

Probably not.

But what did it mean?

Jinx was going to have to decipher the book. He'd

have to take it back to Samara with him, where having it was almost certainly illegal. Should he take Simon back, too?

No, probably not. There were three spells protecting the bottle—the wards around the clearing, the door spell, and the *khththllkh* spell.

Jinx went back up to the thirteenth step, scooped a cat out of the hollow under it, put the bottle away, and said the word to seal it in.

The house felt impossibly lonely, and Jinx needed to talk to someone. Anyone who wasn't a cat. He went outside. The night was cold and starlit. He crossed the clearing. He heard the trees murmur and whisper to each other, and that made him feel better.

Trees didn't get frustrated and upset like Jinx did, and he had to calm himself and slow his thoughts.

Where's Simon? he asked. But although the trees knew what Jinx meant by Simon—he'd taught them that—they didn't know where he was, amid the vastness, any more than they knew where a particular porcupine or werewolf was.

He told them about what he had seen in the bottle.

Wizard's magic, said the forest.

Yes, said Jinx. *But how do I find out what's happened to Simon?*

He is not dead?

I can't tell. I have to read the red book. He explained to the trees what a book was—a spell for sending thoughts through time and space.

Perhaps he's gone dormant.

I don't think humans go dormant, said Jinx.

Wizard's magic, the trees murmured.

Could the Bonemaster do something like that? Jinx almost asked, but then he decided it would be annoying to hear the trees say "wizard's magic" again, as if that explained everything.

Instead he asked the trees if they'd seen Elfwyn, and he showed them the idea of Elfwyn. But they had never noticed her.

They weren't much help. But there was one thing he could ask them.

What does it mean to be a Listener?

A Listener. There has always been a Listener. No, for many circles of years there was no Listener. The Listeners have deep roots. The Restless have no roots. Yes, they do. The trees' argument with each other was a soft rustle, like wind in spring leaves.

It was also not very informative.

That girl you showed me before, the one who the tree branch reached down to touch . . . was she a Listener?

The Listener, yes. The last Listener.

Why was she the last?

The last? But not the last. You are here, Listener, the trees murmured.

What do Listeners do? said Jinx. *Besides listen, obviously.*

They reach deep. Their roots explore. Their roots reach to the very base of the world. The joining. They grow high into the sky. They burn.

They what? said Jinx.

The flame. The wick. The Listener. Fire and ice.

Would you mind saying something I can understand? said Jinx.

To listen is to understand.

No, it's not, actually. What do you mean by burn? I don't want to burn!

You burn already, Listener. We have noticed this. The Restless always burn. But the Listener burns more.

Jinx was somewhat relieved to hear that he was already burning. It meant the trees might be speaking figuratively. They did sometimes, especially when they were trying to get across ideas that Jinx, not being a tree, couldn't really understand.

Yes. To burn is to die, but also to make room for new life, said the forest.

That did not sound encouraging. In fact, it sounded downright bad. And the trees weren't going to explain it any better. Jinx could tell they weren't. He lost patience.

You know, you could try a little listening yourselves once in a while, he said. *Are you saying this Listening stuff is going to kill me? What is it, anyway?*

Listen.

No, said Jinx. He turned angrily and stalked back to the clearing, through Simon's ward spell.

Oh . . . the ward spell. It was all that was protecting Simon's clearing from the Bonemaster.

He felt his way into the ward spell. He understood now how he learned magic. He explored inside the spell and made it stronger. There was no way the Bonemaster could get through it, when Jinx was done. Neither could anybody else. Wait—there were people Jinx wanted to let in. The Wanderers. Ermentraud, who looked after the animals. And Elfwyn. Oh, and Simon and Sophie, of course. Jinx told the ward to let them through. But no one else. Then he went back into the house. Simon was nowhere to be found, the trees were getting weirder, and Elfwyn was probably off getting herself killed in some stupid revolution. He needed to find Sophie, and fast.

❧ ❧ ❧

Jinx was already back in the market square, the Crimson Grimoire hidden inside his shirt, when he noticed footsteps echoing his own. He turned around and looked up at Wendell.

"Did you know someone was following you?" Wendell asked, politely. "Not me. Someone else."

Jinx's heart sank. "No, I didn't."

"Well, they were." He pointed back toward the Eastern Crescent. "Moving through the shadows and along the rooftops. They followed you right up to the door of that house you went into."

"Um . . . oh," said Jinx.

"Just thought you'd want to know," said Wendell.

"Right," said Jinx. "Thanks."

They walked back to the Temple in silence.

18

The Preceptress

Jinx was in the Hutch library, sitting at a table with an enormous stack of books in front of him. This was to hide the fact that he was studying the Crimson Grimoire. He still couldn't make anything of the language, and this struck him as really unfair. He wasn't good at spells—he wasn't good at a lot of stuff—but he *was* good at languages.

A shadow fell across the page. Jinx looked up and met the cold gaze of a grim-faced gatekeeper.

"You are to accompany me at once," she said. "The Preceptress has summoned you."

Someone had followed him to Simon's house. Did they *know* it was Simon's house?

Jinx closed the illegal book slowly.

"At once," the gatekeeper repeated. "Leave your books here."

Not a good idea. Jinx waited till the gatekeeper turned around, then he hid the red book under his shirt. There was no time to do anything else. He followed her through the Hutch to the locked iron door. The gatekeeper opened it with an enormous skeleton key.

Jinx hadn't seen the Temple from this end before—it felt old and grand, and for a moment he had a sense of himself as very temporary and unimportant. People didn't matter; the Temple mattered. The Temple only needed people as vessels, to carry knowledge.

They went down a corridor and up a broad marble staircase, past paintings of stern old scholars in dark robes. Jinx felt as if he was marching to his execution. Maybe he should have left the Crimson Grimoire behind.

Scholars moved quietly through the halls, their robes brushing the floor. The gatekeeper scowled and opened a door. Jinx took a deep breath and went in to meet his doom.

The room was full of scholars. Behind a great polished desk at the far end sat the Preceptress.

She looked every bit as formidable as she had when he'd last seen her. She did not look like a woman who forgot things. Like, for example, faces.

Don't let her get a good look at you, Simon had said.

There was a wide, empty expanse of floor, covered with a rich red carpet. In the center of it stood Satya.

Jinx went over to Satya—still a good safe distance from the Preceptress. "What's this all about?" he whispered.

"Shh," she said. Jinx could see that she was frightened.

"You have forgotten to bow, Zinks," said the Preceptress.

Jinx put his hand to the front of his shirt and bowed, clutching the hidden book tightly. He was still about twenty feet away from the Preceptress.

"So, Zinks, you understand why you have been summoned here?"

"No," said Jinx. Her thoughts were blurry at this distance, but her eyes were knife sharp. He felt certain she could see the book hidden under his shirt.

"We are promoting you to scholar."

"Oh."

"Is that all you have to say?"

"Well, I haven't been here long enough," said Jinx.

"We have received reports that you both show promise," said the Preceptress. "In particular, Docent Omar has said that you raised some unusual points about government and the formation of nations. Therefore, he nominated you for scholarhood. You will endeavor not to disappoint us."

"Uh—sure," said Jinx. "Right. Of course."

"Their robes," said the Preceptress, turning to a red-robed man standing beside her.

He came forward bearing folded garments and, with a bow, presented one to Satya and then one to Jinx.

"You will put them on," said the man.

"Here?" said Jinx, looking around at all the watching scholars. The illegal book had slid down his shirt and been stopped by his belt.

"Over your clothes," the man specified.

Jinx shrugged into the robe. It smelled of soap. It came down to the floor and a little farther, pooling around his feet.

"You will need to hem that," said the Preceptress. "All right then. You are now both scholars, with the rank and title of Questor. You will not return to the Lectors' Square."

"Can we at least go back to the Hutch to visit?" Jinx didn't want Wendell to think he'd abandoned him.

"I see no reason why you should want to," said the Preceptress. "You must devote yourselves to your studies now, and prove that you are not unworthy of the trust we have placed in you. You may go."

They went. Jinx wasn't sure if the Preceptress had recognized him or not.

As soon as they were out of the room, Satya dragged him into an alcove behind a statue of a pudgy scholar.

"What do you think you're doing? Arguing with the Preceptress like that!"

"I wasn't arguing," said Jinx. "I was just asking her—"

"The preceptors are already suspicious enough of both of us," said Satya.

"Suspicious about what? Why'd they promote us, then?" said Jinx.

"How should I know? So they can keep an eye on us!" Satya frowned at the stone scholar's bare feet. "Why'd they promote us so *soon?*"

"I don't know," said Jinx. "Omar said we were both doing okay with the Fallacies and stuff."

"It just doesn't feel right," said Satya.

"Why are you scared?"

"I'm not."

Jinx didn't contradict her. He'd learned from Elfwyn that people don't necessarily appreciate being told how they feel. But Satya was definitely afraid . . . of something.

⌒⌒⌒

At last, Jinx was free to do the things he'd been sent to Samara to do. But none of Simon's tasks seemed as important now as finding Sophie.

He searched the Temple frantically for her. He went through corridor after corridor, up and down winding staircases, through lecture halls and libraries. He saw hundreds, thousands of red-robed scholars. Not one of them was

Sophie. It was maddening.

When he had time to spare from looking for Sophie, he searched for the Eldritch Tome. He didn't find it. He found a few books he thought might be about the bottle spell. They were all in Qunthk—that indecipherable *khththllkh* language.

The main library was vast. Jinx had trouble finding anything among the long streets and alleys of books. There was a system, of course, but Jinx didn't understand how it worked. He was used to Simon's system, which was to cram as many books as possible into the shelves and stack the rest on the floor.

He did not find any books on KnIP, the Samaran magic Simon wanted him to learn.

There was a whole neighborhood—two streets and an alley—of books about the Urwald. Jinx looked for anything about elves, or werewolves, or, most especially, Listeners. He found nothing about elves, except a book with draw-ings of cute little people with peaked caps and belled shoes. These did not look like the elves Jinx almost remembered seeing.

He found only one book that mentioned Listeners, but it seemed to consider them an amusing legend, on a par with witches who rode broomsticks and girls who inadver-tently turned their brothers into swans.

There were many books about werewolves, but none

that mentioned werewolves having names or wearing spectacles. The authors all seemed to think werewolves were a kind of animal. For example, here was a book called *Differentiation in Werewolf Types of the Central Urwald*. It talked about hides, limb lengths, claws versus hands, and the shapes of werewolves' ears. Who had written this nonsense, anyway? Jinx flipped the book over to check the author's name.

Sophie Maya Simon.

Jinx took the book up to a librarian.

"Excuse me, Scribe Aboyomi," he said, remembering to bow. "Do you know the lady who wrote this book?"

She looked at the spine. "No."

"But—isn't she a scholar here?"

"She may have been, but it could have been ages ago. Centuries, even."

"The book looks new." Jinx remembered that, a few years ago, Sophie hadn't known the difference between kinds of werewolves, and had asked Simon about it.

"Well, I don't know the author," said the librarian.

She didn't have clear, distinct thoughts like Omar, but they were clear enough for Jinx to see that she was lying. The name "Sophie" in her mind was locked in a grim, dank cube of foreboding.

"Do you know who might know?" Jinx tried to keep the anxiety out of his voice.

She frowned. "Why is it so important?"

Jinx heard a sound and looked up. Satya was studying book titles on a shelf nearby. He lowered his voice.

"Because it's a really interesting book and—um—" Jinx couldn't think what to say. "I just wondered about the lady who wrote it, that's all."

Aboyomi had that puff of suspicion that they all did when he asked about Sophie—hers was a blue-green color—but then there was a little click, like she had just made up her mind.

"Ask Professor Night," she said. "Urwald Studies Department."

And she turned around firmly and went back to shelving books with great precision.

Jinx took the book back to the table where he'd been working. Satya followed him, and sat down.

"You've got to stop asking everybody if they've seen this Sophie person," she whispered.

"I'm not asking everybody. I hardly ask anybody."

"Anyway, they don't know where she is," said Satya.

"They do know," said Jinx. "They're just not telling."

He would have liked to add "and it's not your flippin' business." But he was trying not to turn out like Simon.

Simon. He looked at the pile of books on the table. Somewhere there had to be an answer to why the tiny Simon in the bottle had gone all funny.

Satya took a book from the stack. *"Theories and Techniques in Deathforce Magic?"*

"I must've picked that up by accident," said Jinx.

Satya flipped through it, past pictures of a pile of skulls, a stack of bones, and a man being held upside down over a vast cauldron. "What is deathforce magic?"

"I guess you'd have to read the book to find out," said Jinx.

"If you didn't already know," said Satya. "You know what you're not, Zhinx?"

Jinx shrugged.

"Devious. You don't do devious." She looked all around, then lowered her voice. "They're watching you. You've got to be careful what you read."

"I'm just interested in magic as theory," said Jinx.

"Well, try and be interested in something else till they get used to you being here."

This was too much. "Supposing you mind your own business."

He felt bad right away for saying it, but he *had* to find out why the Simon in the bottle had stopped moving.

She flickered purple annoyance at him. "They're watching me too, and they're going to be suspicious of me because we kind of hang around together sometimes."

"Yeah? Well, you know what you can do about that." Jinx opened a book and glared at the page. He liked Satya,

217

but she had no right to boss him around.

He waited for her to go away. Instead, she picked up another book.

"Why do you have books in Qunthk? Can you actually read them?"

"Not exactly," said Jinx. "Can you?"

"No. It's famously impossible to learn, because the words are all stuck inside each other. What are all these pictures of bottles?"

"What do you mean, 'stuck inside each other'?" said Jinx.

"That's how you make a sentence in Qunthk. Instead of stringing the words one after another, you split the first word and put the second inside it, and split that and put the third inside, and split that—"

"Oh wow," said Jinx, looking at the hopelessly long words on the page. It was like being handed a key. He could feel the words unfolding themselves.

"Hardly anyone can read Qunthk except a native speaker," said Satya.

"Where do native Qunthk speakers live?"

Satya frowned. "That's funny . . . no one's ever said. Anyway, you should put those books back. They look like magic. What are you doing with them?"

Jinx shrugged. It would have been nice to confide all his problems in somebody. But he couldn't. Not even a little bit.

She leaned forward. "Listen, Zhinx, I'm Samaran. I know what they do to magicians here. And to people who even try to be magicians. And it's not nice."

"What?" Jinx couldn't help asking.

"They boil them in oil."

Oh. Jinx wondered whether that would be better or worse than dancing in red-hot iron shoes.

"I'm not doing magic," he said. "Look, I've got a lot on my mind right now."

"And you think everyone else doesn't?"

She flipped her hair, and left.

~ ~ ~

The Urwald Studies Department was in a corridor where the pillars were carved to look like trees. Here and there were sculptures of what Jinx guessed were meant to be trolls and werewolves. Professor Night had an office, but he was never there. Jinx went back again and again.

Finally one day he saw the door open and heard a man muttering to himself in heavily accented Urwish.

"Excuse me, Professor—"

Professor Night looked up. "Ah! An Urwish speaker! Come in. What's your name?"

Jinx told him.

"Sit down, sit down. So, interested in the Urwald, are you?"

"Yes," said Jinx.

"I've seen you at my lectures, of course. What is it that

attracts you to the Urwald?"

Jinx hadn't attended any of Professor Night's lectures, but he didn't think it would be tactful to say so. "Um, trees, I guess."

"Trees?" A little pink puff of disappointment.

"Er, and monsters of course," said Jinx. "Werewolves, like different werewolf types of the Central Urwald?"

"Ah, fascinating," said the professor. Then he started talking about werewolves, and Jinx didn't get a chance to say anything for some time.

When Professor Night ran out of steam, Jinx asked, "Do they talk?"

"Werewolves? Oh, no, of course not. They're expressions of our primeval, wild selves."

"Oh. Do they talk to each other?"

"Now, that's something that's never been written about. There's not much still left to be written about werewolves, but I believe you've hit on something, young man. Perhaps you should pursue it."

"I'm *trying* to pursue it," Jinx didn't say.

"You certainly speak Urwish very well," said Professor Night. "Not many young people would devote such attention to an artificial language."

"What's an artificial language?"

"A language that was invented. Made up. There is no genuine Urwish language because, of course . . ." The professor paused, as if for effect. "There is no Urwald."

"What?" said Jinx.

"There is no Urwald."

"Of course there's an Urwald!" said Jinx. "I—um, I've read books about it! Lots of books."

"The Urwald is a metaphor," said Professor Night. "For the unfettered mind, which is full of darkness and monsters and fear and—oh, who knows what?"

"Trees," said Jinx.

"Trees," said Professor Night. "A very salient point. How could the number of trees that supposedly exists in the Urwald exist anywhere? And in such density? They would block out the sun."

"But, um, there used to be—like, a hundred years ago, didn't there use to be people who would come here from the Urwald to study?"

"No, no. Now, there was a group of young scholars at that time—nihilists; do you know what nihilists are? These scholars were obsessed with exploring altered consciousness, and learning about magic, and all sorts of frightful things. And they called themselves"—the professor spread his hands dramatically—"*the Urwalders!* But that was just to impress people with how dangerous they were. They weren't actually from there, because the place doesn't exist."

"But—" said Jinx.

"Take the matter of the Listeners, for example."

Jinx tried to keep his voice casual. "What about them?"

"Supposedly, they share a sort of unity with the trees, and there's some nonsensical legend about their roots going much deeper than those of the trees—but no doubt a clever lad like you will spot that as a metaphor for the collective unconscious."

Jinx didn't say that a clever lad like him couldn't understand such gibberish. "Do you know, um . . . anything else about Listeners? At all?"

"Well, it's a symbol that hasn't been used much in the literature. There's some mention of Listeners representing balance, but it's hard to see how they could be both roots and balance, isn't it? Balances move. Roots do not. The metaphor simply doesn't work."

"What if it's real? What would it mean?"

"If it were real?" Professor Night frowned. "Well, there have been scholars who have posited that the Urwald was real. Urwald Realists, we call them. But on the whole, I think that theory has been adequately refuted. As you get ahead, young man, you will continually learn that what you learned before is untrue."

"What if *you* get ahead, and find out that what you just said about the Urwald isn't true?" Jinx asked.

"There is no call to be rude, young man."

"Sorry, I just meant, like—"

"Do not say 'like' so much, please. It lends an uneducated air to your speech. Any worker bee in the marketplace might say 'like.'"

"Sorry," said Jinx again. "But what if you were promoted to preceptor and found out that—"

"I have no desire to become a preceptor," said Professor Night. "There are only thirteen preceptors, and no one knows how they are chosen. And since they generally cease to study and to write books, I think becoming a preceptor could hardly be regarded as a promotion. Now then, was there anything else you wanted to ask me about?"

"Yes." Jinx felt suddenly very nervous. He brushed his hands on his robe and realized they were sweating. If Professor Night wouldn't tell him the truth, he didn't know what he would do. "I'm looking for a friend of mine. I wonder if you know her. Sophie Maya Simon. I mean *Professor* Sophie."

Professor Night looked at the door, as if to make sure no one was listening. He spoke in a low voice. "A friend of yours, you say? Aren't you rather young to be a friend of Sophie's?"

Jinx almost sighed with relief. Professor Night hadn't denied that Sophie existed. "She's a family friend. But we haven't seen her in, like, ages. So you know her, then?"

"Of course I know her. She was a professor in my department. How could I not know her? It's odd, now I

223

think of it, Sophie herself developed an interest in Listeners, three or four years ago. But of course she was unable to pursue it, with so little source material." Professor Night shook his head. "You have your whole life ahead of you, Zhinx. You could go far—even become a professor yourself someday. Don't ruin your chances by associating yourself with someone like Sophie."

"Where is she? Is she alive?"

"I've heard nothing to the contrary. She's in prison."

Jinx felt his heart twist. "Why? What's she in prison for?"

"For consorting with a dangerous wizard."

"That's all?"

"It's enough, Zhinx. I'm talking about the evil Simon Magus. Have you heard of him?"

"Only sort of," said Jinx. "I mean the name's familiar. But why—"

"Simon Magus was actually admitted as a scholar at the Temple, if you can believe it. This was some years ago, when there were fewer precautions in place. He used his position at the Temple to steal magical knowledge—possibly for the Mistletoe Alliance—and he murdered a scholar who heroically tried to stop him."

"But Sophie didn't kill anybody, did she?"

"No, but she *married* him."

"I see," said Jinx. "So that's why they put her in jail?"

"No. They actually allowed her to come back to the Temple after that disgraceful behavior. It certainly isn't the sort of indulgence that would have been shown to *most* of us, but Sophie was always a great favorite of the Preceptress Cassandra."

"What's she in jail for, then?" said Jinx, trying to control his impatience. It was hard to sit still with the thought of Sophie locked up in some prison. She must have been there all the time he'd been in Samara, and he hadn't known!

"A year or so ago, the wizard Simon returned from wherever the Mistletoe Alliance had hidden him. He charged into the Temple, sending firebolts everywhere, and then fled through the marketplace, killing two coffee sellers. I saw it; I was there."

"Was there anyone with him?" said Jinx, who remembered that day perfectly well, only without the firebolts and dead coffee sellers.

"No. But Professor Sophie disappeared the same day, and wasn't seen for two weeks afterward. When she returned, of course she was arrested."

"Why?"

"Well, it was presumed that she helped him escape, that she knew where he was, and that she had been hiding him."

Jinx remembered the first time he had ever met Sophie.

She'd said something like "They don't like me coming here." But surely the scholars couldn't know Sophie was going to the Urwald if they didn't even believe the Urwald existed.

"What's going to happen to her?" said Jinx.

"I assume she will, in the fullness of time, be tried for her crimes."

"And then what?"

"She will be executed."

"In the fullness of how much time, exactly?"

"That I do not know. The wheels of justice may turn slowly or rapidly, depending."

"Do they let people into the prison to visit?"

"Zhinx," said Professor Night. "Forget about Sophie. She can't help you."

"I was thinking more about whether I could help her," said Jinx.

"She made her own bed—or heap of straw, rather—and must lie in it. As for you, you have a bright future, if you can avoid sullying it with unfortunate connections. You have the opportunity to go far. But only if you learn to control this adolescent hotheadedness and cultivate the right people."

"I see," said Jinx. He had no doubt Professor Night had cultivated Sophie, back when she had been one of the right people.

Sophie was in prison. And they were going to execute her. Jinx remembered how she'd insisted Simon teach him to read, how she'd convinced Simon that Jinx was smart enough to be a wizard. How she'd always—well, very nearly always—spoken kindly to him.

He had to see her. He had to find a way into the prison. He had to get her out.

Wendell would be able to help him.

19

Jinx's Plan

Going back to the Hutch was easy. The gatekeepers stepped politely aside for Jinx—scholar robes made a difference. Jinx knocked on the door of room 411.

Wendell stuck his head out. "Oh, it's you."

Then he did a horrible thing. He bowed.

"Cut it out," said Jinx. "That's just weird."

He pushed past Wendell into the room and sat down on what had been his bed.

Wendell sat down on his own bed, and looked at Jinx as if waiting to see what he wanted. There was that orange puff of hurt, and Jinx realized he somehow hadn't gotten around to visiting Wendell at all. He'd meant to.

"So, like, how have you been?" said Jinx awkwardly.

"Pretty well, Questor Jinx," said Wendell, apparently determined to be annoying. "The classes are fascinating."

"No, they're not, and you hate them." Jinx hesitated. It felt rotten to ask Wendell for help right away, when he hadn't even bothered to visit him before.

An uncomfortable silence reigned.

Finally Jinx said, "Look, I need your help."

Wendell smiled, and the orange puff of hurt vanished. "With what?"

"Do you know where the prison is?"

"Sure," said Wendell. "You pass through Crocodile Bottom, and over the river, and it's on a hill in the marshes on the other side. Why?"

"I need to get in there."

"Do magic, then," said Wendell.

Jinx was startled. Then he realized it was meant to be a joke—do magic, and you'll go to prison. He tried to laugh.

"You remember the friend I was looking for? Sophie?"

"She's in prison?" Wendell was genuinely worried. "Oh, that's bad. Well, obviously."

"Do you think they'd let me in to visit her?"

Wendell frowned. "I don't know. Normally, no. I mean they don't let worker bees in to visit. Obviously. They wouldn't let me in. But you've got the robe."

"So they'd let me in?"

"No, I mean not automatically. Well, you don't act right, obviously. You can't be freaking every time someone bows to you—"

"I didn't freak," said Jinx.

"You kind of have to act like you're a king or something, you know. Look down your nose at people. Like—"

"Like the Preceptress?"

"Exactly." Wendell looked at Jinx doubtfully. "If you went to the prison and pretended you were on Temple business, and that the preceptors had sent you, and if you acted really important—oh, Grandpa's arse." He shook his head. "You couldn't do it."

"I could try," said Jinx, stung.

"And then if they caught you, you'd be in prison too," said Wendell. "And they'd, you know, do something awful to you."

"Like they're going to do to Sophie," said Jinx.

They sat for a moment in silence, staring at the floor.

"What's she in prison for, anyway?" Wendell asked.

"It's kind of complicated," said Jinx.

And instantly the orange puff of hurt was back. Gah! Why did Wendell have to be so—breakable?

Then it occurred to Jinx that he was asking a lot of Wendell. He hadn't *asked* him to help get into the prison, but he more or less expected Wendell would, and that meant that Wendell could end up getting arrested too.

"Look, there's a couple things I haven't told you," said Jinx.

"Seriously? Only a couple?" said Wendell.

"I'm, um, okay, I'm not really from Angara."

"I know that," said Wendell. "I may be stupid, but I'm not dumb."

"Okay. Right. Well."

Jinx told Wendell nearly everything. It was a relief, actually.

"So wait a minute, you're really some kind of apprentice wizard?"

"Yeah."

"Cool. So why'd you bother coming to the Temple?"

"To learn stuff. That part was actually true. Well, and to find a book."

"What'd you want to learn stuff here for? When you could be home learning magic?"

"I'm kind of trying to learn magic here," said Jinx.

"But it's illegal here."

"I know."

"And this place you're from—you're really from the Urwald?"

"Yeah."

"So this Sophie isn't really a friend of yours—"

"Well she is sort of—"

"—she's actually married to the wizard you work for, and he's the evil wizard Simon Magus?"

"Yeah."

"And you can really do magic?"

"Kind of." Not much, with no trees around.

"Can I see some?"

Jinx hesitated. "It's against the law."

"So is helping you sneak into the prison."

Good point. Jinx set one of the stray socks on the floor on fire. Wendell jumped, and stared. An unpleasant smell of burnt wool filled the room. It might attract attention, Jinx realized, and he drew the flame out of existence.

"Wow," said Wendell. "Can everyone in the Urwald do that?"

"No," said Jinx. "Just magicians."

"I want to go to the Urwald," said Wendell. Then his face fell. "But I have to stay in the Hutch." He shrugged this problem away. "Okay. The first thing we have to do, we're going to have to teach you to act like a scholar."

"Okay," said Jinx.

"Maybe Satya can help," said Wendell, brightening.

Jinx hesitated. "Or not."

"Why not?"

"Well, I kind of—" Jinx stopped, then plunged on. "Don't really want to trust her with all this, okay? It's sort of secret."

"Obviously. But we can trust Satya."

Jinx needed Wendell's help. He was going to have to accept Satya's as well. "Don't tell her the whole story, then. Don't tell her about Simon or the magic. And don't tell her where I come from."

~ ~ ~

"Think autocratic," said Satya. "Think superior. Think imperious."

They were practicing in an upstairs room at the Twisted Branch. There were lots of upstairs rooms, full of people doing things—in one, some people were playing music on instruments made of wood; in another, they were arguing loudly in a language Jinx hadn't heard before.

It had been hard to get Satya to come along, because she really was afraid to go out in the city. But she was enjoying Jinx's acting lessons immensely.

Jinx walked up to Wendell, who was pretending to be a prison guard—

"Don't walk, *stride*," said Satya.

Jinx *strode* up to Wendell—

"Halt, you!" said Wendell. "No one enters here."

"Let me in," said Jinx. "I'm from the Temple—"

"Don't say 'let me in,'" said Satya. "That's like you're asking him for something. Don't ask him, tell him."

"I think you should call me 'fellow,'" said Wendell. "When Professor Night goes into the marketplace, he always calls the worker bees 'fellow.' Except the women he calls 'woman.'"

"Right. Think like Professor Night," said Satya. "He's the Third Truth—*No one has ever been wrong since the world began.* He hasn't."

"And tilt your head back more," said Wendell. "Not like you have to look up at me 'cause you're shor—not as tall—but like you have to look up so you can look down."

"I can never remember all of that!" said Jinx.

"It's acting," said Satya, flipping her hair. "When you're acting you don't remember stuff, you *become* it. Don't pretend to be an arrogant scholar. Be one."

Be one. Right. Jinx tried again. He filled his head with rightness and Night-ness. He had never been wrong. It was unimaginable that he could be. Whole worlds didn't exist if he said they didn't. He strode across the room to Wendell, resisted the urge to push him in the chest, and glared up at him as if he was surprised Wendell dared to exist. "Out of my way, fellow!"

Wendell and Satya looked at each other and nodded.

"That was much better," said Wendell.

"Only I think you should say 'stand aside,'" said Satya. "It sounds more scholarly."

"Not all scholars are like that," said Jinx, thinking of Omar and of Sophie.

"No, of course not," said Satya. "But you're going to be. Because your life depends on it."

Wendell led Jinx through Crocodile Bottom to the river-bank.

"Not too close," Wendell warned. "Sometimes the crocodiles come up and drag people in."

They looked across to the marshes opposite. A high, bald hill rose in the middle of the marshes, and a fifty-foot-high curtain wall surrounded the hilltop. Jinx could see guards in watchtowers.

"There's no door," he said.

"It's around the other side," said Wendell. "The road winds around, so they can see anybody that's coming a long time before they get there."

"Oh," said Jinx.

"You realize we're not going to be able to break your friend out of there, or anything like that?" said Wendell.

Jinx thought of Sophie, locked inside those stark stone walls. "We have to."

In the intervals of being taught by Wendell and Satya how to act like a scholar, Jinx searched for the Eldritch Tome and worked on learning Qunthk. He searched in vain for anything at all about Listeners, or about KnIP. Rather to his surprise, he had Satya to help him. She was a lot slower at learning Qunthk than he was—she worried too much about the rules of it—but she was very good at libraries. She seemed to be able to zip right through the streets and alleys and come up with the book she wanted every time.

She plopped down next to Jinx with a stack of books. She peered over at the Qunthk book he was reading.

"What's that word there?" she said, pointing.

"'Roots,'" said Jinx.

"How did you know that?"

"'Roots' is the only word that makes sense there," said Jinx.

"But it's talking about a human sacrifice," said Satya. "This spell you're reading about requires a human sacrifice!"

"The roots are instead of the sacrifice." When Simon had done the bottle spell on Jinx, he hadn't sacrificed anybody.

"What are they the roots of?"

"A tree, I think," said Jinx.

"But that's weird," said Satya.

"What?"

"Well, if it's that easy, if all it takes is roots, then why would anybody bother sacrificing humans? I mean, I'm assuming the humans object."

"Well, you know—the roots might object, too."

"How could roots object?"

"Trust me. They could," said Jinx.

He remembered the roots Simon had used for the bottle spell, and how they had smelled of betrayal.

"What is it that you're looking for, exactly?" said Satya. "You're always searching the shelves."

She wasn't suspicious. She was eager, a kind of red glow. . . . Satya liked books a lot. And she knew the library better than he did.

"Something about KnIP," said Jinx. "There's nothing about—"

Silver coils of fear. "Zhinx, don't ask about that. Please don't ask about that."

"But I need—"

"You haven't asked the librarians, have you?"

"No, but—"

"Please don't."

Jinx wanted to ask her what she was afraid of, and what she knew. But he didn't want to touch her fear—it was so strong it was scaring him.

"All right," he said.

"If there's anything *else* you're looking for—"

"A book," said Jinx. "There's a book that these books mention. But I can't find it."

"What's it called?"

Could he trust her? There was definitely something odd about Satya. But Jinx *needed* the Eldritch Tome.

He told her the title in Qunthk.

"What's that even mean?"

"The Eldritch Tome."

No particular reaction showed in her thoughts.

"But I've already looked at all the books in Qunthk," said Jinx. "It's not there."

"There are a lot of ways to hide books in a library. If it's here, I'll find it." She dropped her voice. "After all, knowledge should be free to everyone. Right?"

Where had Jinx heard that before? Suddenly he had a feeling he'd been wrong to trust Satya.

But he nodded and said, "Right. Thanks."

⁓ ⁓ ⁓

Autocratic. Superior. Imperious. Jinx tried to be all of that. But walking around with his nose in the air just made him trip over his feet.

"It's more like you're *thinking* as if your nose is in the air," said Wendell. "The only time the Preceptress ever looked at me, she had this expression like I was something stuck to the bottom of her shoe."

So Jinx tried to look at Wendell like he was something stuck to the bottom of his shoe. Satya and Wendell burst out laughing. He probably wasn't doing it right.

But ready or not, Jinx couldn't put off going to the prison any longer. He was worried about those wheels of justice that Professor Night had mentioned—there was no telling when they might start turning quickly. It was time to go.

Walking alone through Crocodile Bottom, Jinx found

it a lot less friendly than usual. It was because he was wearing his Temple robe. Children stared. Adults scowled, and a boy about Jinx's age actually spat at his feet. Jinx turned, ready to fight, and the boy fled down an alley.

Jinx stalked on, enduring the scowls.

There was no bridge across the river. Jinx approached a woman sitting in a canoe at the water's edge.

"Excuse me," he said. "Could you please take me across the river?"

The woman frowned at him from under the brim of her wide straw hat. "Why are you wearing scholar's robes? You don't sound like a scholar."

Oops. Arrogant! Right. "I am one," said Jinx, haughtily. "How much to cross the river?"

"Two snakes."

Jinx thought that was a lot, but decided he was too arrogant to argue. He got in and they started across. It was hot in the sun, and he trailed a hand in the cool water.

The woman reached out her paddle and whacked Jinx's arm back into the boat. At the same instant a long green snout shot out of the water right where Jinx's hand had been. Oh right. Crocodiles.

Jinx was like Reven in the Urwald, not taking the dangers seriously.

When they reached the other side Jinx paid the woman. He turned and looked up at the prison. It loomed, gray-black and horrifying, and even in the hot sun it made Jinx shiver. If he managed to get inside, he might never be allowed out again.

But Sophie was in there. So he started up the long, curving road.

It looped back and forth, overlooked by the guard towers atop the high walls. It was a long, hot walk, and Jinx was thirsty when he got to the top of the hill.

Now to be imperious, arrogant, and superior.

There were two guards in gray uniforms standing at the great iron door of the prison. They wore swords and held steel-tipped halberds, which they lowered, crossed, in front of Jinx.

"Remember," Satya had said. "People will believe you are who you pretend to be . . . as long as you don't give them any reason not to believe it."

"State your business," said the taller, older guard.

"Bring me a drink of water, fellow," said Jinx.

The guard looked at Jinx doubtfully.

"At once!" Jinx rasped.

The guard turned to the younger man. "Fetch him some water."

It worked! Jinx struggled not to let surprise show in his face. A moment later the young guard was handing him a mug of water. The man's expression was somewhere between dislike and respect.

Jinx drank it straight down. He gave the empty cup to the guard, remembered in time not to thank him, and said, "I'm here to see a prisoner."

"On whose orders?" said the older guard.

"On whose orders? On the Preceptress Cassandra's orders, of course. I am not accustomed to having Temple business obstructed by mere guards."

The guard bridled, but he was a little afraid, too, a tiny purple puff of fear. Jinx was grateful to Satya and Wendell for the acting lessons.

"What's your name, fellow?" Jinx demanded.

"There's no need for that, sir," said the guard hastily. "I just thought you were a bit young, that's all." He inserted a key in a lock, and the prison door creaked open.

And Jinx was inside.

"Take him to Felix, Seth," the guard said to a man inside, who was very large and looked like he could easily carry Jinx under his arm. "Temple business."

Temple business. The new guard—Seth—nodded at Jinx to follow him, turned sharply on his heel, and led Jinx down a cold, creepy-feeling hallway. Behind him Jinx heard the grate of the key in the lock—he was locked in now, and the only hope he had of ever getting out again was to keep pulling off this act successfully. Arrogant, imperious, superior.

"What's this, Seth?" Felix was a roly-poly little man

behind a desk, with a face like an annoyed kitten's, but his thoughts were deep and red and angry. He was a dangerous person, Jinx thought. Much more dangerous than the giant Seth.

"Temple business," said Seth.

"I'm here to see our prisoner," said Jinx, not giving Felix a chance to speak. "The preceptors sent me."

"A little chap like you?" said Felix.

Jinx looked down his nose at Felix—fortunately, Felix being seated made this easier. "Conduct me to her at once and I'll forget you said that."

"Which prisoner is this we're talking about?"

"The woman Sophie," said Jinx.

Felix smiled at Jinx, a little, dangerous smile. His thoughts were full of suspicion. "Take him, Seth."

Jinx couldn't believe he'd gotten this far.

He followed Seth up and down corridors, lengthwise and crosswise, turning left and right. He was sure they passed the same corner at least twice and that Seth was deliberately confusing him. Jinx's heart was in his throat. Surely Seth was about to grab him, arrest him, and throw him in a cell.

He tried to focus on remembering where each staircase and barred door and passageway was. The place was a maze. It was also completely windowless and impregnable.

Finally they came to a long corridor of iron-barred cells.

"Down here," said Seth.

Jinx stopped. "Leave me. I will speak to the woman alone."

"How do you expect to find your way out again?" said Seth.

"You will wait for me. Not here. Down there." Jinx pointed back the way they had come. "When I am ready to leave, I will summon you. Go!"

He grabbed the torch out of Seth's hand, leaving him to stumble away as best he could in the dark. He turned without waiting to see if Seth had obeyed him, and swept down the line of barred cells with his head held high. He walked fast, in a hurry to get away before Seth heard his heart thumping in terror.

He passed one iron gate after another, and behind each he saw a pile of straw, a bucket, and nobody.

The whole corridor seemed to be empty. He was beginning to suspect Seth had tricked him. Now Jinx was trapped, walking down a probably dead-end corridor with enemies at his back.

In the very last cell, there was something that looked like a heap of old clothes in a corner.

20

KnIP

Jinx stood there looking at the heap until it resolved itself into a person—who didn't notice he was there.

He stuck the torch into an iron ring in the wall. "Sophie?"

She looked up, confused—it *was* Sophie. Her hair was a dull tangle and her eyes, which used to have shooting stars in them, now looked like a clouded-over night.

"Jinx?" She reached a hand through the bars. "Are you real?"

Jinx grabbed her hand.

"You *are* real," she said. "I've imagined so many strange things, but you're real."

"Uh-huh," said Jinx. He had this horrible sensation

behind his eyes like he was going to cry or something. Sophie looked awful, pasty and thin and lifeless. It was as if someone had tried to make a fake Sophie out of mud and sticks and had gotten it all wrong.

"Listen, I don't know how long I have—" Jinx said, in Urwish.

"You're wearing a scholar's robe."

"Yeah, because I'm a scholar. We have to figure out how to get you out of here."

"There's no way out." All her thoughts were like a thick gray cloud that covered the whole sky.

"There has to be," said Jinx.

"I expect they'll have a trial for me eventually," said Sophie.

And then they'd execute her. "We have to get you out before then."

"They might find me innocent." Her voice sounded gray, too.

"Do you think that's what's going to happen?"

"No," said Sophie. The sky was darker than ever. She looked past Jinx, down the hall, as if searching for someone.

"So tell me what we can do to get you out," said Jinx, desperately. He'd expected to find Sophie smart and quick and ready to figure it all out and tell him what he needed to do.

"I don't know," said Sophie.

Her mood was contagious. What was the good of all his planning to get in here when he couldn't get Sophie out?

"Is—is Simon all right?" said Sophie, still looking down the hall.

"Um, he . . ." Jinx fumbled over the question. "He gave me a letter for you."

"A letter?" Sophie showed signs of life for the first time. "What does it say?"

"I don't know. He told me he'd turn me into a toad if I read it." Jinx drew the letter out of the inside pocket of his robe.

Sophie actually smiled. "I suppose he couldn't come himself."

"Well, there's a price on his head," said Jinx. And then, realizing that Sophie might not consider that a good enough excuse, "And he doesn't know you're in prison. I only just found out myself."

Sophie had brightened considerably now. Amid the deep-gray clouds of her mind, Simon was like a glow of sunlight trying to break through. This struck Jinx as a really bizarre way for anybody to feel about Simon.

For the first time in his life Jinx was embarrassed to be seeing into someone's mind. "I'll just walk down the corridor a little bit while you read it."

He went far enough that he couldn't see her feelings

anymore, and then he leaned against the cold stone wall and thought.

He had seen nothing at all that suggested there was a way to escape from this prison. You might as well try to escape from the solid-stone dungeon under Bonesocket. He didn't dare tell Sophie how worried he was about Simon; he needed her brain to come up with an escape plan. If he told her Simon had gone off to look for the Bonemaster ages ago and not been heard from since, she'd go all gray and half-dead and useless.

He went back. Sophie was still poring over the letter. She was glowing brightly now, a sort of happy silver sunshine.

"You're not done yet?"

She folded the letter and smiled. "I was rereading. Goodness, Jinx, you've grown. What have you been doing? And why are you a scholar?"

Jinx told her, as quickly and quietly as he could, what he'd done since he'd seen her last. It was pleasant to be speaking Urwish to someone, and not to have to worry about them finding out who he really was.

"You fell off a cliff onto rocks? How were you not killed?"

"I was! But Simon had my life in a bottle and he put it back."

A blue-brown puff of worry at that. Sophie didn't like

magic. Jinx went on, though, and told her about his trip to Keyland, and his quarrel with Reven and Elfwyn—

"Wait—you turned a man into a tree?"

"It was an accident," said Jinx.

"This Reven, your friend—"

"Enemy."

"Some people would say Reven has a point," said Sophie. "About the monsters, and the poverty—"

"He doesn't."

"I'm not saying he does," said Sophie. "But it's one point of view. You know, he doesn't sound like he'd be a bad king."

"He can be a good king all he wants as long as he stays out of the Urwald," said Jinx. "You know what he wants? He wants to turn us into more Keyland."

He went on to tell her about his adventures, skimming over the fact that Simon had gone to hunt the Bonemaster. He left out the destruction of Cold Oats Clearing, too. It would only upset her, and she might guess where Simon had gone. But he did tell her about Malthus.

"I've never heard of werewolves talking or wearing spectacles." Sophie frowned. "That doesn't mean it's not possible, of course."

"He told me to think about balance."

"And have you?" said Sophie.

"No, I've been busy with other stuff. What about

elves?" said Jinx. "I think I talked to elves too. Only they kind of put a spell on me and I don't really remember much."

"Elves are dangerous. You shouldn't be talking to elves. And—"

"Do you know anything about Listeners?" Jinx asked.

"Only that they're supposed to have roots deeper than the Urwald. But I'm not sure if that's meant figuratively. And there haven't been any in a hundred years."

"But I'm one," said Jinx.

"Really?" No surprise at all from Sophie. "I told Simon you might be. I've tried to research Listeners here—"

"There's nothing," said Jinx.

"There's very little. And of course my colleagues wouldn't find my sources reliable."

"The werewolf told me I had to find out about Listeners. Oh, and the trees showed me this kind of vision of a girl who was the last Listener," said Jinx. "What happened a hundred years ago? That's when the doors to Samara were shut, too—the Bonemaster said."

"I don't see how there could be a connection," said Sophie. "But there were incidents. Crimes. There was a gang of young scholars misusing magic and trafficking in monsters. I'm surmising this. Nothing's been written. All the portals were shut—"

"You mean like the door to Simon's house?"

"That's the only one left. That nice old wizard who used to live there—"

"Egbert the Onion?"

"Even when he thought he was an onion, he was a very *kind* onion," said Sophie. "I think years ago, before he got sick, he must have figured out how to unlock the portal. These friends that helped you get in here—you shouldn't trust them, Jinx."

Jinx shifted uncomfortably. Maybe he had been wrong to trust Satya. But without her acting lessons he'd never have made it past the guards. "They're okay. Wendell's great. And anyway I can—" Jinx stopped himself. He wanted to tell Sophie that he could see what they were feeling. But that wasn't the sort of thing people liked to know.

"Jinx, you can't trust anyone from the Temple."

"*You're* someone from the Temple," said Jinx. "And I *can* trust Wendell."

"And tricking your way into the prison by pretending to be on an errand for the preceptors . . . that was a terribly dangerous thing to do, Jinx."

"So let's not waste it," said Jinx. "Let's figure out what we're going to do to get you out of here."

"Yes. There's—no," said Sophie.

"No what?" said Jinx, frustrated.

"It's too dangerous, and it wouldn't be right."

"Okay, fine, forget it then," said Jinx. "What?"

"KnIP," said Sophie.

"But you don't know any KnIP," said Jinx.

"Of course not. Magic is a terrible crime. But Simon knows KnIP, somewhat. He's a user, and he's done some creating, but he's not a creator adept."

This was so much more than Jinx had ever heard about KnIP—and he was hearing it from Sophie, of all people, who made a point of knowing as little about magic as she possibly could—that he could only stare.

"I don't know if anyone but a creator adept could create a door," said Sophie.

"You mean, like, a door out of the prison?" said Jinx.

"That would probably be much easier than a door into the Urwald," said Sophie. "Because it wouldn't require breaching a dimension."

"You sure know a lot about magic all of a sudden," said Jinx.

"In *theory.*"

"So is there anybody who knows enough KnIP to make a door?"

"It might have to be several doors. There are probably a lot of walls between here and outside. And it would have to be done quickly enough for us to get out before anyone knew what was happening."

"So where can I find out more about KnIP?" Jinx asked.

The glowing sun told him the answer before she did. "From Simon."

Jinx took a deep breath and tried for as light a tone as possible. "Simon's away right now."

Instantly a blue-brown pool of worry. "Away where?"

"He wants to get some witches and wizards together to help keep the Bonemaster locked up." Which was technically true.

"Oh, well, we'll wait for him to come back, then."

"I really don't think we should," said Jinx. "They might decide to have your trial any day, right? How does KnIP work, anyway?"

"Knowledge is power," said Sophie.

"I know that," said Jinx. "But how—"

"That's how it works. All magic requires power, doesn't it?"

"Yeah," said Jinx. "Oh! You mean . . ." He thought. "Okay, I know that's how the door into Samara works. You know it's there and so it opens for you."

"But a creator actually *uses* knowledge," said Sophie. "As power. The same way an Urwald wizard uses—I don't know, flames or chalk figures or dried leaves."

Or lifeforce. "So, like—how does that work? Using knowledge as power?"

"Simon can tell you," said Sophie.

"Aren't there books or something?"

"Oh! Yes, I forgot." She reeled off three Samaran titles, which all sounded like they were about something else. "They're in the library, hidden among books about other things. They're pretty abstruse, I'm afraid. Simon can tell you more."

She just wouldn't stop mentioning Simon. It was starting to make Jinx feel like a liar.

"If I read those books, will I be able to do KnIP?"

"You'll need Simon to help you," said Sophie. "Don't worry, Simon knows."

"But . . ." He hesitated, not sure how to put this. "What if Simon—well, what if he doesn't come back in time? I might have to figure it out for myself."

"Couldn't you go and get him?" said Sophie.

"Sure," said Jinx. "Yeah. That's what I'll do. I'll go and get him."

He couldn't really say anything else without her realizing something was wrong.

"Oh, and Simon wants this book called the Eldritch Tome," he added. "Do you know where it is?"

"Not everything Simon wants is something he should have," said Sophie.

"He kind of really needs it."

"Does it have something to do with the Eldritch Depths?"

"What are the Eldritch Depths?" Jinx remembered

253

hearing the name somewhere.

"Where the elves live," said Sophie. "Or *exist*, rather. The legends say it's part of the ice, half of the ancient balance, supposedly, in the Urwald. The other half is fire. It—"

Footsteps sounded in the corridor. Jinx jumped to his feet and tried to look imperious as Seth's huge form hove into view.

"Jinx, about KnIP," Sophie whispered hastily. "Remember that knowing is having confidence in the infinity of possibility. What isn't true now may be true in the future. And don't underestimate the preceptors. They may have *let* you—"

She broke off as Seth arrived.

"Boss wants you out," said Seth.

"I told you I would summon you when I was ready, fellow," said Jinx.

"Sorry. Visits limited to one hour."

"I shall report this to the preceptors," said Jinx.

A little pink nervous ripple from Seth at that, but he was more afraid of Felix than of the preceptors. "Sorry. I have to do what the boss says. Come along, please."

Jinx turned to Sophie. "I will certainly check the veracity of what you've told me, woman, and if I find any error, it will be the worse for you when I return."

He hoped she got the message: he would return. He

gave her a haughty nod and preceded big Seth down the corridor.

～ ～ ～

The first thing Jinx did when he got back to the Temple was find the books Sophie had mentioned. One was filed under Ancient History, one under Botany, and one under Physics. The books weren't just abstruse. They were complete gibberish.

Here was an example:

What is known is a matter of time, and time is a matter of what is not yet known.

What was that supposed to mean? Jinx shut the book in disgust. He'd read each of the three KnIP books twice, and he was getting nowhere with understanding them.

And so finally, Jinx went back to Simon's house.

He'd been putting it off because he was so much hoping that Simon would be there, and so certain that he wouldn't be, that he dreaded actually going into the house and finding it empty.

It was after midnight when Jinx reached the blue-violet door to Simon's house. He put out his hand to lift the latch. But the latch didn't move.

KnIP, he reminded himself. He *knew* the door would open.

But it wouldn't.

He tried the door-opening spell he'd learned at the Bonemaster's house. The door did not open.

He worked his knife along the crack of the door by the lock. Nothing.

He tried prying the door open. The knife blade broke.

He kicked the door.

Then he had a feeling, just for a second, of thoughts close by, and he spun around fast and was just in time to catch a glimpse of a dark form running away across the rooftops.

Jinx didn't know what to do. There was no visible lock, and no way to remove the latch or the hinges. And he was pretty sure, from the feel of things, that whoever had locked the door had done it with magic.

He was trapped in Samara.

～ ～ ～

If he couldn't get back to the Urwald to find Simon, then Jinx had to learn KnIP, and fast.

Back at the Temple, he tried desperately to create KnIP spells. He tried knowing things that weren't true. But he . . . knew they weren't true. So the spells didn't work.

He couldn't risk going back to visit Sophie again to ask her for help—not when he was being followed. He couldn't get into the Urwald to look for Simon. He told Wendell what he'd found in the KnIP books, but Wendell just frowned and looked concerned. He wasn't much help with book-related stuff.

Jinx sat in a tree in the yard of the Twisted Branch. People walked past, laughing and talking. They didn't have Jinx's worries. He had to rescue Sophie, find the Eldritch Tome, figure out what had happened to Simon, teach himself KnIP . . .

Somehow Simon had managed to learn KnIP. Who had taught him? Egbert the Onion? If he'd just learned it from those stupid books, then he was a lot smarter than Jinx was.

Jinx leaned his face against the tree trunk and felt the tree's lifeforce pulsing through it. He thought about the Urwald. If only the prison was in the Urwald! He'd get Sophie out easily.

He found himself telling the old tree about the Urwald.

Then in the darkness he became aware of thousands of trees—millions of trees—a vast forest, stretching on forever. The roots drank from the Crocodile River, they dug deep into the rich, moist soil of the hill where the Temple stood—

Really? There was a forest here? How long ago? Jinx asked.

The tree was confused by the question—time was different for a tree. Time was a circle of seasons, even in Samara. Time was always now.

But this particular now? Perhaps fifty thousand years ago.

Jinx couldn't even imagine that much time . . . time enough for a forest to become a desert. In the tree's memory, he could sense the lifeforce the ancient forest had had . . . and now it was gone from the world.

What if the Urwald's lifeforce were lost from Jinx's world? If Reven cut down all the trees? Then the place would become like Samara—hot, dry, and magicless.

But no—Samara wasn't magicless. It had KnIP.

"Hey, what are you doing?" Wendell stood under the tree, looking up at him.

"Thinking." Jinx said a silent farewell to the tree, and jumped down.

"About that KnIP stuff?"

"Yeah. Well, actually . . ." Jinx looked around to make sure no one was within earshot. Then he told Wendell what the tree had shown him.

"So wait a minute, you mean you taught a tree how to talk?"

"No, it already knew how," said Jinx.

"Cool. Is that magic?"

"No," said Jinx. "It's easy if you kind of listen and stuff."

"So all you Urwalders can talk to trees?"

"No—"

"Just magicians?"

"Not really," said Jinx. "I mean I've never met anyone else who could do it. But—"

"So it's a kind of magic that you invented," said Wendell.

"It's not magic. Other people could do it if they tried." But Jinx found himself wondering for the first time if Listening actually was a kind of magic.

"Maybe if you asked the tree what Sophie meant, it'd tell you," Wendell suggested.

"Trees don't think like that."

"But it was talking about time, right? Same as Sophie was. Well, it's probably something I wouldn't understand. Oh, hey, I got another guiding job."

He glowed blue happiness.

"That's nice," said Jinx.

"It was those same merchants I guided before—well, no, it's different merchants, but those first merchants told these guys they should ask for me! Can you believe it?"

"Yes," said Jinx, amused.

"So they came here looking for me," said Wendell. "It's only for a few days, starting a week from Thursday."

"That's great," said Jinx. "Um, listen, is there a way to find out when Sophie's trial is?"

Wendell frowned. "They don't announce that kind of thing. I mean not in advance. They sort of spring it on people."

"Oh."

"Makes it more terrifying, obviously. And then they get

through it quick and do the boiling right after, in public. It's very effective."

"I guess boiling would be," said Jinx.

"I mean effective at keeping people scared. The whole way they do it. But generally it kind of leaks out, a day or two ahead of time."

"Leaks . . . oh, you mean gossip?"

"Yeah."

"Could you sort of listen for the gossip?" Like hooking into the Witchline.

"Oh! Yes! I can do that."

~ ~ ~

Jinx sat in the library and stared at the stupid book.

> **What is known is a matter of time, and time is**
> **a matter of what is not yet known.**

Gah! That was about as useful as what Sophie had said. What was it? "What isn't true now may be true in the future." And "Knowing is having confidence in the infinity of possibility."

And Wendell had said to ask the tree, which wasn't useful, because "the future" didn't mean the same thing to trees. . . .

All right. What if you did think of time the way a tree did? Not from the dead-and-gone past to the unknowable future, but in a circle, ever present? Then you could know something was true in the future . . . no, you could know that something *could* be true in the future. . . .

Jinx stared at the library table in front of him and, holding his breath, knew there was a hole in it.

A small hole, the size of a cup, appeared in the table.

That was it! He could *know* it because it was possible in the future! That was all there was to it.

Only it turned out that wasn't all there was to it. Because when Jinx tried to make a bigger hole, he couldn't. He knew and knew and knew, but the hole got no bigger.

He tried knowing there was another hole next to the first one. That worked. Then a third. And a fourth. Now there was a hole about eight inches wide, and shaped like a four-leafed clover.

"Hello, Zhinx."

Jinx grabbed a book, meaning to hide the hole, but it was too late. Satya was coming down the aisle between two bookshelves carrying a small blue volume and sipping a cup of tea.

She set the cup down on the hole Jinx had made in the table. The cup sat there, on empty air.

"What are you staring at?" she said.

"Um, nothing." Jinx had to fight the urge to reach his hand up through the table and grab the cup from underneath.

"We're allowed to have tea in the library." She handed

him the book. "Take a look at this."

The title was *Internal Force Ratio of Torque Functions.*

"Uh, yeah?" said Jinx.

Satya smiled. "Open it."

The book was handwritten in tiny, cramped script. Jinx had to put his head close to even make out that it was Qunthk.

Satya turned back to the title page.

There, in ordinary-sized writing, were the words, in Qunthk:

The Eldritch Tome

"Oh wow," said Jinx. "Where did you find it?"

Satya's thoughts stepped behind each other. They slid around. She smiled. "Over there, with a bunch of other books with 'torque' in the title."

She wasn't lying, exactly. Jinx had an idea that that *was* where she had found the book, but that that wasn't the whole story. Maybe someone had told her to look there. He wondered who.

Anyway. He had the Eldritch Tome. If he deciphered it, it would tell him how to undo the deathbindings, what strange thing the Bonemaster had done with his own life, and maybe even what had become of Simon. It seemed to Jinx that he could never thank Satya enough for finding the book. The trouble with having grown up with Simon was that it didn't provide you with a lot of resources, politeness-wise. What would Reven have said in this situation?

Just that, probably. "I can't thank you enough."

Satya beamed. But she was still frightened—of something. She picked up her floating cup of tea and left.

Jinx stuck his hand through the table to make sure there was really a hole. Yes, of course there was. He'd *known* there was.

That's it, Jinx thought. For Satya, there was no hole in the table. KnIP spells only work if you know they're there.

And it was just as well, because the librarians would probably take a dim view of people making holes in their tables. When Jinx tried to make the hole go away, he couldn't.

～ ✒ ✒

The trouble with the Eldritch Tome was that it was unreadable. Not just because of the tiny print and the strange language. It was, as Sophie would say, abstruse. Way more abstruse than any other magic book Jinx had ever read. It went along like this:

Let life equal death, and let living leaf
equal cold stone. Take leaf to life, and
dearth to death, and seal the whole at
the nadir of all things.

Jinx couldn't figure out what this meant. Maybe if he managed to rescue Sophie, she'd be able to explain it to him. After all, Sophie was pretty abstruse herself.

Jinx practiced KnIP for the next couple of days. He got pretty good at creating spells—tiny spells. He didn't have enough power to do more because he didn't have enough knowledge.

The more KnIP he did, the more clearly he saw his own knowledge—a woven ball that kept adding to itself, sending out threads that connected to other threads and looped around and caught old bits of knowledge and connected them to new bits and created completely different bits out of the connections.

And he saw other people's knowledge. He would've expected Satya to have more than Wendell. But she didn't. They both had quite large amounts.

But the adult scholars had more. Jinx figured it was just because the weaving and the connections had been going on for longer.

Even Professor Night had more knowledge than Jinx did. But Omar, Jinx's teacher from the Hutch, had more than Professor Night. Jinx was rather pleased by this, because he liked Omar.

The preceptors had huge amounts of knowledge. They walked around in great glistening interwoven glowing spheres like dense matrices of golden wire. It wasn't twice as much knowledge as Jinx had, or five times as much. It was a thousand times as much.

How could a person ever know that much?

〜 ✂ ✂

Wendell had gone to do his guiding job. Jinx hoped he wouldn't miss any gossip about Sophie's trial. As for Jinx, he had to find a way to get back to the Urwald.

There was no getting around it—if knowledge was the power that made KnIP work, Jinx just didn't have enough. Sophie couldn't escape from prison through a hole the size of a coffee cup—not unless Jinx turned her into a snake, and he definitely didn't have enough knowledge to do that. Plus she would hate it.

He needed Simon.

It was two o'clock in the morning. Jinx went up the street of close-set doors. He put down the Eldritch Tome and tried the door to Simon's house. It was shut as tight as before. Jinx thought into a possible future in which the door opened, and he knew that the future existed, and therefore he knew the door opened. Quickly, before the certainty could escape from him, he tugged at the door.

It gave a little bit—what was stopping it this time was an ordinary lock, Jinx thought, not a magical one. Okay. Jinx *knew* there was a hole in the door. The hole appeared, and he reached through it and found a bolt. Which was odd. There had never been a bolt there before.

Jinx slid back the bolt, picked up the Eldritch Tome, and stepped into the house. It was pitch dark.

He heard a hasty sound from the room beyond, like a book being shoved onto a shelf. He moved toward the sound. The person in the book room was absolutely silent—but there. Jinx could see a blue-green cloud of fear. They were afraid of him? Good.

"I can tell you're here," Jinx said. "Whoever you are."

Surprise, purple and pink, mixed with the blue-green fear. Then someone burst out of the room and shoved past Jinx, knocking him down. The Eldritch Tome went flying. The door to Samara opened and the footsteps ran out through it.

Jinx scrambled to his feet and looked out onto the empty Samaran street. There was no sound and no sign of anybody. Hastily he felt around on the floor for the Eldritch Tome, and was relieved when his hand closed on it.

Rattled, Jinx shut the door and latched it. His heart thudded in his ears. Someone had managed to get into Simon's Samaran house. What had they found, and what did they know?

Jinx went all through the Samaran part of the house, searching for thoughts and feelings. Nothing. He was alone.

Well, there was no way he was hiding the Eldritch Tome under the sofa cushions now. Clutching it tightly, he opened the KnIP-hidden door into Simon's Urwald house.

Cats approached him, mewing and yowling. Jinx

could tell from their complaints that Simon hadn't come home.

Jinx checked the Farseeing Window. He didn't bother with the aviot, because he wasn't interested in Reven right now. The window showed him nothing but the night darkness of the Urwald. He checked Simon's bottle. The Simon figure was still lying on its side. Still breathing. Jinx locked the Eldritch Tome under the thirteenth step, beside the bottle.

The house felt hugely empty and bereft, except for the cats. It was hard to believe it had ever had Simon in it. Jinx wondered if it had felt this way to Simon when Egbert the Onion died.

But Simon couldn't be, well, dead. As nearly as Jinx had been able to understand from the Crimson Grimoire, Simon's lifeforce would become less visible when Simon died.

There had to be an explanation. And Jinx knew where he would have to look for it.

And he had to look *now*, because without Simon, Jinx wasn't going to be able to rescue Sophie. He needed Simon. Simon would know what to do.

He went and put on his warm Urwald clothes. He looked around for food and found some hopelessly desiccated apples and a chunk of extremely unlikely-looking cheese. That was odd. He didn't remember the cheese from his last visit. Someone must have been in the house since then.

He looked out the window. It was pitch dark. He ought to wait for daylight before he started, but the house was cold and he was too nervous to sleep.

He went out the front door, and began his journey to the Bonemaster's house.

21

The Paths of Fire and Ice

Jinx walked through the woods, off the path, in the dark. The last time he'd been in the Urwald, it had argued with him. The trees had told him he wasn't listening, and he'd mentioned that they didn't listen much themselves. The trees had said that Listeners burned.

But now the trees murmured and whispered. The Urwald's lifeforce filled and surrounded him. It calmed and warmed him. He felt safe, even when monsters passed by him in the dark and he had to stop and do a concealment spell.

At dawn he reached a path. He noticed there were a few seedlings growing on it, which was a thing he had never seen before.

He asked the trees *About this burning stuff you mentioned before . . . is there any way I can keep from burning?*

You burn already, Listener. Seeds cannot grow without fire.

Right. I know that, said Jinx. *Or anyway some can't. Lodgepole pines, for example. But I'm not a seed.*

Seeds are everywhere.

The forest was being cryptic and no help at all. Still, Jinx preferred it to Samara, which had had a great forest's lifeforce and lost it.

Listeners leave, and gain knowledge, said the trees. *Knowledge is power.*

What? Jinx tried to get the trees to explain, but they murmured and grumbled to each other. They had no idea they'd said anything important.

He walked on, careful not to step on any seedlings.

~ ~ ~

Jinx stopped once, in Badwater Clearing, to buy some of what passed for bread there.

At least the people in Badwater Clearing didn't slam their doors on him. Maybe the rumors about him hadn't reached this far into the Urwald. They gathered around and watched him as he picked stones and husks out of the bread. Jinx saw curiosity, interest, suspicion—and grim gray clouds of Urwish fear.

"You don't like our bread?" a woman demanded.

"No, it's okay," Jinx lied. "It's good."

"Maybe not what fancy-dressed rich people are used to," said another woman.

Jinx bit into the bread. It was stale and took a lot of chewing. He swallowed painfully. It felt gritty in his throat.

"You shouldn't insult him," said a girl. "He's a very powerful magician."

With a start, Jinx recognized her. It was the girl who'd called him "sir" in Cold Oats Clearing.

"Hilda! How did you get here?"

"Walked, sir."

"You got away," said Jinx. "Was everyone else—"

"Thirty-two people were killed, sir," said Hilda.

Jinx thought about how much power the Bonemaster must have gotten from killing thirty-two people. "So how many got away?"

"Twelve," said Hilda. "Me and Silas came here—"

There was a general *harumph* through the crowd.

"Silas being my cousin," said Hilda. "He's four."

"He's not even her brother," someone muttered.

"Where did the others go?" said Jinx.

"I don't know. We went in different directions, because we figured nobody was going to take us all in."

"Wait, are you the evil wizard who destroyed that clearing?" a man asked.

Before Jinx could answer, someone else said, "Of course he ain't, it was the Bonemaster that done that."

271

"How do we know he ain't the Bonemaster?"

"He can't be, he's just a kid."

"He can't even be a wizard."

"He lifted an enormous fallen tree off our house," said Hilda. "By magic."

They all looked at Jinx with a deep purple awe that was rather gratifying.

"*We* had someone disappear in Bone Canyon last month," said a man.

"Did you go looking for them?" Jinx asked.

"Why would we need to do that?" asked the man. "The Bonemaster got her."

"Well, to see if she was really dead. And to let the Bonemaster know you weren't going to stand for it," said Jinx. "If everyone banded together—"

People began giving him angry looks.

"Trolls could've got her," another man said fairly.

"Yes, we don't know for sure."

But what they really meant, of course, was that they didn't want to end up like Cold Oats Clearing.

"Wait a minute," said Merva, the woman who'd perpetrated the bread. "You ain't the boy that turned an army of trolls into rocks, are you?"

"No," said Jinx.

"We heard about somesuch happening over that way." She gestured to the east. "Folks are strange over there."

Jinx gave up on trying to eat the bread. "People there

are about like people here," he said. "We're all Urwalders."

"Are you sure you didn't turn trolls into rocks?" said Merva. "Because the boy I heard done it had the same name as you."

"Sort of thing we could ask the Truthspeaker," someone said.

"Yeah, if the Truthspeaker was here, she'd know."

"I'm sure I didn't turn anyone into rocks," said Jinx. "Listen, there are people in the east trying to cut down the Urwald—"

"I told you they were strange over there," said Merva to a man standing next to her.

"It's not Urwalders doing the cutting, though," said Jinx. "They're—"

"You just said we were all Urwalders," said the man next to Merva.

"We are!" said Jinx, getting frustrated. "But these other people are from Keyland, which is outside the Urwald—"

"There's an outside to the Urwald?"

"'Course there is, it's where them Wanderers come from," said another woman.

"What makes it outside of the Urwald, then? Why ain't it the Urwald?" Merva demanded.

"Because there are no trees there!" Jinx said. "Or at least hardly any. So the Keylanders come into the Urwald and cut down ours."

The people of Badwater Clearing looked at each

other and shook their heads.

"Well, like I said, folks are strange over that way," Merva said.

Jinx did not have time to waste trying to pound new ideas into the Badwater people's heads. So he took his leave of them.

He had just started down the path when a voice said, "Hey, wait up, um—what's your name again?"

Jinx stopped. A boy with the scraggly beginnings of a red beard came trotting up. Jinx had seen him hovering behind Hilda, listening.

"Jinx. What's yours?"

"Nick. Listen, are you sure you didn't turn anyone into stones?"

"Completely sure," said Jinx.

"Oh." A little blue cloud of disappointment.

Jinx made a decision. If people were going to talk about him, it might as well be the truth. "I turned one guy into a tree."

"Why'd you do that?"

"He was cutting down trees," said Jinx. "He was one of a whole bunch of Keylanders that were cutting down the Urwald. But nobody cares."

"Like the Bonemaster," said Nick.

"What?" said Jinx, confused.

"Nobody cares about the Bonemaster. I mean not

enough to do something. It's like we just keep quiet and hope he doesn't kill us next, right? You heard what he did to Cold Oats Clearing, right?"

"Yeah. Are you from there?"

"No, but Hilda is." There was a purple glow around the name "Hilda." "And she's told me all about it. It'll keep happening unless we all stand together and fight back."

"Yup," said Jinx.

"There's not much *we* can do," said Nick. "But if *you* can turn people into trees, then—"

"I can't," said Jinx. "Not the Bonemaster. He's . . . well, kind of powerful."

"You've been places, right? Are there people in other clearings that have talked about fighting back?" said Nick.

"Um—I'm not sure." Jinx didn't want to discourage Nick when the guy was just talking himself into fighting.

"Sometimes I think about going somewhere else. Folks in Badwater Clearing are mad because Hilda won't get rid of Silas."

"Won't abandon him in the forest, you mean."

"Right. I can understand her thinking. He's all she's got left. We've talked about going to Cold Oats Clearing, but we can't live there alone, can we? We'd need more of us—it's not safe to be just three people in a clearing. And one of them only Silas."

"I think it would be a really bad idea to go there with

just the three of you," said Jinx. "Listen, that Truthspeaker that people were talking about . . . have you seen her?"

"Seen her?" Nick looked confused. "No. It's just a tale that's been going around. There's this girl that only speaks the truth, no matter what. Anything she tells you, you can believe."

The rumor had gotten it wrong, but it sounded like Elfwyn. "You don't know where she is?"

"No, I don't know if she's even real. I mean a lot of things you hear are just tales."

Drat. So the story could be old, and not news about Elfwyn at all. "Look, I have to get going."

Nick looked crestfallen.

"You understand that there's a country called Keyland and that the people there want to cut down the Urwald?" Jinx asked.

"Oh, sure," said Nick, though there was a purple-pink tangle of confusion around his head. "It's not the Urwald, and this is the Urwald, and we don't want the trees cut down."

"And we're Urwalders," said Jinx. "And the Urwald is our country."

"We're Urwalders," Nick repeated. "Got it."

"Do you think you could try to explain it to those idio—to the people in your clearing?"

"Sure," said Nick. "And listen, if—well, if you're ever

looking for people that are willing to band together against the Bonemaster—well, it's not much, but you can count on me and Hilda."

It was evening when Jinx reached the edge of the Canyon of Bones. He could see the stone cliffs of the island a mile away, and Bonesocket standing out black against the sunset.

The Bonemaster was an extremely dangerous wizard, and he didn't like Jinx.

And as soon as Jinx climbed down into the canyon, and moved away from the trees, he would lose his power source. But he had an idea.

I need to take some power with me, he told the trees. *May I?*

It is your power. How will you take it? The Restless, they always take. It is all right. It is his power. It is our power. It is the Urwald's power. He is the Urwald.

Jinx took this for permission.

He lit a stick on fire and set it down in a clear spot on the path. Then, drawing the Urwald's power up through his feet, he made the fire bigger. And bigger. A roaring green column of flame shot up into the twilight. Then Jinx drew the fire down into himself. He would carry it with him.

Thank you, he told the Urwald.

It is your power.

"Excuse me. What exactly are you doing?"

Jinx recognized the werewolf's voice. He turned around. "Hello, Malthus."

They were not on the Path.

"I hope you're not doing what I think you're doing," said Malthus.

Jinx wanted to say it was none of Malthus's business what he did. But even with the amount of fire that he had inside him now . . . you just didn't say that kind of thing to a werewolf.

"You're going to face the Bonemaster?" said Malthus. "You're not ready."

"Neither is he," said Jinx.

"He's a tough old wizard with all the deep power of ice behind him. You are, forgive me, scarcely more than a cub." Malthus tapped his lower lip with a pencil. "Do you not see the problem with this?"

"Don't worry about me," said Jinx.

"I'm not," said Malthus. "Not as such. I'm worried about— Pardon me. Do you mind standing a bit downwind?"

"I just had a bath yesterday!"

"It's not that. It's that you, ah, smell like dinner."

Jinx took several steps away from the werewolf. "What did you mean about the deep power of ice?"

"I'd better draw you a picture." The werewolf whipped out a notebook, and Jinx didn't see where it came from. Malthus had no clothes—just fur—and hence no pockets, as

278

far as Jinx could see. "Could I have a light?"

Jinx found a stick and lit it.

Malthus drew two parallel lines, from the top of the page to the bottom. "Here, you see, we have the Urwald. Not the Urwald *qua* Urwald, you understand, but the Urwald in a magical sense. You might say these two paths represent fire and ice, or lifeforce and deathforce. They have existed as long as the Urwald has. Did you think about balance, as I told you to?"

"Kind of," said Jinx. "I've been busy."

"Fire balances ice. Life balances death. Picture these two paths proceeding downward indefinitely," said Malthus.

"Downward?"

"Yes. The amount of power that can be drawn on is virtually limitless. Lifeforce and deathforce. Fire and ice. Do you understand? Do you mind not standing so close?"

"I guess," said Jinx, stepping hastily away. "I mean, yeah. You're saying the Bonemaster has this deathforce power, which is ice? And I've got lifeforce power? So like, I'm on one of the paths and he's on the other?"

"Precisely. One could say you are each other's chosen nemesis. Except that neither of you, I suspect, has a clue as to what you're doing. Nonetheless, he'll do it better, because he's been doing it longer."

"I know what I'm doing," said Jinx. "I'm going to find Simon."

"It would be much better not to."

"Why?" Jinx felt suddenly cold, despite the fire inside him. "What do you know?"

"Nothing," said Malthus, "except that up here"—he tapped the upper part of his diagram—"if the two forces meet, there tend to be explosions."

"If that's what it takes," said Jinx. "I have to find Simon. And rescue him, if he needs it."

Malthus's golden eyes flashed green in the firelight. "I've never understood humans. Now, werewolves are much more practical. When one of our number is in trouble, we eat him."

"That *is* practical," said Jinx.

"In this way, werewolves survive."

"Some of them, anyway," said Jinx.

"That's the point. But enough chitchat about how our cultures diverge. I'm sure it's very interesting, but I'll eventually succumb to the urge to eat you, and that would be, on the whole, disastrous. As would your present plan. Any explosions will harm you more than him."

"I have to rescue Simon, so that I can rescue Sophie," said Jinx. "Because they're—" What were they exactly?

"They are your pack." The werewolf raised his eyebrows. "Yes, you stand to lose everything. Heroes generally do lose everything."

"I'm not a—"

"Wicks are nearly always heroes or villains. Mind you, a few have led nice quiet lives."

"So fire is good, and ice is evil?"

"Whatever gave you that idea? They're forces, that's all."

"But if ice is death, then—"

"Death isn't evil," said Malthus. "Life doesn't end in evil. Many people end their lives as delicious meals for werewolves."

"Then I might be the villain?" said Jinx.

"You might. But in werewolves' tales, the Listener is a hero. A Listener's job is to keep things balanced, steady. The Urwald needs this. You can do far more good by not trying to rescue your Simon—by surviving, that is. I suggest you go home."

"Sorry, but no," said Jinx. "People aren't like werewolves."

"Not at all like werewolves," said Malthus. "Humans are frightfully affectionate folk. Take your stepfather. He abandoned you in the forest when you were scarcely whelped."

"Yes, but—"

"He could just as well have killed and eaten you himself. Lucky for werewolves that humans are so squeamish."

"How did you know about that?"

"My aunt followed you," said Malthus, with a furry shrug. "Both of you wandering so deliciously in the dusk—she couldn't decide whether to try for the pair, and risk getting neither, or wait till the tough, stringy stepfather abandoned the tender tidbit. Then that wizard came along and cheated her out of a good dinner."

"Right, well, that's the wizard I'm going to look for now," said Jinx. "So if there's nothing else—"

Malthus sighed, a rather canine sound with a slight howl to it. "There is something else. If I can't dissuade you—please, please, don't take the Urwald's fire with you."

"I need it."

"There's a very good chance that when your power meets the Bonemaster's, that fire will kill you. There may come a time when you can face him with all that fire inside you and survive. But that time is not yet."

Jinx looked at the werewolf's thoughts. They were mostly a disturbing level of hunger, hedged around with a golden-green determination not to eat Jinx just now—but other than that, Malthus seemed perfectly sincere.

"Whose side are you on, Malthus?"

"The Urwald's," said the werewolf promptly.

Is that true? Jinx asked the trees.

True? True, sighed the trees. *Who can say what the Restless mean?*

Is it true what he said about the lifeforce and the deathforce, and fire and ice and all that?

There have always been wicks, said the trees. *Wicks of fire, wicks of ice.*

"Excuse me," said Malthus. "Are you talking to the trees?"

"Yeah," said Jinx. "D'you mind?"

"Not at all," said the werewolf. "I consider it a very good sign. But I'll just be running along. You grew a bit abstracted there for a second, and a werewolf does tend to pounce in those situations, even if he regrets it afterward."

As he spoke, his upper body slid downward, his snout lengthened, his arms became legs. He turned and ran off into the dusk. Jinx had missed what happened to the notebook.

Can I trust him? Jinx wanted to ask the trees. But trees weren't very good with that sort of question. Jinx had to decide on his own.

He looked toward Bonesocket. Going there *without* the Urwald's power seemed crazy. And why should he trust a werewolf?

Well. When someone freely admits that they want to eat you, they're probably not going to lie about a little thing like power and explosions.

Reluctantly, not at all sure he was doing the right thing, Jinx let the Urwald's power seep back down through his feet. He felt the mighty green fire inside him diminish until it was no more than the flame that was always there.

It took about half an hour to clamber over the rocky ground to the spot where the Bone Bridge crossed the stream and sloped up the cliff to the island.

It was more ladder than bridge, really, with the spaces between the bones. Jinx felt sick looking at it. This was the exact spot where he had acquired his fear of heights.

But this wasn't like last time, when he'd been captured by the Bonemaster and forced to climb the Bone Bridge or die. Jinx had more power now, and more knowledge, and he even knew one or two more spells. And it was his choice whether to climb the bridge or not.

He remembered Witch Seymour's advice. He thought three times about what he was going to do. Was it wise to confront the Bonemaster in his own lair?

Nope. Definitely not wise.

He began the long, terrifying climb.

22

The Truthspeaker

"Jinx, is it?" The Bonemaster stood waiting at the top, smiling his kindly smile. His thoughts were twirling, flickering knives, flashing black and silver.

If you didn't know better, thought Jinx, you might mistake him for a benevolent old wizard, long white beard, pointy hat, and all.

Jinx felt his heart clench. He hadn't meant to be afraid of the Bonemaster. He really hadn't.

"I saw your message," said the Bonemaster. "A word of advice: we don't announce ourselves with bursts of green fire nowadays. That sort of thing is"—he made a gesture of distaste—"overstated. Vulgar."

"Not like destroying a clearing and turning all the people in it into skulls and bones," said Jinx.

"It's all in how it's done," said the Bonemaster. "Taste is terribly important. Won't you come inside?"

"Where's Simon?"

"Come inside, and you'll find out," said the Bonemaster. "Besides, I couldn't think of sending you away without dinner—if I send you away at all. You're quite clearly exhausted, hungry, and one might say, in no shape to do battle."

"I want you to tell me where Simon is," said Jinx. "Have you seen him?"

"Oh, yes." The knives went flick, flick, flick. "And in a sense, quite recently."

"What do you mean 'in a sense'?" Jinx demanded.

"Really, Jinx, I don't care for your tone," said the Bonemaster. "Manners. Now, will you come inside?"

"You can answer my question out here."

"There's someone inside I'm sure you'll want to see. And it would be such a waste to kill you here," the Bonemaster added.

Jinx could feel the fire inside him—his own fire, which wasn't much. The Bonemaster undoubtedly had more power. From where he was standing, Jinx couldn't sense very much, and he couldn't be sure if Malthus had told him the truth about that ice stuff or whatever it was. But Jinx had come here to find things out, and for now, the best way to do that was probably to go along.

"All right," he said. "Let's go, then."

～✒✒✒

Jinx stepped into the great hall of Bonesocket. The heavy door creaked shut behind him.

"Where's Simon?"

"Really, Jinx," said the Bonemaster. "One begins a social visit with 'So how have things been' or 'What have you been doing lately.'"

"I know what you've been doing. Killing people. How did you escape from Simon's wards?"

"It really wasn't difficult at all," said the Bonemaster. "With the aid of an extremely careless wagoner—"

"—who you murdered?" said Jinx.

"—I obtained a bit of deathforce power and was able to part Simon's crude spell with little difficulty. Dinner will be ready shortly. Would you care for a cup of wine in the meantime? Or, no, on an empty stomach, perhaps some cider?"

He waved his hand. There was a clattering in the kitchen, and two flagons—made of silver, not of skulls— came sailing down the hall. The Bonemaster caught one in each hand.

"You choose," he said, offering them both to Jinx.

Jinx took one randomly. "You killed thirty-two people in Cold Oats Clearing."

"They weren't important," said the Bonemaster. "Except insofar as their deaths provided me with a considerable amount of power."

"Of course they were important," said Jinx. "They had people they cared about, and who cared about them."

"You think so? Even Simon didn't care about them. He pretended to, but he was really just offended that I took something that was his—even if he didn't want it."

Jinx was dismayed by this use of the past tense to describe Simon.

"Useless, dismal little Clearing lives," said the Bonemaster. "Scratching at the earth and fearing the world outside. But I made them worthwhile—converted them into power they never had when they were alive."

The Third Truth, Jinx thought. *No one is ever wrong.* The Bonemaster thinks he's doing good. Weird.

"And you killed a woman from Badwater Clearing," Jinx said.

The Bonemaster frowned, as if searching his memory, though the knife blades were razor sharp and twirling easily. "A woman . . . ? Ah, yes. She came to sell me bread. It was terrible bread."

"It probably was," said Jinx. "But you can't kill people for that."

"No? We shall have to agree to disagree."

"Where's Simon?" said Jinx.

"You're not drinking your cider."

Jinx set the flagon down on a table.

"Really, Jinx, this is tedious. Have you come all this way to discuss Simon?"

"Not to discuss him. To rescue him."

The Bonemaster laughed lightly. "Oh, we *are* going to do battle. Excellent. I'm afraid it will be rather brief, and the ending inevitable, but your deathforce will be worth far more if it's won in battle. Although." He took a sip of cider. "I see you have your lifeforce back in you. Simon let you keep it?"

"I kept it."

"For me. How kind. Perhaps I'll bottle it, if I succeed in restraining you alive. It all remains to be seen, doesn't it? But for now, let us dine."

He turned and called up the stairs, "Time to set the table, my dear."

Jinx felt a jolt of horror. There couldn't be very many people the Bonemaster called "my dear."

Elfwyn came halfway down the stairs, froze, and stared at Jinx.

Great, Jinx thought. Now I have to rescue her, too.

Elfwyn's emotions were a green blob of alarm, quickly washed over and obliterated by a roiling purple thundercloud of fear. Her face remained impassive.

"Oh, it's Jinx," she said.

She turned and waved a hand toward the kitchen, and plates, cups, and silverware came tumbling end over end through the air and clattered down in a heap on the table.

"Not quite as gently done as it could have been, my dear," said the Bonemaster. "Remember that the setting down is the real test of a summoning spell. It requires finesse."

Elfwyn brushed past Jinx and went and set the table. Jinx went over to help her.

"What are you doing here?" he asked her.

"I'm the Bonemaster's apprentice. Bonemaster, tell the boy not to ask me questions, please."

Concentrating on lining the spoon handles up (the Bonemaster was very particular about that), Jinx caught her eye and mouthed, *I'll get us out of here.*

She ignored him.

"Ah, excellent," said the Bonemaster, coming to sit at the head of the table. "One day, my dear, you'll be able to make the plates and spoons arrange themselves, but everything in small steps."

He nodded toward the kitchen, and platters and bowls of food came sailing gently through the arched kitchen doorway and settled themselves on the cloth without spilling a drop.

"You see how it's done, my dear? Just a little pause before descent, to adjust the spell. Please, sit down."

"I don't want to sit down and eat with someone who's killed hundreds of people," said Jinx.

"You've done so on many previous occasions." The Bonemaster turned to Elfwyn. "My dear, is the food poisoned?"

He's using her curse, Jinx thought. Like Reven did.

"Of course not," said Elfwyn, in a bored voice. "Why would you waste his life by poisoning him? There's no power in that. Don't be stupid, Jinx. You have to eat."

If Jinx hadn't been able to see her emotions, he would have been hurt by her coldness. Actually, he was kind of hurt by it anyway. He sat down.

And ate, because he was extremely hungry. There was fricasseed chicken, and mashed sweet potatoes, and roasted beets, and pea soup, and it was all, as usual, very good.

"The advantage to me of bottling your life," said the Bonemaster, swirling wine in his cup and gazing at it thoughtfully, "is that I'll get much more power from your trapped life than I would from your transformed death."

"But you could also bottle his death, couldn't you, Bonemaster?" said Elfwyn.

"Oh, yes. But that produces only slightly more power than deathforce magic—and, of course, is less decorative."

Jinx remembered the tunnel lined with bones down in the dungeon.

"Bottling my life would take a human sacrifice," said Jinx. The Bonemaster wouldn't sacrifice Elfwyn, would he?

"Oh really?" said the Bonemaster. "Is that what Simon did? This Simon you're so eager to rescue? I'm not surprised. What human did he sacrifice?"

Jinx cursed himself for opening his big mouth. He'd forgotten the Bonemaster's tendency to find useful clues in almost anything you said.

"Perhaps he didn't sacrifice anyone," said the Bonemaster. "There's a way around most things in magic, if you know where to look."

Jinx busied himself with his chicken.

"Perhaps he used ghast-roots," said the Bonemaster. "Which, of course, also come from a human sacrifice."

A little red wavelet of disgust from Elfwyn.

"There must be other ways besides ghast-roots," said Jinx.

"Oh really? Have you been reading about the bottle spell? You know, the book that Simon stole from me contained only the human sacrifice version. I suppose Simon worked out the ghast-roots. Or he read more books. Perhaps *you've* read more books. You can read, can't you?"

"Pretty much," said Jinx. "But I think *you* can't do the bottle spell at all without your book. It's not possible, is it?"

"I think that it's not," said Elfwyn.

The Bonemaster frowned at her.

"I'm sorry, Bonemaster. He asked me a question."

Jinx hadn't been asking her at all, of course. And she

knew that, he thought. She really was learning to manage her curse.

The Bonemaster turned back to Jinx. "How do you know I didn't go to Simon's house and recover my book?"

"Because—" Jinx shut himself up.

"Because you've seen the Crimson Grimoire recently? Perhaps you have it yourself. But you wouldn't have brought it here. You left it at Simon's house, perhaps.

"What a pity I can't get into Simon's house," the Bonemaster continued. "I went, of course. And noted your mysterious absence. But the ward spells around Simon's clearing are extremely strong. More so than I'd expect from such a mediocre wizard as Simon. Perhaps he had help.

"It was while I was there that I had the good fortune to encounter my new apprentice. She was staying in the house—apparently the wards had a rather sentimental intentional flaw that allowed her to pass through. She wasn't able to extend the exception to me, however. Of course I asked her to bring me the required objects, the book and the bottle, but alas, they were behind a bespelled door, through which she could not pass."

The Bonemaster paused, and the knives in his thoughts gleamed bright pink with suspicion. "Unfortunately she is making little progress with the door spell."

"But I was going to come here anyway," said Elfwyn.

"Does Simon have other books about the bottle spell,

Jinx?" the Bonemaster asked.

"No."

"Ah. A direct response, no evasion. So he's read the books somewhere else, then, and so, perhaps, have you. Your skin is a bit darker than I remember. As if you'd spent time somewhere sunny. What was it you said before—a place with no trees?"

"Where's Simon?" said Jinx.

"You know, Simon said to me, 'I've sent the boy where you'll never find him.' I paraphrase—his actual language was appalling. I surmised that he meant Samara, of course. I don't know why he thought I would want to find you."

"When did he say that?" Jinx demanded.

"Oh, let me see. . . ." The Bonemaster looked up as if in thought, and the knives spun hungrily. "It was quite a while ago. January, I think."

"Where did he say it to you?"

"Why, right here, of course. He kindly came to visit his old master."

"And what did you do to him?"

"Well, it's interesting," said the Bonemaster. "Now that we've eaten, why don't you come upstairs, and I'll show you."

Purple-green horror from Elfwyn.

"What happens if I go upstairs?" Jinx asked her.

"I don't know." She sounded bored.

The Bonemaster looked at her and the knives glimmered with suspicion. "My dear, I don't think this conversation need involve you. You may go into the laboratory and practice your potions.

"And stay there until I call you, dear," the Bonemaster added, as Elfwyn left the room without so much as glancing at Jinx. "No matter what you hear."

23

Jinx's Magic

The Bonemaster led Jinx to a heavy wooden door. "Won't you go in?"

Jinx put his hand on the latch. But instead of opening the door, he felt his way into the room with his mind. There were no colored clouds of emotion in there. He searched harder—no wiry golden ball of knowledge either.

He turned to the Bonemaster. "There's nobody in that room."

"Ah. Unexpected powers, eh? So you know there's nobody in there? But, as it happens, you're wrong."

"What is in there?" said Jinx. "Because I can tell it's not Simon."

"And again: wrong. Open the door."

"Stop playing games and tell me what you've done with Simon."

"Open the door."

Jinx clenched his free hand around the hilt of his broken knife. He felt the fire inside him—and he felt, also, the other power in the castle. Deathforce power. It came from the Bonemaster's recent murders. He reviewed quickly the few spells he knew—levitation, fire, door-locking, concealment (not much use here) . . . oh, and KnIP, of course.

He lifted the latch and opened the door.

The room was in darkness. The Bonemaster shoved Jinx inside, followed him, and shut the door. Jinx felt a door-locking spell snap into place. The Bonemaster lit a candle and handed it to Jinx. The candle flame grew brighter and brighter, until it lit the whole room. . . .

. . . Which was mostly filled with an enormous slab of ice. It stood on end and reached nearly to the ceiling. Through it, Jinx could dimly see the curtains and the window on the opposite side of the room.

"What's this supposed to be?" said Jinx.

"What you insisted on seeing."

"This isn't Simon," said Jinx. "It's ice."

"One problem with young people," said the Bonemaster, "is their tendency to make snap judgments."

Jinx went closer to the slab. He could feel cold radiating

off it. He saw tiny bubbles deep in the ice. He reached out a hand and touched it.

There was a loud *crack* and Jinx was thrown across the room, the candle flying out of his hand. He hit the wall and lay there for a moment, trying to figure out whether he was dead.

"Ah. I should have mentioned. It's best not touch it," said the Bonemaster.

The wizard summoned the candle from where it had fallen, lit it, and set it down on the floor.

"When you're feeling up to it," he said, "do have another look."

Jinx got shakily to his feet. He glared at the Bone-master—the knives were whirling in the wizard's thoughts and dripping blood, gently. The Bonemaster smiled. "Whenever you're ready."

Jinx approached the ice slab again. When he'd touched it, it hadn't felt like ice. It hadn't been wet. And it didn't melt or steam. It had felt like a cold beyond cold—a cold from the other side of death.

Cautiously, Jinx walked around to the other side. Now he could see the Bonemaster and the candlelight, blurrily, through the slab. He walked around to the front again. So okay. So it was a big slab of ice.

The knives in the Bonemaster's thoughts twirled in a rhythm Jinx was beginning to recognize as amusement. Jinx started back around the thing again. There was no—

Wait. What was that?

"Ah. You see it, do you?" The knives spun more quickly, flashing like flames.

Jinx shifted his head slightly. You had to look from exactly the right angle. It was the figure of a man, life-sized, and—Jinx jerked his head back in surprise, and then had to shift around to find the right place to look again. It was Simon. He was standing on one foot, his arm raised, as if he was running forward and trying to throw something—or cast a spell?

He was slightly transparent.

"What did you do to him?" Jinx demanded.

The knives in the Bonemaster's thoughts had slowed and were flashing different colors now, a lazy display that reminded Jinx of one of Simon's cats, purring.

"I shifted him slightly. He's no longer quite here."

"He's not dead!" Jinx said.

"No? Interesting. What does his homunculus look like, back home in the bottle?"

Jinx glared at the Bonemaster. "It is not interesting. Bring him back."

"But why should I? He tried to harm me. Quite foolishly, because I've bound his death to mine. And yours, of course. He seemed to think your death wasn't part of the deal, but it is."

"He knew that," said Jinx. "Knows it, I mean."

"He seemed to think he'd undone it in some way.

299

Really, he has an insufferably high opinion of his magical abilities. And with very little—"

"Shut up!" said Jinx. He drew his broken knife. "Bring him back or—OW!"

He dropped the knife, which had grown red hot, and looked down at his burnt hand. Then he charged at the Bonemaster and punched him in the stomach.

The Bonemaster fell back, hitting the door with a clunk. Jinx jumped on him. Or tried to—he hit an invisible wall. The Bonemaster had thrown up a ward. Jinx tried KnIP—he *knew* the ward wasn't there—but the ward stayed. And a second later he was flying up to the ceiling, where he stuck.

He struggled. His clothes were frozen. The ceiling was about ten feet up from the floor and if Jinx managed to wriggle out he'd fall a long way—and have no clothes on.

The Bonemaster got to his feet and glared up at him. "That is hardly the way to enter into negotiations."

Jinx fought an urge to spit on him—it wouldn't help. "Let me down."

Jinx was just above the door. And outside the door, he realized suddenly, was a green glow that he had always associated with Elfwyn. He wondered how long she'd been standing there.

He felt his way into the Bonemaster's spells. He knew levitation, of course, and he could see now how clothes-freezing worked. He couldn't undo it, though—the fire inside him was no match for the Bonemaster's power.

He could sense the golden sphere of Elfwyn's knowledge, outside the door.

"Let me down," Jinx said, more loudly.

"Unfortunately this seems to be the only way in which we can have an intelligent conversation," said the Bonemaster. "Or intelligent on one side, at least. Do you wish me to bring Simon back?"

"You're going to tell me I have to bring you his bottled life."

"No, no. I thought of that. But you would refuse, of course. After all, once he's completely dead, you would inherit—oh no, I forget. There's a wife of some kind, isn't there?"

"What do you mean by 'completely dead'?" Jinx was getting very uncomfortable hanging up here.

"Well, some would say he was, in a sense, very nearly dead now."

"And now you're going to tell me you can bring him back if I give you the bottle," said Jinx.

He had a sinking feeling the Bonemaster really was going to kill him. It was hard to tell much about the feelings of a person whose thoughts were made of cutlery, but there seemed to be a flipping back and forth, an indecision.

As if the Bonemaster hadn't quite decided whether to kill Jinx or not.

He thought Elfwyn, do something! But of course she didn't hear him.

"If you won't bring me the bottle, then there's very little reason for me to keep you alive," said the Bonemaster. "I'm sure you understand."

Jinx tried *knowing* that Elfwyn could hear him, and tried thinking at her again.

It didn't work. You couldn't do just anything with KnIP, apparently. There must only be certain spells.

His shirt was starting to feel tighter. Probably because he was hanging from it.

He was having difficulty breathing.

"Of course, there's an outside chance you could do something worth Simon's life," said the Bonemaster. "But given that you'll undoubtedly refuse—"

Jinx had a sensation of strangling. Beneath him, the Bonemaster became blurred and fuzzy. White flashes appeared on the edges of Jinx's vision. He tried to call out, to yell for Elfwyn. He summoned all the breath he could and managed to gasp out "EGGGGhhh . . ."

The green glow outside the room turned to purple alarm. Elfwyn pounded on the door.

"Bonemaster! Bonemaster!" she yelled.

The Bonemaster turned and frowned at the door. Jinx

felt the strangling sensation increase. He managed to draw on the fire inside himself and unlock the door. It burst open and Elfwyn stumbled into the room. She ran up to the Bonemaster and grabbed his robes. "Come quickly, there's a—"

She stopped and looked up at Jinx. Her thoughts pulsed purple and red terror, which just for a second showed in her face. Then she said in a bored voice, "Haven't you killed the boy yet, Bonemaster?"

"Never mind the boy," said the Bonemaster. "I told you not to interrupt me."

They were both starting to look like dark blurred shadows to Jinx. What was the Bonemaster doing to him, and how could Jinx undo it? Desperately he groped his way into the Bonemaster's spell. . . . It was one he'd never seen before.

"Oh, but I broke a retort," said Elfwyn. "And I spilled some of that acid that you said eats flesh? And I— He's turning purple, Bonemaster."

"Yes, well, he's very stubborn, my dear," said the Bonemaster.

"I don't like purple," said Elfwyn. "Couldn't you put his shirt back like it was?"

His shirt! That was it, the Bonemaster was shrinking Jinx's shirt, squeezing the life out of him. Quickly, Jinx used KnIP. He *knew* that his shirt was the size it had been before. It didn't work. Thinking fast, he *knew* a slash down the front of his shirt. He felt the fabric give slightly, but the slash failed to appear.

With his dimming vision, he could see the golden wires of Elfwyn's knowledge, wound all around her. He reached for her knowledge, and drawing on both it and his own, he *knew* that his shirt was torn right down the front.

That worked. He could breathe again. His tunic kept him from falling.

"How interesting," said the Bonemaster. "What an unusual spell. Now, my dear, have you manufactured any other disasters that I'm meant to come and inspect when I'm in the middle of an important conversation? If not, I suggest you leave us."

Jinx hoped she wouldn't.

"I wanted to watch you kill the boy," said Elfwyn.

The Bonemaster's knives sparked pink suspicion again. "I haven't decided whether to kill him. And I had rather thought you were fond of him, my dear, when you were here last summer."

"Oh well, that was ages ago," said Elfwyn. "Boys are boring."

Jinx was too out of breath to object to this.

"Undoubtedly, my dear. But this one has access to important knowledge, which I want." The Bonemaster frowned up at Jinx.

Jinx wondered whether to set him on fire. He decided against it—the Bonemaster could put the fire out, and then he might start the clothes-squeezing thing again or do worse things.

"These books you've read about the bottle spell. I assume they're in Samara?"

Jinx didn't say anything.

"I want the books," said the Bonemaster. "You'll get them for me. And you'll bring me books about Samaran magic as well. Let's say—oh, how many books do you think there are?"

"I don't know." It sounded like the Bonemaster was going to let him go.

"Bring me all of them, then," said the Bonemaster.

"And what do I get?" said Jinx.

"Your life. But since you will already have taken that and gotten far away—Simon's life, as well. Will three days suffice?"

"Suffice for what?" said Jinx.

"To go to Samara, fetch the books, and return."

"No," said Jinx. "I need five days."

"You haven't got five days. You have three days. No time for hatching little plots and schemes. You go to Samara, you fetch the books, you return here."

"It'll take me a day and a half just to get back to Simon's house."

"Indeed? That's where the portal to Samara is located? How interesting."

Drat. "And then I need one day to apply for entry into the library," Jinx improvised. "And one day to apply for permission to remove the books."

"Magicians don't ask for permission." The knife blades wavered, considering. "Four days. You have until Tuesday."

Jinx thought about what would happen if the Bonemaster learned KnIP. The Bonemaster had a large golden ball of knowledge, much more than Jinx did, though Jinx hadn't been able to draw on it for his spell. It hadn't been touchable somehow. With KnIP the Bonemaster would be even more powerful and even more deadly. Was it right to give the Bonemaster more power, just to get Simon back?

Stupid question. Of course it wasn't right. And of course Jinx was going to do it.

Or at least agree to it, till he could think of something else.

"All right," he said. "But I'm not actually going to give you the books until you show me you've got Simon."

"I have already showed you."

"I mean alive. I mean you bring him alive, to me, at Simon's house, in four days, and I'll give you the books then."

The Bonemaster looked up at Jinx dangling from the

ceiling. "You're in no position to make demands."

"And I want to take Elfwyn with me," said Jinx.

"I think you'll find she doesn't want to go," said the Bonemaster. "You'll bring the books here, and I will examine them. And if I find that they are genuine, that they are informative, and that they don't explode, then I will release Simon to you."

Jinx pretended to consider this for a moment. "All right."

The knives purred again. "Elfwyn, my dear, fetch him down."

❧ ❧ ❧

"I would invite you to stay the night," said the Bonemaster, "but under the circumstances, it's best if you set off at once."

He opened the front door and whistled.

He frowned, perplexed. He whistled again. Then he stepped out into the night.

Jinx turned quickly to Elfwyn. "Come with me."

"I don't want to," said Elfwyn. Then she dropped her voice and whispered, "Wait for me at the bottom of the bridge."

"But what if he doesn't let you go?"

"Don't worry. I'll get away." She raised her voice and said, "I want to stay here."

The Bonemaster came back inside. "Off you go then, Jinx. Watch out for the ghoul."

Jinx hated the Bone Bridge and hated how hard it was to make himself go to the edge of the cliff. The bridge swung and swayed as he climbed down it backward, clutching the cold bone rungs, but at least he couldn't see the ground in the dark.

At the bottom he waited for Elfwyn.

And waited.

He shivered on the cold rocks. What was taking her so long? The Bonemaster had been suspicious of her. Maybe he'd done something to her.

Jinx would have to go back and find out.

Just then he heard the sounds of someone climbing down the Bone Bridge. He looked up and saw a figure black against the starlight. Elfwyn. She got to the bottom of the bridge and looked around. "Jinx?"

"Right here."

She hugged him. "Oh, I'm so glad to see you! When I got to Simon's house and you weren't there—"

"When was that?"

"A month ago. You're not supposed to ask me questions."

"Come on." Jinx took her hand. "Let's get out of here."

She pulled away. "Let's stay here. I don't want to come back over the rocks in the dark."

"Come back over the—we're not coming back! You're escaping. Come on."

"No I'm not." Grim green determination. "I'm staying."

"You can't stay here with the Bonemaster!"

"Yes I can. He's teaching me magic."

"Get someone else to teach you magic! He taught Simon magic, and you saw what happened to Simon. By the way, what did happen to Simon?"

"I don't know. And stop asking me questions. You can say something without making it a question, you know. And it's not so easy to find someone to teach you magic. And I have to learn from him or I won't know how to defeat him."

"He's teaching you deathforce magic."

"No he's not." Elfwyn shifted uncomfortably. "Well, I don't *use* deathforce, anyway."

"You can't stay here," said Jinx. "He's suspicious of you already." He told her about the pink glow on the knives.

"He's just a little suspicious," said Elfwyn. "Not very. I can handle it."

"But it's really—"

"—dangerous. And whatever you're doing probably isn't dangerous at all." Elfwyn held a hand up. "Don't tell me what it is. I don't want to know the answers when he asks."

"Well, there are some parts I can tell you." Jinx had been thinking about this while he waited. The Bonemaster already knew about Samara and the Temple. "I needed Simon because I can't rescue Sophie without him."

He told her about the prison. He left out things he thought the Bonemaster didn't already know about—KnIP, and the Eldritch Tome. "Simon knows enough magic to get her out. But I don't."

"But you've got to try anyway," said Elfwyn. "Just like I have to stay here and learn all I can about the Bonemaster."

"You shouldn't! Simon says the Bonemaster's not an easy wizard to fool," said Jinx.

"Maybe not, but I can do it if anyone can."

"Elfwyn, did you—you didn't see what he did to Cold Oats Clearing."

"Yes, I did," said Elfwyn. "On my way back. That's what made me realize that I had to come here. Nobody else can get close enough to find out how to defeat him."

"Elfwyn, he hasn't bottled your life, has he?"

"No. That was a question."

"If he hasn't, he's going to. It's the price of apprenticeship."

"I told you. I don't think he can do the spell," said Elfwyn. "He hasn't put any more people in bottles. I looked."

Because Simon stole the Crimson Grimoire, Jinx thought. And the Bonemaster wants me to bring him more books—so he can bottle Elfwyn.

He hadn't sensed the icy power that Malthus the werewolf had talked about. But then there was that big slab of—well, not exactly ice, but something. He wondered if the Bonemaster even knew about the ice and the wicks and all the stuff Malthus had gone on about. After all, Jinx hadn't known.

"I don't know what he did to Simon," said Elfwyn. "Until you came here tonight, I didn't even know Simon was here. Er, sort of here. But it doesn't look like it has anything to do with the bottle spell, does it?"

"No. Listen, um . . ." Jinx couldn't think how to put this. "I know you've gotten better at managing your curse, which is, um, great. But there's no way the Bonemaster's not going to get you tell him, well—everything."

"That's why he trusts me," said Elfwyn. "Some people trust me because of my curse. *You* could try trusting me."

"But—"

"I'm not trying to talk you out of what you're doing, am I?" said Elfwyn. "I'll try to figure out what he's done to Simon. You'll be back in four days, right?"

"I hope so," said Jinx, wondering how he was going to manage it and what books he was going to bring instead of magic books. "Listen, what hap—"

"Don't ask me questions!"

Jinx huffed in annoyance. "Well, I was just wondering what happened with Reven."

"He's an idiot."

"Glad you finally figured that out," said Jinx. "Wha—well,

311

supposing you tell me whatever you're willing to tell me."

She glanced up the Bone Bridge, nervously. "Reven's fighting a war. He has that Sir Thrip creature and Lord Badgertoe on his side—and a bunch of other sirs and lords. There're a couple dozen of them, and some of them sided with the king but most of them sided with Reven. And then the lumberjacks are on his side—"

"Because he promised to let them cut down the Urwald," Jinx guessed.

"Yes. And those people we met in the forest, at the Edge—"

"And Lady Nilda." Jinx remembered the girl on the horse.

Purple-green waves of anger from Elfwyn. Jinx decided he wouldn't say anything else about Lady Nilda.

"She's an idiot too," said Elfwyn. "Anyway, Reven invited me to stay and be his court magician—"

"But he doesn't have a court."

"No, all he's got is a war," said Elfwyn. "So I left."

Jinx could see the Lady Nilda-shaped thoughts around Elfwyn's decision to leave.

"So is he— I wonder if that means he won't invade the Urwald. Since he's busy with his war." Jinx told her what Witch Seymour had said, that Reven might divide the Urwald up among his followers.

"Oh, he does want to do that," said Elfwyn. "And he might not wait till his war is over. Because if he held the

Urwald, then he'd have people loyal to him along one border of Keyland and he could attack from that side. It all has to do with military tactics," she explained. "Reven knows a lot about military tactics."

A cold blue anger surrounded the name "Reven." Definitely no more pink fluffy thoughts.

"But he can't conquer the whole Urwald." Jinx might not know military tactics but he knew one thing: "The Urwald is huge."

"Huge and empty," said Elfwyn.

"It's not empty."

"There aren't enough people to defend it if Reven invades," said Elfwyn. "There aren't enough people to even *notice* if Reven invades."

She looked nervously up the bridge again. "I'd better get going. The Bonemaster might notice I'm gone. And the ghoul might come back."

"Where *is* the ghoul?"

"I threw flesh-eating acid at it," said Elfwyn. "I thought you might need to escape, so I wanted it out of the way."

"You killed it?"

"I don't think so," said Elfwyn. "They're hard to kill."

"Then it's going to tell the Bonemaster you threw flesh-eating acid at it!"

"I'll say it was an accident," said Elfwyn. "It'll be my word against the ghoul's, and I'm not sure they can talk."

Jinx didn't like the sound of that. He didn't like the

sound of any of it. And short of dragging her away kicking and screaming—or trying to, anyway—there was nothing he could do about it.

Jinx wished her good luck, and watched her climb back up the Bone Bridge.

~ ~ ~

He'd been counting on Simon to have all the answers—and instead Simon just turned out to be another huge question. Jinx was going to have to rely on his own magic to help Sophie.

And Jinx's magic amounted to this: a few wizards' spells that he wasn't very good at, although apparently he could learn new ones if he got a chance to feel around inside them. (He thought he might be able to do the clothes-freezing spell now.) A little bit of KnIP, but he wasn't sure how KnIP really worked, or what the rules were. He'd figured out one rule tonight: KnIP spells couldn't undo wizards' spells.

And listening to the trees—Jinx supposed Wendell was right about that being magic.

And he had lifeforce power that he could draw from the Urwald—which was useful for wizards' spells, but not for KnIP, as far as Jinx could see. Did he have that because he was a Listener? He supposed so. Malthus might know, but the idea of asking advice of werewolves still just seemed weird.

And the business of being able to see people's thoughts. Dame Glammer had told him that was deep Urwald magic.

Jinx's magic was a peculiar mishmash of half starts, a mix of things he didn't really understand. It was mostly different from the stuff Simon had tried to teach him, and different from the magic Jinx had read about in books.

And Jinx's magic was all he had to save Sophie.

24

Jinx Gets Caught

Jinx hurried through the streets of Samara, anxious for news of Sophie. Anything could have happened while he'd been gone. He tried not to think about the exact details of "anything."

He opened the door to his room in the Temple. There was a folded paper lying on the floor. He unfolded it and read:

Jinx,
    Wendell wants you to meet him at the
Twisted Branch right away.
               —Satya

Sophie! Jinx thought. Wendell must have heard something about her trial.

Jinx was halfway to Crocodile Bottom when something occurred to him: He didn't know *when* Satya had left the note. Wendell might not even be at the Twisted Branch anymore; he might be back at the Hutch.

Down by the river, things felt cool and alive and right. The babble of voices in many languages and the sound of someone playing a tongue-drum came through the trees as Jinx approached the Twisted Branch.

Jinx had to wait around for nearly an hour—one of the barmaids told him that Wendell had left that morning with his merchants, and would be bringing them back for supper. Jinx wanted to ask her if she had heard anything about a trial coming up soon. But he was wearing his Temple robe, and that made clouds of mistrust gather everywhere he went. She wouldn't tell him.

He bought some lamb-and-onion stew with flat Samaran bread. But he was too worried to eat.

Finally Wendell came in, followed by a knot of men in bright yellow robes who Jinx guessed must be the merchants.

"Hang on a second," Wendell said, when Jinx hurried up to him. "I have to get these guys settled."

Jinx went back and sat next to his untouched stew. Wendell spoke to a barmaid, asked questions, answered questions, and chatted with the merchants, who grinned and listened and clearly hung on his every word. Finally the merchants trooped upstairs. Several barmaids followed with trays of food.

Wendell hurried over to Jinx. "Thank Gramps you're back! Where were you? I looked for you yesterday, and then I looked this morning, and then I was busy all day taking these guys around the silk market."

"Is there news about—" Jinx began.

"Tomorrow."

"What?"

Wendell looked around him, and lowered his voice. "The trial's tomorrow morning. It'll probably last till around noon, and after that—"

"Boiling?" said Jinx.

Wendell nodded.

There were several loud stomps overhead.

Jinx felt his stomach go cold with despair. He had to get Sophie out of the prison tonight. But how?

He looked at Wendell and saw him standing in the midst of a sphere of glowing, interconnected golden wires. Knowledge.

Jinx took a deep breath. "Could you come to the prison with me?"

"Sure," said Wendell. "But I have to get rid of my guys first. And they're going home tomorrow, so I want to get paid."

The stomping overhead grew louder.

"Let me explain what I want to do," said Jinx.

"No—not here. Tell me when we get there." Wendell looked up at the ceiling, which was shaking. "Oh, Grandpa! They're arguing."

"Those are your merchants?" The stomping was heavy and rhythmic. "It sounds like they're going to knock the building down."

"Yeah, that sometimes happens. Vernese people never argue aloud, 'cause words are sacred. They stomp. I'd better go. I'll meet you over there, when the moon sets. It'll be darkest then."

"What time does the moon set?"

"Just before two." Wendell held up two fingers as he backed away. "Meet me on the south side."

Wendell hurried upstairs.

Imagine knowing how Vernese merchants argued and what time the moon set. Jinx wondered how on earth the Temple had managed to convince Wendell he was stupid.

Jinx ate his stew, which had gotten cold. After a couple of minutes Wendell ushered his merchants down the stairs and out the front door, stomping all the way.

Jinx needed to think. He went out into the yard, where the merchants had separated into two groups and were stomping at each other. He leaned up against a tree. He wondered if Sophie had been told that her trial was tomorrow, and if she was frightened. How could she not be?

He thought about the inside of the prison, as he knew it from his one visit, and about where he could make holes to get out.

One thing was for sure—if he managed to get Sophie out, he couldn't possibly return to the Temple. Ever. Which meant he needed to retrieve the Crimson Grimoire, the book Simon had stolen from the Bonemaster. It was in his room at the Temple.

He skirted around the stomping Vernese merchants and set out for the Temple.

Strait Street was quiet, and Jinx could tell that he was being followed. The follower went in and out of range—sometimes Jinx could see a blue-green cloud of suspicion and sometimes he couldn't. The cloud was behind him, sometimes on the right, sometimes on the left. Then it was up above, on a rooftop. Jinx had difficulty managing not to look up.

Then a moment later the follower was down on the street, in the shadows of an alley.

Oh. So there were two of them.

Jinx walked faster.

There were no people around. Nobody to interfere. The man in the shadows was keeping quite close now, his mind always within reach of Jinx's sight. The one on the rooftops was still bobbing in and out of Jinx's range.

Up ahead Jinx could see a pool of light. If he could get that far . . .

Figures lurked in the shadows ahead. Jinx heard footsteps behind him; he broke into a run. The people ahead of him moved, blocking the alley. Jinx ducked and charged straight toward them. They reached out to grab him and he dodged to the left, and almost made it.

Something hit him hard in the back. A sack was thrown over his head. Jinx punched and kicked at everything around him, but rough hands caught hold of him. Then he was up in the air, still kicking and punching.

There were screams and grunts from beneath him. He fell, hitting the cobbled alley so hard he couldn't breathe for a minute. People fought above him. Jinx rolled to avoid getting trampled. He clawed the bag from his head, staggered to his feet, and ran back the way he had come.

Something tripped him, and he fell sprawling. Before he could move, ropes were pulled tight around his wrists and ankles. He yelled until someone stuck a rag in his mouth. He was blindfolded, thrown over someone's shoulder, and jounced along in the dark, headed who knew where.

~ ~ ~

They were going down a steep spiral staircase. Jinx would very much have preferred not to be doing it hanging upside down and blindfolded. The air was dank and moldy. It would have been nice not to have had the Bonemaster's secret catacomb full of skulls and bones in his memory.

Finally they reached the bottom. Jinx was set down on his feet, but they were bound so tightly that he fell right over.

"Cut his bonds." It was a woman's voice, and Jinx recognized it. "We are not afraid of children."

The ropes pulled tighter as someone sawed through them, and Jinx's hands and feet were free. He pulled off the blindfold and took the gag out of his mouth.

He was in a round room, lit by flickering torches. The Preceptress was looking down at him.

"So this is our errant scholar," she said. "Hm. I didn't think the Mistletoe Alliance was really dead."

She was flanked on either side by a preceptor. Their faces were sinister in the torchlight. And each of them was at the center of one of those insanely outsize preceptor-ish spheres of knowledge. The spheres hummed and buzzed in a way most people's didn't. Jinx hadn't noticed that before.

There were two men lurking behind them—the thugs who had caught him, Jinx guessed. Scholars didn't dirty their hands.

"Stand up," said the Preceptress.

Jinx did, painfully.

"What were you doing at the Twisted Branch?"

"Eating dinner," said Jinx. "Isn't that allowed?"

"You could have eaten at the Temple," said the Preceptress.

322

"Scholars who don't stay in the Temple are dangerous."

"Is that why you've been having me followed?" said Jinx.

"There is no need to follow you. Your movements have been noted and reported. The people of Samara are loyal to the Temple. We permitted your visit to the prison. We knew we could capture you whenever we chose—as we have now done. All your efforts have done, you know, is to prove to us that Sophie Maya really is in the Mistletoe Alliance."

"Neither of us is, actually." Jinx looked around the room—no way out but up. He had his back to the stairs.

"When will you people learn?" she said. "We know how to recognize spies from the Mistletoe Alliance. We watch each class of lectors carefully. Surely your leaders have realized that, after so many deaths?"

"I wouldn't know," said Jinx. "I haven't got any leaders."

There was a sudden blurp of surprise from the Preceptress. "You're that boy. The one that came into the Temple with Simon Magus."

Sudden green gleams of interest from all of the preceptors. Jinx had just become someone important. And that was not to his advantage.

There was nobody between Jinx and the stairs. But could he outrun the preceptors and their thugs?

"Where's Simon Magus?" said the Preceptress.

"I would really like to know that," said Jinx.

He sucked the flames from the torches, spun, and rushed up the stairs, stumbling and grabbing at the wall. Behind him, he heard thumps and cries as the thugs and preceptors crashed into each other in the dark. Then someone was coming up the stairs behind him. Jinx climbed faster.

Bam! He hit a door at the top. The thugs were just a few yards behind him. He yanked at the door. It was locked. He tried the door spell on it, but it didn't work—the door hadn't been locked by magic.

KnIP. He *knew* there was a hole in the door. And there was. Not a big enough one, though. There was no time to keep making little holes—Jinx needed more knowledge. He grabbed the knowledge of the thugs behind him and *knew* a bigger hole in the door. There were more footsteps climbing the stairs behind him. The hole in the door was still too small—maybe twice as wide as the cat flap back home.

Jinx stuck his head through the hole, and painfully squeezed his shoulders into it. It was a tight fit and he had to wriggle like a snake. It felt like his ribs would crack. Someone grabbed his robe. There was a ripping sound, and he fell through and landed on stone pavement.

"Let him go," came the Preceptress's voice. "We know where to find him."

Which was more than Jinx knew. He had no idea what part of the city he was in. Nothing looked familiar.

The houses were far apart and there were no lights. Jinx started walking toward the west, hoping that would take him to something he recognized.

He walked for a long time before he realized he was being followed. Again.

Well, he had had enough. He wasn't interested in having any more people jump on him, kick him, or throw sacks over his head.

He stopped beside an abandoned house with empty staring windows and an old wooden door hanging off a single twisted hinge. He backed up to the wall, his fists clenched.

His follower moved along the wall toward him. Jinx could see the thoughts—determined, suspicious, faintly annoyed. Scared. His follower was scared. Well, fine.

The follower came closer. And closer still—Jinx could hear his footsteps now. He waited.

25

The Prison

Someone grabbed Jinx's arm. Jinx grabbed the grabber, dragged him to the ground, and fell on top of him.

Oops. *Not* a him.

"Hey! Let go of me!" cried Satya.

Jinx let go. "You attacked me."

"I was just trying to talk to you." Satya picked herself up and brushed herself off. "You can't go to Simon's house. They're watching it."

"How—"

"They've always watched it off and on," said Satya.

"Actually, I was going to ask how you knew—"

"Simon? I remember him from when I was little," said Satya.

"You're in the Mistletoe Alliance, aren't you?"

"Hush! Don't say that name. You never know who's listening."

"Has the Mistletoe Alliance been following me?" said Jinx. "And knocking me with sticks and throwing sacks over my head and stuff? Because—"

"A press gang grabbed you, and the preceptors snatched you away from them. The Company couldn't care less about you—"

"Who's the . . . never mind," said Jinx.

"But we have to protect Simon's house," said Satya.

"Because you keep your books in there?" Jinx guessed.

"The preceptors' spies watch it."

"And you do too," said Jinx, bitterly. "And you locked me out of it."

"*I* didn't. But it had to be done. They've never been certain that house has anything to do with us—"

"But Simon owns it, doesn't he?" It felt weird to be asking a Samaran about Simon.

"Yes, but it's not really there, or something. Something to do with magic," she said dismissively. "The preceptors think a different house is there, which belongs to Sophie's aunt. But of course, with you going there all the time—"

"Three times, total," said Jinx.

"—that's how they made the connection between you and Sophie. You can't go back to the Temple either."

"Well, duh," said Jinx. "I just escaped from the

327

Preceptress. About Sophie, listen: Can you help me get her out of prison tonight?"

"No." Hard blue thoughts. "I can't risk my mission."

"She's going to die tomorrow if I don't get her out tonight."

"Sophie knew the risks," said Satya.

"The risks of what? Being married to Simon?"

"No," said Satya, scornfully. "Of being in the Company."

"But Sophie's not in the Mi— the Company," said Jinx.

"Of course she is," said Satya.

Jinx remembered something Professor Night had said. "She's in it because of Simon?"

"No, Simon's in it because of her," said Satya. "She's been in it since she was younger than I am."

Jinx felt hurt that Sophie had never told him.

"Then why haven't you guys tried to get her out?" he asked.

"We can't. The cause is bigger than she is," said Satya. "We'll all die in it eventually."

"Don't you care?" said Jinx.

"Of course I care," said Satya. "That's what I just got done telling you. We can't risk showing the Temple that the Company still exists."

Jinx couldn't imagine believing in something so much you would die for it. Could he?

He thought about Reven, and the Bonemaster. Would Jinx be willing to die to save the Urwald? He didn't know.

"Look, I'm not in your stu— your Company, and I'm going to go in and get her out of there," he said. "Will you help?"

"No."

"You won't have to risk your mission. Nobody will even see you. Here's what I want to do."

Satya listened. "You know enough KnIP to make a hole in the prison wall?"

"A small hole," said Jinx. "But with your knowledge to draw on, and Wendell's—"

"You're involving Wendell? What if he's seen? He'll never be able to go back to the Hutch."

"I don't think he'll cry too hard over that," said Jinx.

"No, I suppose not," said Satya.

"Will you help? Please?"

A long, purple-and-blue struggle twisted and turned around Satya's head.

"As long as no one sees me," she said at last. "And as long as I can go back to the Temple right afterward."

"Actually, I'll need you to watch Simon's house," said Jinx. "Or the Company should watch it, I guess, because you'll need to come down to the river and tell us when it's safe to go there."

"You're hiding Sophie in her own house? But that's not safe at all!"

"I can get her from there to a safe place very easily," said Jinx. "Trust me on that. All I need is for the Mi— the Company to help her get to the house."

"You mean you'll take her to the Urwald?"

Jinx was surprised. "You know about the Urwald?" Suddenly Jinx remembered Sophie saying "They don't like me coming here." She must have meant the Mistletoe Alliance, not the preceptors.

"Of course."

"Well, can the Mi— can those guys at least guard the house till we get there?"

Purple-blue whirring thoughts from Satya—worry, uncertainty, and, always, a silver coil of fear.

"I guess it's the least we can do for her," she said at last.

"Just about exactly," said Jinx.

Jinx waited in a tree beside the river. The tree murmured about the current tickling its roots, and Jinx wondered if Satya was ever going to show up. Maybe she'd changed her mind.

Silently, a boat drifted under the overhanging branches. Satya looked all around.

Jinx lowered himself from the tree into the boat. The

boat rocked and Satya gave an exasperated sigh.

"That's not how you get in a boat. Just keep your hands inside." She steered expertly away from the bank.

Jinx did. He remembered the crocodiles.

He looked at Satya. "Flipping your hair is part of your Satya act, right? You don't do it away from the Temple. What's your real name?"

"Satya is my real name," she said, dripping ice.

"And making friends with two guys from Angara makes you look less suspicious, right? Because no one would ever suspect Angarans of being in the Mi—"

"*Company.*" A little blue twinge of guilt. "Wendell is a very nice person, for your information. Anyone would want to be friends with him. And I knew you weren't Angaran. You're not good at deception."

"I am too!" said Jinx. "I got into the prison, didn't I?"

"They probably let you get in," said Satya. "You're a terrible liar, you know. That's why I trusted you. The preceptors would never have a spy who was such a lousy liar."

Jinx thought of Elfwyn and wondered if he'd caught being a lousy liar from her. Except that Elfwyn was actually a pretty good liar, as long as no one asked her a question.

When they reached the other side, Satya paddled up a small inlet among overhanging trees—and crocodiles, Jinx didn't doubt. The boat clunked against wood. Satya climbed out.

"There's a dock here," she said.

"Are there crocodiles on it?" said Jinx.

"Of course not," said Satya.

Jinx didn't see why it was an of-course-not, but he climbed out. Satya tied up, and they headed for the prison.

He thought about how Satya had found the Eldritch Tome for him in the library, hidden in the cover of a different book. And Sophie had told him how to find the KnIP books, disguised as something else.

"Does the Mi— the Company hide books in the Temple libraries?" he asked.

"Hush."

Wendell was waiting for them. Jinx recognized the little red-orange blurp of happiness at seeing Satya.

"Okay, what I need you to do is—" Jinx started.

"Speak Herwa," Satya said.

Jinx switched to Herwa. "I'm going to make a hole in the prison wall—"

Surprise from Wendell.

"—and I need to use your knowledge to do it. Then Wendell and I will go in, so that I can use Wendell's knowledge if I need to make any more holes, and we'll get Sophie, come out this way, run down to—"

"Don't say the place," said Satya.

"—to meet Satya," Jinx told Wendell. "Okay?"

"No problem," said Wendell.

But there was a problem.

It wasn't using Wendell's and Satya's knowledge—that came easily, and with three golden spheres' worth of power Jinx was able to dig his way quickly through the six-foot-thick wall of the prison, making a person-sized hole.

The problem was, he was the only one who could see it.

"It's right here!" he said.

"I can't see it," said Wendell.

"Me neither," said Satya.

"Look." Jinx stuck his hand into the hole, then his arm, all the way to the shoulder.

"At what? You're hitting your hand against solid stone." Satya reached out and touched the opening, and her hand stopped as if it had hit a wall.

Jinx remembered that before he had *known* there was a door to Samara in Simon's house, it had felt like solid stone to him.

Well, it didn't matter about Satya. She wasn't going in anyway. But Wendell had to get through.

"Look, you have to *know* there's a hole here."

"It's not that I don't believe you," said Wendell.

"It doesn't matter what you *believe!* You have to *know* it!"

"Keep your voice down," Satya whispered. "You'll have to go alone."

She was right. There was no time to waste.

"If I don't come out, get out of here and go somewhere else and—"

"You don't have to tell me," said Satya.

Jinx nodded to both of them and ducked into the hole.

It was more like a tunnel, really. Jinx had chosen the spot because he thought it was close to one of the passages that Big Seth had taken him through on his last visit. And it did lead into a passage of some kind. But the right one, or not? It seemed to be going crosswise to how he remembered.

Without trees to guide him, Jinx didn't really have much sense of direction.

He stumbled along in the dark, feeling for minds. He came to another passage, and turned, and then another.

Then there were thoughts up ahead. A green knob of suspicion, a few yards away.

A guard! Jinx froze, and stopped breathing. And the green suspicion suddenly moved away.

That seemed wrong to Jinx, and wrong in exactly the wrong way. The guard must have heard Jinx, and be going for help.

Except shouldn't a guard be able to handle an intruder on his own?

Uncertain, Jinx started walking again, as silently as he possibly could.

There was another mind moving toward him, coming

up from behind, tracking him. A mind that was mostly an orange blob of worry. Now, why would a guard be worried?

He wouldn't. Jinx stopped and let the orange blob catch up to him.

"How did you get in?" Jinx whispered.

"Shh," said Wendell.

They came to a staircase and crept up it.

Another mind up ahead—stern red thoughts that reminded Jinx of Felix, the warden. And then that mind, too, got up and walked away.

"They're letting us get in," Jinx said. "It's a trap."

Wendell said nothing.

"You should leave," said Jinx.

"Shh," said Wendell.

They walked on.

Then there were thoughts just above them—a blue-brown cloud of anxiety, edging into gray despair.

Jinx knew that mind.

He walked faster. Smack into a wall. He groped around for an opening. Now that he'd found Sophie he felt he had to get to her immediately—who knew how early they'd come to take her to the trial?—and the passages weren't cooperating. Finally he found a stairway going up.

A moment later he and Wendell were hurrying down the corridor of empty cells toward Sophie.

"Jinx!" Red joy. Then she frowned. "Who's this?"

"This is Wendell," said Jinx. "You can trust him. We have to get out of here."

"Where's Simon?" Sophie demanded.

"Home. He couldn't come. We—"

"What do you mean, he couldn't come?" Building white fury.

Jinx did not have time for this. "Sophie, they know we're in here. We have to go *now*."

"My trial is tomorrow, and he couldn't come?"

"He didn't know," said Jinx. "Could you please shut up so I can concentrate?"

"Yes, do, please, Professor," said Wendell urgently.

Sophie had a very large sphere of knowledge for Jinx to draw on. It was almost easy to remove a bar from her cell, and then another.

"Now you can squeeze through."

"I'm not *that* thin yet," said Sophie.

Jinx had never realized before just how exasperating Sophie could be. "I made two bars disappear. These two."

Sophie pressed against the bars. But it was clear she was meeting cold iron.

"You have to *know* they're not there," said Jinx. "Just like you do with the door into the Urwald."

"And to do that, I have to believe you can really do KnIP," said Sophie.

"You think I'm still seven years old and can't do anything."

"No, of course I don't think that. But I'm a scholar, I'm supposed to be skeptical."

"Excuse me," said Wendell. "There's a—"

"Just a moment, please. I have to concentrate," said Sophie.

"But—" said Wendell.

Sophie frowned at the bar and, with a great brown push of determination, put her hand through it. A little purple blop of surprise—and she stepped through the bars. "There! That was very clever of you, Jinx."

"Now let's go," said Jinx.

He grabbed her arm, turned around, and saw that the corridor down which they had come was in flames.

High, green flames. They completely blocked the corridor. There was no way out.

"That's what I was trying to tell you," said Wendell.

26

Battle

Jinx tried to draw the flames into himself, but they just grew higher. This wasn't wizard magic, this was KnIP. Jinx tried *knowing* the flames weren't there, but even drawing on Sophie's knowledge, he was no match for the preceptors.

Because the preceptors were there, behind the flames, all thirteen of them. Jinx could see the vast golden knowledge, overlapping, crowding, filling the corridor.

"Can't you make the flames disappear?" said Sophie.

"No," said Jinx. "The preceptors have got too much power."

The flames crackled toward them. Rivers of light and

shadow climbed the walls. There was no smoke—the preceptors didn't want to choke themselves, Jinx supposed. But there was plenty of heat.

"Can you make a hole in the wall behind us?" said Sophie.

"No good, Professor," said Wendell. "This is an outer wall, and we're about fifty feet up."

The flames were still marching toward them. Jinx, Wendell, and Sophie backed up until they were pressed against the dead end of the passageway.

"So, Sophie. You're craftier than I thought." It was the Preceptress's voice. "All this time you were pretending not to study magic, you were busy becoming a creator adept."

"What's this green fire?" said Sophie, shouting over the roar of the flames. "Is this KnIP? Are you using magic? What about the law?"

"We make the laws," said the Preceptress. "Laws are for other people."

"Why—"

"We'll ask the questions," said the Preceptress. "How did you learn KnIP, after you refused my offer of a preceptorship?"

"You have to let these boys go," said Sophie. "They haven't done anything."

"The boy deserves to die as much as you do." The flames began to edge along both sides of the corridor. "He came here as a spy for Simon Magus, and he is positively foul with magic."

The flames reached to the ceiling. Things were becoming uncomfortably warm.

"If you let him go, he'll go far away," said Sophie. "He'll never return here. I can promise you that. And—"

"And we should accept your promise? After you've betrayed our trust for so long?"

The green, dancing fire was completely opaque. Jinx couldn't see the preceptors, but he could still sense that huge mass of knowledge. And knowledge was power.

"Sophie, keep talking to them," Jinx said quietly. "I've got an idea."

The flames grew hotter still, and bright, bright green. Jinx heard Sophie arguing. He moved closer to the preceptors, closer to the flame. He felt his eyes getting too hot, and then his face.

Now he was just a few feet from that enormous store of knowledge, and he began to draw on it. And draw on it. It was a vast amount of power. It was as great as the Urwald's, but it was a very different kind of power, a doing instead of a being kind. He reached out a hand for it, through the flames, and felt it wind and intertwine with his own knowledge.

Now then.

Jinx backed away from the flame fast. His hand was

burned and blistered. Wendell immediately started whack-ing him on the head.

"Hey!" said Jinx.

"Your hair's on fire," said Wendell.

Jinx grabbed Wendell and said in his ear, "I'm going to make a door, and you absolutely, totally have to *know* that it's there."

"Okay," said Wendell.

"I mean it," said Jinx. "You have to *know* it's there."

"Sure."

Sophie was yelling at the preceptors, stuff about how they didn't let knowledge out of the Temple because they wanted to preserve their power, and how they kept magic illegal so that they could be the only magicians in Samara. The flames had crept all the way around now, completely surrounding Jinx, Sophie, and Wendell. And the circle of fire was drawing inward.

The sleeve of Wendell's shirt caught fire, the green flames dancing upward. Wendell's hair was on fire now, and Sophie beat at his head. Her hair was on fire, too. Distractions! Jinx gripped the preceptors' rolling, unwieldy knowledge and concentrated as hard as he had ever done in his life.

He turned to the dead end of the corridor and *knew* the Urwald was there.

A tear appeared in the flames. It wasn't a door exactly,

it was nothing like so neat. It was a round, ragged rip in reality.

"Do you see it?" he demanded.

"Yes," said Sophie.

"What?" said Wendell.

"Just grab him," said Jinx, and he and Sophie dove through into the Urwald, dragging Wendell between them. They rolled on the ground, putting out their burning clothes and hair.

~ ~ ~

"Ouch," said Jinx, sitting up.

"Wow, is this real?" said Wendell.

"Realer than anything," said Jinx. "And it's really dangerous, so don't do anything stupid."

Orange puff of hurt. Jinx sighed. "I don't mean *stupid* stupid, I mean unfamiliar-with-the-Urwald stupid."

"The prison's still there," said Sophie.

And it was. There was a hole in the air, a couple feet above the Urwald floor, and through it Jinx could see the green flames.

"I can see it now!" said Wendell. "You made some kind of—door through the world, or something."

"We need to get out of here," said Sophie.

"They can't get through, can they?" said Wendell. "They don't know the hole is there."

"They'll know when they take the flames away," said

Jinx. "And don't find our bodies."

"But *I* didn't see the hole," said Wendell.

"No offense," said Jinx, "but they're better at this than yo— than we are."

Yes, the preceptors were better at KnIP than Jinx. They were creators adept, and he was just some kid feeling his way through magic that was much too hard for him.

At least, that was how it had been back in Samara.

But this was the Urwald. Jinx felt its power breathing and flowing through him. He wasn't some lowly scholar here. He was the Listener. He was the Werechipmunk. He was the Urwald.

I need a ward spell, he told the Urwald. He'd never done the spell, but he'd strengthened Simon's, with the Urwald's help. *Do you remember?*

Wizard's magic. Strong and tall like trees. Yes. The Urwald remembered.

Around this portal, then, said Jinx. *Over and all around.*

"What's he doing?" said Wendell.

"Hush," said Sophie.

Jinx knew he learned magic best from the inside, and he'd seen the inside of Simon's ward spell. He and the Urwald grew the ward the way a tree grows, reaching and crawling deep into the soil, stretching high toward the sun.

Inside the portal, the green flames vanished. The preceptors appeared, standing in the prison hallway.

"How did they do that?" said Sophie. "KnIP spells can't be undone."

"I guess the fire must be different," said Jinx. "You kind of draw it in, maybe."

The preceptors crowded at the end of the corridor, milling around, two feet in the air. Their thoughts were a purple-black blur of confusion—as if they were wondering where the corpses were.

Unfortunately they didn't stay confused for long.

"They've made a portal," a preceptor snapped.

"I can't see it," said a preceptress.

"Surely they've been dashed to bits if they made a portal in this wall. It's fifty feet down to the courtyard."

"Unless they made a portal to somewhere else."

"They don't have the power for that."

"Nonetheless, I think they did," said the Preceptress. "In fact, I *know* they did. And I *know* where."

"Where?"

The Preceptress paused for a moment, as if considering whether to answer.

"We should get out of here," said Wendell.

"No," said Jinx.

"They're in the Urwald," said the Preceptress.

And a moment later all thirteen preceptors were climbing through the hole in the air and tumbling out onto the forest floor.

Sophie and Wendell backed away. Jinx did not. He stood watching them as they recovered from their stunned surprise and got to their feet.

"So it is real," said a preceptor.

Jinx remembered his acting lessons. People would believe he was who he pretended to be. Arrogant. Imperious. He drew himself up to his full height, such as it was.

"I could have killed you all just then," he said. "But I chose not to. Yes, this is the Urwald."

"Thank you," said the Preceptress. "We've been trying for years to open a portal to the Urwald. But we couldn't do it, because none of us *knew* the Urwald."

She took a step toward him and hit an invisible wall.

"What's this?" she said. "Some sort of ward? I *know* it's not there."

"Then you're wrong," said Jinx.

The other preceptors were pushing against the ward, their faces pressed grotesquely flat against it.

"Cool," said Wendell.

"Very nice, Jinx," said Sophie.

The preceptors were busy summoning their vast golden knowledge, which was all crowded into a few square yards with them. They were creating portal and door and window spells in the ward, but nothing happened. Knowledge was power, but the Urwald was a different kind of power.

"KnIP won't work against it," said Jinx. "So don't

waste your time. You can't get through the ward. But trolls can. And werewolves. And all the other things you've read about. They're all real in the Urwald, and they'll be along soon."

Won't they? he asked the trees.

We have no control over the Restless.

You always say that, said Jinx. *But I think you do.*

We will see what we can do.

"Shouldn't we leave then?" said Wendell.

"Nah. I can do a concealment spell." Jinx nodded at the preceptors. *"They* can't."

"Of course we can," said the Preceptress. "There is much more to KnIP than a mere professor like Sophie has been able to teach you."

They were still feeling around the ward spell, figuring out that it encased them like a dome.

"Go back through the portal," said Jinx. "And I'll close it, and no one will get hurt."

"Idiot boy. You can't close it now," said the Preceptress. "We *know* it's there."

Nobody called Jinx an idiot except Simon, and Simon didn't really mean it—or, well, meant it in a way Jinx was used to. "Shut up and get out of the Urwald," he snapped.

"We'll figure out a way to get through your so-called ward," said the Preceptress. "And even if we don't, we can simply make another portal somewhere else . . . once we *know*. Ladies and gentlemen, please *know* the Urwald."

"Trees, numerous," said a preceptor. "Spaced at distances of approximately one to fifteen feet."

"Height, up to and including three hundred feet," said a preceptress.

"Deciduous and coniferous. Diameter at chest height up to eight feet."

"Shut up," said Jinx. Their babbling was nothing like knowing the Urwald, but it might well be *knowing* it.

"Fauna, reported: trolls, werewolves, various."

"The place assuredly exists," said a preceptor, "and is not merely a metaphorical expression of our fears and anxieties."

"Inhabitant, observed," said a preceptress, pointing at Wendell. "Adolescent male."

"Ah, one of the locals," said the Preceptress. "A genuine Urwalder. Charming in his savage innocence."

Wendell opened his mouth to speak, then shut it with a small glow of satisfaction.

But Jinx was getting really worried. "Stop *knowing*! Get out of here, now."

"Climate, apparently cool to temperate, with frequent precipitation," said a preceptress.

Jinx needed to do something—but what? He'd been lying when he'd said he could have killed the preceptors. He didn't know any spells that would actually kill anybody.

347

There was fire, but he couldn't burn the Urwald.

"Estimated value of trees, per unit, up to two hundred seventy aviots."

There was a green gleam of greed with these words, and Jinx remembered what Reven had said. Urwish lumber would be worth a lot in Samara.

"Two hundred seventy?" a preceptor said. "Look at that one over there. Five hundred aviots, at least."

The Terror is back, said the Urwald.

Jinx thought of Reven. But the Urwald explained.

The Terror. Thirteen terrors. They must die. The trees murmured to each other along their roots. *We must kill these intruders.*

And Jinx had a horrible feeling that by "we" the Urwald meant him.

"Jinx? What's the matter?" said Sophie.

I can't kill the preceptors! Even if I knew how—

We know how.

They'd fight back, Jinx said. *I don't know what spells they can do, but they might know some that can cross the ward. They'd kill my friends.*

"There must be thousands of trees like that one in this forest," said a preceptress, pointing at the 500-aviot tree. "We're looking at hundreds of thousands of aviots here."

Suddenly the air was filled with a stink like rotting meat.

"Millions of aviots," said a preceptor.

Greed attracts trolls.

Jinx grabbed Sophie's and Wendell's arms. "Don't move, and don't speak."

He drew the concealment spell around them just in time. The forest filled with trolls—tusks and claws, matted fur and rolling bloodshot eyes, and that terrible troll stench. Even though he knew he was invisible, Jinx had trouble standing his ground as the trolls tromped past, missing him by inches. He kept an extra tight grip on Wendell—Sophie at least knew that the concealment spell would work, but Wendell might do anything.

Jinx couldn't see the preceptors through the mass of trolls, but he could hear their cries and screams. He felt sick.

Then suddenly there were werewolves, too, seething among the trolls, leaping and snapping.

You did call them, Jinx said shakily, to the trees.

There was snarling and roaring. Jinx could no longer hear the preceptors. The heaving mass of monsters surrounded the concealment spell on all sides. The creatures knocked and smashed and bit and growled, and they kept just missing Jinx and his friends. Then an enormous troll fell directly in front of Wendell, and Wendell stumbled backward.

"No!" Jinx grabbed Wendell, and the concealment spell broke.

Concealment spells kept you from being noticed. And now Jinx and his friends were being noticed by masses of monsters. The creatures came at them, snickering and slurping. Jinx, Sophie, and Wendell pressed close together in the shrinking circle.

"Stop!" Jinx yelled. "Where's Malthus?"

The werewolves looked at Jinx, and at each other. None of them was wearing spectacles. But there were jagged lines of green-gold puzzlement. At least he'd confused them.

"You can't attack us!" said Jinx. "The Urwald needs me! I'm the Listener. Ask Malthus! And you can't have my friends, either!"

"You *know* these werewolves?" said Sophie.

"Unfortunately, no," said Jinx.

The werewolves muttered and growled to each other. The trolls laughed and advanced on Jinx and his friends, slavering and snarling.

Jinx really didn't like setting people on fire. But the alternative was to be eaten. He ignited the trolls' matted fur, one fire after another—green flames and red, purple and blue, as fast as he could.

Then there was a loud collective roar, and the werewolves turned on the trolls.

Flames, said the trees. *Fire. Burning.*

The Urwald was not pleased.

The trolls yowled and roared and thundered away, some

of them burning, some of them not. The werewolves pursued them. Jinx watched them go and, when they were almost too far away to sense, he sucked the flames out of existence. He concentrated hard on this. It was very important not to let any fires catch in the Urwald.

"Grandpa's arse!" said Wendell.

"That's all of them, anyway," said Jinx.

"Not quite," said Sophie.

Jinx turned around and looked up at an enormous, yellow-tusked troll.

The troll was missing an arm.

"You!" said the troll.

Jinx hadn't known trolls could talk. Even trolls that used to be human. Even trolls that used to be his stepfather.

"Get lost, Bergthold," said Jinx.

"You *know* this troll?" said Sophie.

"Unfortunately, yes," said Jinx.

"Owe you." The troll reached out and grabbed Jinx by the arm, and lifted him into the air. Jinx kicked and flopped, too disoriented by the swinging to summon fire.

Sophie whacked the troll with a heavy stick. "Let Jinx go!"

Bergthold knocked Sophie casually aside. She rolled over, out of Jinx's line of sight. He struggled frantically, trying to see what had happened to her. He still couldn't find the fire.

Bergthold gave Jinx a shake. "Owe you for my arm."

"You do *not!*" Jinx gasped. "You tried to kill me. All I did was cut off your arm. We're even. Not even even!" His own arm was agonizing. "I owe you!"

"Never did you no harm."

"You beat me and starved me and abandoned me in the forest!" Jinx kicked at the troll, but couldn't make contact—he was too far from its body.

And Sophie—what had happened to Sophie? Where was Wendell?

Then Jinx saw them, circling to get behind the troll. Jinx looked away quickly. This couldn't end well.

"Gave you a start in life," said Bergthold, in the tone of someone who had never been wrong since the world began. "Thanks I get? Chopped my arm off."

He swung Jinx suddenly forward and opened his mouth wide, his yellow tusks and sharp yellow fangs gleaming. The smell of rotten meat was overpowering. Jinx kicked and hit with his free hand and tried to gouge at Bergthold's eyes. Bergthold's mouth closed on Jinx's captive arm. There was a horrible crunching sound. Then Jinx and the troll were tumbling to the ground. Jinx was in a sick red haze of pain. He had a very blurry sense of what happened next, but it involved Sophie, Wendell, sticks, a large rock—and a werewolf.

Jinx had the fuzzy feeling that he ought to do something

352

magical, but he was in too much pain to think straight. But he needed to help his friends, and he really couldn't do anything useless and embarrassing like faint. Which he promptly did.

27

Rumors of War

Jinx awoke to the creak of wagon wheels and the smell of dye, wool, and sugarplum syrup.

"Try not to bleed all over the broadcloth bolts, wizard boy," said Tolliver.

"Gooseberry Clearing is closest." Quenild's voice, speaking Urwish.

"Then take him there, please," said Sophie.

"No way," said Tolliver. "They'd eat him or something. They're all cretins in Gooseberry Clearing."

"Hey," Jinx objected weakly. "'M *from* Gooseb'ry Clearing."

"See? Proves my point," said Tolliver. "Anyway I

notice you didn't stay there."

Jinx didn't answer. He was feeling very sick. Too sick to even mind that Sophie was fussing over him, or to count how many arms he had.

"They won't be able to help him in Gooseberry Clearing," said Quenild.

"Where can you take him, then?" Sophie said.

The Wanderers switched abruptly to their own language.

Sophie leaned over Jinx. "What are they saying?"

Jinx didn't feel up to translating the whole thing. "They need to be in Bragwood b'fore th' war starts. They know a place 'long th' way."

"What war?" said Sophie.

Jinx had no idea, and anyway answering seemed like too much work.

"King Bluetooth of Keyland's declaring war on Rufus the Ruthless of Bragwood," said Tolliver, switching back to Urwish. "We met the messengers with the war declaration back thataway. We gave 'em bad directions, sent 'em up toward the Boreal Wastes. But someone'll probably set them straight."

"Ours," said Jinx.

"Hush, Jinx," said Sophie, laying a hand on his good arm.

Jinx meant that the Urwald belonged to itself and its

people, and that kings shouldn't send messengers to declare wars across it. But he was much too tired and dizzy to explain.

"They told you they were carrying a war declaration?" said Sophie. "I'm surprised."

"Nah, we guessed," said Tolliver. "We've been expecting it for ages, ever since ol' Ruthless let that Keylish boy king escape. What else was Keyland going to do?"

"We don't like wars," said Quenild. "Bad for business."

"What are they saying?" came Wendell's voice, in Samaran.

Sophie began translating for Wendell. Jinx realized muzzily that he hadn't actually slept in three days. So he did.

❧ ❧ ❧

"Better now, chipmunk?"

Jinx opened his eyes blurrily. The world was full of Dame Glammer's face.

He tried to back away. "How many arms have I got?"

Dame Glammer cackled, which was not helpful.

Jinx looked down. His right arm was a mass of bandages. He tried to move it, and couldn't. He panicked, then realized that was because it was strapped tightly to his chest, bound with the shreds of his Temple robe. His arm hurt. A lot.

"Broken in two places," said Dame Glammer. "And

torn up, right from one end to the other. Can you move your fingers? I won't be a bit surprised if you can't."

Jinx tried. Pain shot through his arm. He gasped.

"You're lucky you have an arm at all. I never did see a chickabiddy come out of a troll's mouth in one piece before.

"The Wanderers brought you to me. Along with that wife of Simon's that we've all heard so little about, and a very strange young man who doesn't speak a word of Urwish—except your name."

Her eyes gleamed orange, and Jinx was suddenly reminded that Dame Glammer was not on his side. Not on anybody's side, according to Simon. Simon! Jinx remembered the Bonemaster's deadline. He struggled to get up. Dizziness overcame him.

The witch's clawlike hand landed on his shoulder. "Not so fast, chipmunk. We don't want to faint again, do we? We've been doing nothing but faint for two days."

Two days. Simon was surely dead. "What day is it?" Jinx demanded.

"Wednesday, chipmunk."

Wednesday. He was too late to save Simon.

Suddenly Sophie was there. "Jinx! You're awake. Thank goodness." She was speaking Urwish. "This kind woman—"

"Don't trust her," said Jinx in Samaran. "She's not on our side."

Sophie frowned. "But she's helped us."

"She helps the Bonemaster too."

Dame Glammer grinned. "Well, I'll just leave you to talk in your funny language."

"Pardon us," said Sophie, in Urwish. The witch shuffled out. Sophie switched back to Samaran. "The Bonemaster? The evil wizard Simon was apprenticed to?"

"Yeah." Jinx suddenly found he didn't want to discuss Simon or the Bonemaster with Sophie at all. "Where's Wendell?"

"Out digging a new vegetable patch for the witch. Jinx, we have to get you home. I'll go and get Simon."

Jinx felt sudden hope. "Get Simon? He's here?"

"No, I mean go to his house, of course. He'll know some magic way to move you. He can levitate you or something."

"You can't go there alone," said Jinx. "It's too dangerous."

A blue flash of annoyance. "I certainly can."

"No, you can't. You're not an Urwalder. You'll get eaten by something. And it's far, and you don't know the way."

Sophie pursed her lips. "Don't tell me what I can and can't do, Jinx. I'll stick to the Path, and I'll ask directions."

Bright silver glow—she really wanted to see Simon. Jinx felt awful about this. "Look, there's something I have to tell you."

Sophie's thoughts turned to ice-blue fear. "What?"

"Um, Simon isn't exactly there."

"What do you mean, not exactly there?"

"I mean he's, um, well he's kind of . . ."

"Is he dead?"

"Not exactly." Jinx couldn't bring himself to say that he probably was, by now.

"Not exactly?" Sophie's voice rose angrily. "What exactly does 'not exactly' mean?"

"I mean the last time I saw him he was kind of trapped inside a giant slab of ice."

"Tell me exactly what you mean," said Sophie, with iron. "And don't leave anything out."

Jinx told her. He was feeling dizzier, and his arm and head were both aching abominably, so he kept it short.

"And you knew that, and you let me think he was at home waiting for us?"

"I didn't know it when I saw you the first time."

"But you knew it when you came to the prison on Sunday night. And you lied to me."

"Of course I did!" said Jinx angrily. "If I hadn't, you would have gone all gray and hopeless and refused to even try to get out of your cell!"

He really couldn't believe how ungrateful she was being. He was about to tell her so, when he saw the thick brown cloud of pain surrounding her. He shut his mouth.

"We have to—" She looked down at his arm. "Well, *I* have to go and find the Bonemaster, then."

"No way," said Jinx. "That's exactly what you can't do. He—"

"I'm rather tired of you telling me what I can't do, Jinx."

"He'll seriously kill you," said Jinx. "Or else he'll take you hostage to make me do something—like bring him Simon's bottled life."

"Simon's what?" said Sophie.

Oops. "Nothing."

"Simon's bottled life? Are you talking about the Qunthk bottle spell?"

"Kind of," said Jinx.

Dame Glammer came back into the cottage.

"Why on earth did Simon bottle his own lifeforce?" Sophie asked.

"He didn't. The Bonemaster did. The same as Simon did to me that time. And now the Bonemaster wants Simon's lifeforce back. And he wants a bunch of other stuff. Power. Magic. KnIP. Books. A way into Samara."

Sophie frowned. "You've just created a way into Samara."

Jinx looked at Dame Glammer. She had definitely heard and understood "Samara."

"I think we should stop talking about this right now,"

he said meaningly. "But you absolutely can't—I mean please don't go anywhere."

"I have to—"

"No, *I* have to," said Jinx. "Because I'm a magician and you're not. This is magician stuff."

Bright blue determination. "Then I'll become one."

"What?" Jinx was feeling very dizzy, and the room and Sophie had unaccountably started to spin.

"I said I'll become one. Jinx, are you all right?"

It's not that easy, Jinx wanted to say, and anyway it's already too late. But he couldn't seem to say anything, or even think straight. He seemed to be sliding into a black pit and there was no way to stop himself.

Confusing things happened after that. There was a lot of pain in Jinx's arm. But then the pain floated up to the ceiling, and slipped away through the thatch. It was then that Jinx realized that Dame Glammer's cottage was underwater. This worried him at first, because he couldn't swim, but it seemed to be all right. Nixies drifted past, but didn't mess with him. Tall plants wavered in the water. Faces floated by—Dame Glammer, grinning, Sophie and Wendell, worried, and once, oddly, Elfwyn.

Then Jinx got up and walked through the water. He pushed it aside, and it parted. There was a path between high walls of glass. At the end of the path was darkness.

Curious, he walked toward the darkness. It was difficult, like walking through heavy snow.

"Stop right there, boy."

Jinx stopped, surprised. "Simon?"

"Don't come down here." Simon's voice issued from the darkness ahead.

"But I have to get to you," said Jinx. "I was supposed to rescue you."

"Rescue me? You think I can't take care of myself?"

"Well, you weren't doing a great job of it last time I saw you," said Jinx. "You were frozen into a big block of ice."

"You mind your own business, boy. And stay away from here."

"But you're just down the path."

"Nonsense. There is no path," said Simon.

And Jinx realized that Simon was right—the path had been coming into existence only as Jinx walked.

"I want to know what the Bonemaster did to you," said Jinx.

"Even he doesn't know that," said Simon. "And as long as we can keep him from finding out, you might have a chance."

"What about you?" said Jinx. "Have you got a chance?"

"Once he figures out what he's done, he can strike

at you through me," said Simon. "You think I'll let that happen?"

"What do you mean?" said Jinx.

"Never you mind. Go and do what you're supposed to."

Jinx wavered. What he was supposed to do, he was pretty sure, was rescue Simon. He took another step. It was getting even harder to move.

"I'm warning you, Jinx. Three more steps and you won't be able to stop any of this."

"Any of what?" said Jinx. He took another step, and it was nearly impossible, as if he was stuck in deep mud. His feet and legs seemed to weigh a ton.

Simon didn't answer.

"Simon?" One more step, and it was like moving through lead.

No answer. Simon seemed to be gone, but the darkness and the glass walls remained.

And going any farther might break things, things that he was pretty sure weren't supposed to be broken, or at least not yet.

~ ~ ~

Jinx woke up, but couldn't open his eyes. They were gummed shut. He heard voices, and was surprised that one of them was Elfwyn's.

"He's going to be all right, Grandma?"

"Oh yes. Just a spot of infection and a few days of

babbling and screeching—he said the most surprising things—but that woman kept boiling up her brews and making poultices. Went through my cupboards like she owned the place!"

"Good," said Elfwyn. "I like Sophie."

"Where does she come from?" said Dame Glammer.

"Samara. Don't use my curse, Grandma. I know where *that* came from."

"Do you, now?"

"Yes. You cursed me." Grim green determination. "And that means you can tell me how to undo it."

"That's just what I can't do, dearie."

"Yes, you can," said Elfwyn. "You can if anyone can."

"That's what I mean, chickabiddy."

There was an awful pause. Elfwyn appeared to figure out what the witch meant at the same time Jinx did.

"That fool of a mother of yours didn't teach you a thing about witchcraft," said Dame Glammer. "Don't you know where the power for a witch's curse comes from?"

Jinx listened. *He* didn't know.

"Yes," said Elfwyn. "Of course."

"And don't you know what happens to a witch's curse, as time goes by?"

"No," said Elfwyn. Churning orange trepidation. She at least suspected something.

"It gets ingrown," said Dame Glammer. "The curse

was made from your own lifeforce, when you were just a wee chickabiddy. But then what happened? Your lifeforce grew, and changed, and became more your own, and the curse grew and changed and curled into itself and sprouted through itself and wound around itself until it's as much a part of you now as your own lovely voice. More."

"But isn't there some way to take it out?"

"No more than there's a way to take out your skeleton."

"How could you do that to me?" Elfwyn's voice rose angrily. "You knew you were doing it, too! I was just a baby and you cursed me for life and you knew you were doing it!"

Dame Glammer cackled, and Jinx suddenly wanted to jump up and shake her. But he stayed quiet, so he could listen.

"You think it's a curse, chickabiddy? You still think it's a curse?"

"Yes, and yes," said Elfwyn. "There, I answered both your stupid questions, because I had to. I hate you."

"Of course you do, dearie. Now go talk to the chipmunk. He's awake."

Jinx heard the witch's footsteps recede. He managed to get his eyes unstuck as Elfwyn came and sat down on the floor beside him.

"You look awful," she said.

"Thanks." Jinx's mouth felt thick and dry. "Is there any water?"

She brought him some.

He drank it all down in one gulp. "That really sucks about your curse."

"She can't be right," said Elfwyn. "There has to be a way to undo it."

"Is that really—I mean, that's really how witch's magic works, I guess. It uses the lifeforce of the—" He realized his voice was rising into a question intonation, and stopped. "I mean I guess a witch's spell uses the lifeforce of the person that the spell's being done on."

"Wizards aren't supposed to know that," said Elfwyn.

"And that's why it's easier for a witch to do magic on a person."

"Don't tell anyone, please," said Elfwyn.

"All right," said Jinx. "Simon doesn't know—" His dream came back to him, or his hallucination or whatever it had been. "Is Simon, um, well, dead?"

"I don't know," said Elfwyn. "I think not."

"The Bonemaster said he would kill him."

"I don't think the Bonemaster *can* kill him. I think that wherever he put Simon, he can't reach him now."

"That's what Simon said," said Jinx.

"What?" Blue-green confusion.

"I mean I kind of had this dream, and Simon said the

Bonemaster didn't even know what he'd done to Simon."

"That's very weird," said Elfwyn. "Because I think that's actually true. What else was in your dream?"

"Ice," said Jinx. "And a path that I couldn't walk down. Or no, there wasn't actually a path. And—well, to tell the truth I thought it was kind of about death, or something."

"I don't think he's dead," said Elfwyn.

Jinx refrained from saying that Elfwyn also didn't think her curse was permanent. Elfwyn was maybe taking too positive a view of things.

"Anyway, he still looks exactly the same as he did before," said Elfwyn. "He's still inside that ice or whatever it is. The Bonemaster didn't do anything else to him and he didn't even try, and I really think he's got no idea what he's done. That's what I came to tell you."

"How d— I wonder how you knew I was here."

"Oh, that. My grandmother sent a message to me."

"And the Bonemaster let you go?"

"Yes. That was a question."

"Sorry."

"Anyway, I have to go back to him now."

"You can't!" Jinx struggled to sit up. "You really can't, Elfwyn. Supposing you end up like Simon."

"I'm the only one who can find out how to beat the Bonemaster."

Jinx saw that grim green determination and knew he

could argue all day and not talk her out of it. "I bet he let you come here so that you could find stuff out and then he could get it out of you by asking questions."

"Maybe," said Elfwyn. "But you haven't told me anything important."

And I can't, Jinx thought. He would have liked to tell her about the portal, and about Malthus and what he'd said about paths of fire and ice. He would've liked to ask her what she thought he should do about it all. But her curse made her a spy.

There was one thing he had to tell her, though.

"When the Bonemaster does figure out what he's done to Simon—I need to know right away." Jinx remembered the dream Simon saying, "He can strike at you through me. You think I'll let that happen?" What would Simon do to himself to stop it from happening? "I mean really, really right away."

"All right," said Elfwyn.

"Oh, and there's going to be a war. Between Keyland and Bragwood, with us stuck in the middle." He told her what Tolliver had said. "Do you th— I wonder what the Bonemaster would do in a war."

"I don't know," said Elfwyn. "But I know what Reven will do. He'll ally himself with Rufus the Ruthless."

"The king of Bragwood? But that's the guy that killed Reven's stepmother!" Jinx knew that amid all those calculating blue-and-green squares, the dead stepmother was one person Reven had genuinely cared about.

"It's going to be a temporary alliance," said Elfwyn. "Rufus won't know it's temporary, of course. But Reven told me he'd use Rufus to help him fight Bluetooth."

"Reven's hitting through, not at," said Jinx. "Elfwyn, you *can't* go back to the Bonemaster."

But she went.

～ ✦ ～

Wendell wanted to go back through the portal.

"You can't," said Jinx. "You'd be walking into the prison."

The dim gray hallway hung there around knee level, weirdly out of place among the first tentative red leaves of spring. A guard stood at attention, staring directly into the Urwald at Jinx and his companions and not seeing them. Jinx wondered what reason the guard had been given for watching a blank stone wall.

"Why did you make the portal here, Jinx?" asked Sophie. "Wouldn't it have made more sense to make it to Simon's clearing?"

"I don't know why. Here is just where I thought of."

He'd passed this spot with Reven and Elfwyn on his way to Dame Glammer's house nearly a year ago. Come to think of it, they'd stopped here, and built a fire and cooked. He'd found a bit of deadwood, right here, that the

Urwald didn't need, and Elfwyn had come to help him drag it, and he'd said something and she'd laughed. He couldn't remember what he'd said.

"This just seemed like the Urwald," he said, and shrugged.

"But I have to get back to Samara!" said Wendell. "Satya must be worried sick."

"There's another way through," said Jinx. "From Simon's house. If it's not being watched."

"Maybe you should stay in the Urwald, Wendell," said Sophie. "You're a criminal in Samara now."

"The preceptors didn't see me at the prison," said Wendell. "They saw me here and thought I was an Urwalder."

"They might recognize you if they saw you again in Samara," said Sophie.

"Just means I can't go back into the Temple," said Wendell. "I'm out. Done. No way can I go back to the Hutch! Ever."

"That's a shame, dear," said Sophie.

"No it's not," said Wendell. "I mean thank you and all, Professor, but it really isn't."

A blue wisp of sadness escaped Sophie like a sigh. Jinx realized that Sophie could never go back to the Temple again, either. And she'd liked it there.

"They'll be able to get through again," said Sophie.

"They know the portal's there."

"But they won't get through the ward," said Jinx.

He poked and prodded at the ward spell with his mind. It was very strong, and anyway KnIP shouldn't work against Urwald magic. Jinx showed the image of each preceptor to the spell, and reminded it that these thirteen people must not get through.

Not thirteen, said the Urwald. *Not those Restless, no, not the Terror. Nine.*

Nine? Jinx asked. *So four were killed?*

The Urwald murmured and susurrated its satisfaction.

"Four of the preceptors are dead," said Jinx.

"Really?" To Jinx's surprise, there was a little puff of sadness from Sophie. "Which ones?"

"I don't know. The trees don't recognize faces."

"Grandpa's arse," said Wendell. "You killed four preceptors?"

"Those monsters did," said Jinx.

They walked on. Jinx was glad to be back in the Urwald, and glad to have Wendell and Sophie with him. He'd done it—he'd rescued Sophie, with his own incomplete and jumbled magic.

He hoped Elfwyn would be able to find out what had happened to Simon. Jinx felt he ought to be doing that himself, but the truth was the Bonemaster was more likely to tell her. But would she be able to get away again?

There were a lot more seedlings growing on the path. The path seemed to be getting narrower, and here and there a tiny tree had been uprooted by a careless boot or claw.

"Do we have to do this every single time?" Sophie asked, the fourteenth time Jinx stopped to replant one of these.

"Yes," said Jinx. "Could you give me a hand? Since I've only got the one."

And she and Wendell helped him replant the seedling . . . off the path.

The Urwald muttered its disapproval. *Seedlings grow where seeds fall.*

Well, sorry, said Jinx. *But if we put it back on the path, it'll just get trampled.*

Besides, he couldn't resist adding. *The Path belongs to the Restless.*

Not now, said the Urwald. *No, not now. The Ancient Agreement is broken.*

According to who? said Jinx. *I'm the Urwald too, and I say it isn't.*

"Jinx, why are we standing here? It's getting colder, and we want to get home tonight," said Sophie.

They walked on. Jinx listened to the long argument that his words had started, crawling through the roots, rippling through the sap.

They have cut down trees. They have murdered without rea-son and without cease.

The Listener says those are other Restless.

He would say that. He's one of them. One of whom? One of the Restless. But he's not one of those Restless.

He says.

All Restless are the same. He says those Restless aren't Urwalders. The Restless are the Urwald. Some Restless are the Urwald. Are the Restless the Urwald?

Yes, said Jinx. *The Restless are the Urwald. The trees and the Restless. We're all the Urwald.*

This set off another discussion, along and across, over and under the tangled roots of the Urwald.

"Is your arm hurting you, Jinx?" said Sophie.

"What?" said Jinx.

"Are you talking to the trees again?"

"Thank you," said Jinx distractedly.

Finally a decision seemed to be reached, and it came murmuring and gathering in from all sides, from above and below.

If the Ancient Agreement is not broken, then the Restless must tell us so.

I'm telling you so, said Jinx.

They must all tell us.

Some of the Restless can't talk, said Jinx. *I mean you're talk-ing about what, all the thinking beings? Nixies and werebears and like that? Werewolves? Trolls? Ogres?*

Yes.

They must all agree, said the trees. *All of the Restless. The wolves, the bears, the porcupines? No, they cannot agree. But the speaking beings, yes. The trolls, the weres, the nixies, all. You must bring them to agreement, or you must vanquish them.*

What, all by myself? Jinx said. *I'm not exactly the vanquishing type. I mean I'm, like, utterly without claws or tusks of any kind. The Restless aren't going to listen to me, but they might eat me for lunch.*

Jinx thought about the Last Listener, the girl the trees had shown him. He wondered if she'd been asked to do any vanquishing.

"Look at this," said Sophie. "We're home. But who's this?"

28

Jinx's Rules

It was Hilda, the girl from Cold Oats Clearing. She was sitting beside a fire in the middle of the path, just a few yards from where it ended in Simon's clearing. She stood up. Her cousin Silas clung to her skirt.

"Thank goodness you're finally here, sir. We've been waiting for three days." She nodded at the clearing. "A woman comes to milk the goats, but she won't take us through your ward."

"Oh, you poor children!" said Sophie. "The ward should have let you in. Simon would never have set it to keep out unarmed, nonmagical people."

Oops. Jinx had done it. To cover his confusion he said,

"What are you doing here?"

"They threw us out. Me and Silas. And Nick came with us." Hilda nodded at the forest. "He's out hunting."

Sophie took Hilda's arm and drew her and Silas through the ward.

"You kindly advised us against going back to Cold Oats Clearing, sir, so we came here. We knew you'd take us in, seeing as we're relatives."

Wendell was frowning in concentration, as if trying to pick out the Urwish words.

"These are relatives of yours?" said Sophie. "How nice."

"No," said Jinx. "This is Hilda."

"But we are relatives," Hilda insisted. "Simon's my mother's brother's nephew by marriage. And since you're his son—"

Prickly ice. "What?" said Sophie.

"I'm not," said Jinx. "My father's name was Claus and he was eaten by werewolves."

"That's certainly what I was *told*," said Sophie.

"Well, you were told right," said Jinx. "Simon lied to *his* father and said I was his because he didn't want his father treating him like a kid."

"Simon has a father?" said Sophie. "Since when?"

"Since not anymore. The Bonemaster killed him." Jinx's arm hurt abominably and he wished people would stop carping at him. "These aren't my relatives."

"They're certainly welcome anyway," said Sophie.

"Yeah, sure, whatever," said Jinx.

"Can we go inside?" said Wendell. "It's cold out here."

It was colder inside than out, and the cats gathered round and complained loudly that none of the new arrivals was Simon. Jinx thought about all the things that had to be done now—get some firewood in, find food for six people, sort out beds for everyone, look in the Farseeing Window and see what Reven was up to.

He went through the kitchen and up the tower stairs.

❧ ❧ ❧

The window showed black night at first, though it was still daylight outside. Then it lit up and showed the clearing below. Jinx laid an aviot on the windowsill and thought of Reven's aviot.

And there was Reven. Not fighting this time—he was standing on a tree stump, his arms folded, talking. A great mass of people were gathered around him, men and women—hundreds of people, Jinx thought. Maybe a thousand people. And all of them focused on Reven.

There was no way to tell what Reven was saying. But he was smiling. And where were they, all these people? Somewhere open, with no trees, but . . .

. . . lots of tree stumps.

Jinx got a cold feeling in his stomach. Reven was in

the Edgeland. As far as Jinx was concerned, the Edgeland was the Urwald. Reven went on smiling and talking to the crowd. He no longer needed Elfwyn to tell people who he was. They knew.

Well, there was no point in watching Reven talk when Jinx couldn't hear a word. He'd just have to keep an eye on the situation, that was all. He put the aviot in his pocket.

The scene switched back to Simon's clearing. The chickens were pecking and clucking their way back into the shed to roost. And more people had arrived. About a dozen of them milled around, just outside the wards. Jinx recognized them, and was *not* glad to see them.

He hurried down the stairs, jumping over a cat at the bottom and painfully jarring his arm when he landed. He wove through the kitchen, where Nick was skinning something and Hilda was boiling water while Sophie and Wendell bustled about with blankets and things.

He strode across the clearing. The new arrivals pressed as close to the ward as they could get while sticking very strictly to the path. They had bundles piled around them.

There was Cottawilda, Jinx's stepmother; and her husband, Jotun; and their daughter—what was her name? He couldn't remember. And Inga, a girl who'd pushed his face down in pig muck when he was little. And more of them . . . people from Gooseberry Clearing, where Jinx had been born.

"What the flip are you doing here?" Jinx demanded. His arm was agonizing.

"It took us over a week to find you, but then some Wanderer boy who sings to his donkey gave us directions," said Cottawilda. "He said to tell you he was right about Urwalders. Whatever that means."

"Well, now you've found me, you can clear out of here," said Jinx.

"But we need help," said Inga. "Cottawilda remembered she'd got a rich relative who would take us in, so we came here."

Jinx was tired. Everybody suddenly wanted to be his relative. And his arm wasn't hurting any less. "Let me get this straight. You all sent me out into the Urwald to fend for myself when I was six, and I'm supposed to take you in why, exactly? First of all"—he held up a finger on his good hand—"I'm not her relative. Second, I'm not rich. And third, no, I'm not taking you in."

"We took you in when you came through last year," said Cottawilda.

"For money," said Jinx. "That doesn't count. So turn around and go back to Gooseberry Clearing."

"We can't," said Jotun. "It's gone."

"Then go somewhere else," said Jinx. "What do you mean, gone?"

"A wizard came and destroyed it," said Inga.

"The Bonemaster," said Jotun.

"He blasted the houses apart," said Cottawilda. "And turned people into heaps of bones, and there's nobody left but us."

Jinx stared at them. There was that bottle-shaped green fear in all of them, the fear Simon had made when he'd warned people about the Bonemaster, and Jinx knew they were telling the truth. The Bonemaster had destroyed Gooseberry Clearing. Everybody in it, except the handful of people standing in front of Jinx, was dead.

The Bonemaster must have attacked while Elfwyn was out of the way, visiting Jinx at Dame Glammer's. And it had been done because of Jinx . . . to get back at him for not meeting the deadline and bringing the books.

It seemed the Bonemaster no longer thought of Jinx as Simon's stupid apprentice. He had identified Jinx as an enemy, and he had declared war.

Jinx owed these people from his home clearing nothing. Or at least he never used to. But now, in a horrible way, he did.

Wendell came up beside Jinx. "Who are they?"

"People I knew when I was little," said Jinx.

Wendell leaned through the ward and picked up Cottawilda's bundle. "I am carrying you bag at them house," he said in awkward-but-determined Urwish.

Jinx sighed. He told the ward to let them all in—and to

go ahead and let in anybody who didn't have a weapon . . . and wasn't the Bonemaster.

He drew a little more of the Urwald's power into the wards, and strengthened them. And hoped they were strong enough.

～✐ ✐ ✐

Most of the house had been taken over by visitors. Jinx preferred to think of them as visitors. That they had nowhere to go and weren't likely to leave anytime soon was too annoying to think about. It was one thing to say that Urwalders should unite, and another to have whole bunches of them camping in your kitchen.

Still, it was nice to hear voices speaking Urwish around him. The sound was almost as comforting as the murmuring of the trees. But it would have been nicer to have the kitchen to himself again, with Simon and Sophie off in the background, and maybe Elfwyn stopping by for a visit.

He'd told Cottawilda to stop calling herself his stepmother or she was out.

He set another condition, too.

"Where's Gertrude?" he demanded.

"Who?" said Cottawilda. "I told you, everyone was killed by the Bonemaster."

"Not Gertrude," said Jinx. "She already wasn't there when I saw you last year. So what happened to her?"

"If you told me who she was, maybe I could tell you

what happened to her," said Cottawilda peevishly.

"Your daughter," said Jinx. "The baby you had right before you abandoned me in the forest."

The confusion cleared. "Oh her."

"You abandoned her too, didn't you?" said Jinx.

Jotun cleared his throat. "I don't want you taking that tone with my wife."

"I was taking it with both of you," said Jinx. "You abandoned Gertrude too. Didn't you?"

"She wasn't mine," said Jotun.

"That's not what I asked," said Jinx. "But never mind. Find her."

Satya's acting lessons were still coming in handy. But, he realized, he was only partly acting. Maybe he really was a little bit arrogant and sometimes imperious. It wasn't a particularly pleasant realization, but there it was.

"How can we find her?" said Cottawilda.

"That's your problem," said Jinx. "Just find her, or you don't stay."

He realized Sophie was standing beside him. This was really more her house than his. He didn't have a right to give orders, he supposed.

"That seems reasonable," said Sophie.

"She's probably been eaten," said Jotun.

"Find out," said Jinx.

If everybody was going to move into his—well,

Simon's—house, then they were going to have to abide by a few rules. Not abandoning children in the forest was one. And no claiming to be Jinx's relative. Oh, and stay out of the south wing. Those were Jinx's rules.

~ ~ ~

Sophie, Jinx, and Wendell were sitting just below the thirteenth step, in the south wing, where the magic door protected them from visitors. They were contemplating bottled Simon.

"How can you tell he's not dead?" said Sophie.

"He's not translucent," said Jinx. "The Crimson Grimoire said that when the person's dead, their lifeforce goes see-through."

"But he was walking around before?" said Wendell.

"Yup," said Jinx. "It's only since the Bonemaster put him in that block of ice that he's been like this."

"And Elfwyn thinks he's been sent somewhere else?" said Sophie.

"Yeah, but she doesn't know where." He told them about how he'd walked through high walls of ice and spoken to Simon.

"A dream," said Sophie.

"No, 'cause then Elfwyn said some stuff that made me realize it was true. It was something that was sort of . . . shown to me."

"By whom?" said Sophie.

"I don't know. Maybe Simon? He told me not to walk any farther or I couldn't stop—something. He didn't say what."

"Hm. We'll have to find out." Sophie opened the Eldritch Tome. "How did he, er . . . seem?"

"Cranky."

Sophie smiled. She squinted at the Eldritch Tome. She held the book up close to her face, then far away.

"It's kind of abstruse," said Jinx. "And also the writing's really small."

"The abstrusity is meant to slow us down, I'm sure," she said. "It probably makes perfect sense to elves."

"Elves?" said Jinx.

"Elves wrote this, presumably," said Sophie. "Since it's in Qunthk, or Eldritch."

Jinx had a sudden memory of elves speaking a snarly language that he now realized could only be Qunthk.

And they'd talked about wicks, he remembered. They'd said Jinx and the Bonemaster had chosen themselves.

"If it's an elf book, I wonder if it explains anything about . . . the balance and the fire and ice and all that," said Jinx.

"It might, if we can figure it out. What about that red book of Simon's?" said Sophie. "Is it any better?"

"Yes, but I left it in Samara."

"You what?"

"I was going back to the Temple to get it before we rescued you, and that's when the Preceptress caught me. And she recognized me. After that, I couldn't go back."

"But we need that book!" said Sophie.

"I'll get it," said Wendell.

"You can't," said Jinx and Sophie together.

"Sure I can. Where'd you leave it?"

"In my room in the Temple. Under the mattress. You can't go to the Temple, you'll be recognized and anyway, there's no way the gatekeepers would let you in."

"There may be other people I can ask," said Sophie carefully.

"Well, I'll be happy to help out those 'other people,'" said Wendell.

"You don't want to join the Mistletoe Alliance," Jinx told him. "They won't even try to rescue you if you get caught."

"Jinx, we don't talk about the Company," said Sophie.

"I don't care about the Mistletoe Alliance's rules," said Jinx. "They weren't even going to rescue you, you know."

"The Company doesn't rescue people."

"Yeah, I had that explained to me." He turned to Wendell. "Seriously, you don't want to get involved with them. And anyway, I bet there are lots of Mistletoe Alliance spies inside the Temple who could get it." He looked at Sophie. "Aren't there? They smuggle books out and store them in Simon's Samaran house? They change the covers of books to hide them in the Temple library?"

"Not 'lots.' But there may be one or two people who could help us." She frowned. "Jinx, the portal that you made—I don't understand how you did it. You don't really have enough knowledge."

"I used the preceptors'." Jinx described how he'd drawn on the enormous networks of golden wire.

"You can *see* knowledge?"

"Sure." Jinx shrugged. "Everyone can who can do KnIP."

"I don't think so," said Sophie. "And I don't think everyone can draw on other people's knowledge for power, either."

"Oh," said Jinx.

"Exactly how much magic *can* you do, Jinx?"

Jinx told her.

He only left out the seeing-thoughts part, because that was kind of awkward to talk about.

"All of that?" A purple blop of surprise, but only a very small one, Jinx noticed. "That must be very unusual, Jinx."

"But I don't really know it all," said Jinx. "A lot of it's only kind of half there and I don't understand it and stuff."

"We'll figure it out." Sophie peered at the Eldritch Tome, then stood up. "I need a magnifying glass. There's one in the book room."

"But the book room is in Samara," said Jinx, to her back. He heard her go through the KnIP door and into the Samaran house.

"I should be getting back," said Wendell. "I just hope I haven't lost any guiding jobs while I've been gone."

"The Preceptress will recognize you if she sees you again."

"So I won't let her see me. Besides," he said, in the kind of casual off-hand voice that didn't conceal that this was the main point, "somebody's got to find Satya and tell her we're all right."

"That's not worth dying for," said Jinx. "And neither's getting that stupid red book. Look, I'll feel rotten if I get you killed."

"You, get me killed? You saved my life. You got me out of the Hutch."

"You weren't dying there," said Jinx.

"Not where it showed." Wendell picked up Simon and frowned at him. "My family's going to disown me, of course. But that means I never have to eat dinner with Grandpa ever again."

Jinx thought they'd better get one thing clear before Wendell went and got himself boiled in oil for nothing. "Satya's um—" He wasn't sure how to put this. "She's not thinking pink fluffy thoughts about you."

"I wouldn't expect her to. She's not a pink fluffy kind of person."

Jinx was surprised. He had to admit to himself that he didn't know much about pink fluffy stuff, and he wondered if Wendell could be right. Probably not. Jinx was the one who could see such things, after all. And he was pretty sure *he* wouldn't want to waste time following around a girl who didn't think pink fluffy thoughts about him. He thought of Elfwyn. For example. It would be useless him thinking that kind of thoughts about Elfwyn—for example—because she definitely was not thinking any thoughts at him that were at all pink, or the least bit fluffy.

"Yeah, but another girl I know," Jinx said, "she's also not a pink fluffy kind of person, and she still thinks pink fluffy thoughts. About some people."

Wendell shrugged. "Well, sometimes people just aren't themselves. So this is really the wizard you're apprenticed to?"

"Essentially," said Jinx. He took the bottle from Wendell. The tiny, somnolent Simon seemed like the biggest problem he'd ever faced in his life. There *had* to be a way to get Simon back. Maybe Sophie would find something in the Eldritch Tome. But would she find it in time?

There were a few other problems, too. Reven, who was going to invade the Urwald. The Urwald itself, which was taking back the paths and denying the Ancient Agreement. And, of course, the Bonemaster.

"How do I get back to Samara?" said Wendell.

"Oh, there's a KnIP portal right downstairs," said Jinx. "But it goes to the house that the preceptors sometimes have watched, so we'll need to be careful."

"Will I be able to come back here?" said Wendell.

"Hopefully," said Jinx. "We'll figure something out."

"Can't you make another door into Samara from somewhere else?"

"No," said Jinx. "I don't have enough power."

"I figured," said Wendell, with a shrug. "I figured that was why we had to walk here from Dame Glammer's house, instead of you just making a door."

"That wouldn't have worked," said Jinx. "Because—"

"Yeah, I figured it wouldn't have worked."

"Because—" Jinx stopped. Because why, exactly?

It wouldn't take a huge knowledge bomb like the preceptors' to do that. Would it? It wouldn't be as easy as making a hole in a wall, but it should be easier than breaching a dimension. If he could do it, he could travel anywhere in the Urwald in an instant. He could even connect the clearings by a new kind of path.

"Oh, wow," he said.

FIND OUT WHAT'S NEXT FOR

IN HIS NEW ADVENTURE.

COMING JANUARY 2015

Quercus

🐦 @quercuskids
www.quercusbooks.co.uk

For special offers,
chapter samplers,
competitions
and more,
visit . . .

www.quercusbooks.co.uk
🐦 @quercuskids